THAT
SUMMER

THAT SUMMER

JOAN WOLF

WARNER BOOKS

An AOL Time Warner Company

For Patty,
my trusty story consultant

THAT SUMMER

CHAPTER 1

I didn't really believe that my father was dead until I saw him lying in a casket. Realization struck, then grief, and for the first time since I'd received the news, I cried. My mother put her arms around me and patted my back.

"I know, Anne. I know."

"I can't believe that this is happening. I can't believe that I'm never going to see him again."

"I know, honey. I know."

It was just my mother and I, alone in the funeral parlor's Room One, alone with Daddy.

"He was the healthiest person," I said. "He ate well, he exercised, how could he have had such a massive heart attack? He was only sixty-two."

"I don't know why these things happen, but they do." My mother's voice quivered and I reached my arms back around her.

We held each other for a long moment and then we knelt in front of the casket to say a prayer. The blanket of pink and white carnations that covered the coffin read BELOVED HUSBAND AND FATHER.

I looked at the shell of my father that was lying beneath

the flowers and shut my eyes. *Daddy, help us to get through this.*

Finally we stood up and composed ourselves. I had just put a tissue back in my bag when someone came in the back door.

"It's Uncle John," I said, bracing myself to meet the grief of my father's only brother.

The wake was jammed. My father had worked at Wellington Farm here in Midville for the last twenty years, and during that time he had personally broke every youngster that had come through that well-known thoroughbred breeding operation. Everyone in town knew him, from the lowliest stable boys to the millionaire farm owners.

The room was at its most crowded when Liam finally arrived. I saw him over the heads of others as he stepped into the doorway and looked around.

I stopped breathing.

Across the room our eyes met.

I hadn't seen him in two years, but he looked as arrogant as ever.

"It's Liam," I heard someone behind me say.

He started across the room and people automatically made room for him as he passed. My heart began to slam. Then he was standing in front of me and holding out his hand.

"Annie. What can I say to you? I'm so sorry about Pete."

He was the only person I had ever allowed to call me Annie.

I put my hand in his and he bent and kissed my cheek. I recognized the smell of him. "Thank you, Liam," I said. "It was quite a shock."

I took my hand away and at that moment my mother came up to us. "Liam. It's good to see you."

He turned his cobalt blue eyes toward her and said how sorry he was.

"Thank you, Liam. It's going to be hard getting used to living on my own."

"Annie is staying with you, isn't she?"

I said, "I took a month's leave from my job to help Mom get settled."

"How did you manage that?" he asked.

"A vet who practices in Florida during the winter is a friend of Dr. Ritchie's and she came north for the summer to work for us. Florida is dead in the summer. So, when I asked about taking an unpaid leave for a month, Dr. Ritchie agreed. The visiting vet can take my spot."

A faint line appeared between his black brows. "I always thought that when you graduated you would come back here to practice."

Just what I need, I thought. *A chance to see Liam all the time.*

"This job in Maryland was a great opportunity," I said. "I was lucky to get it."

His frown didn't lift, and he turned to Mom. "Please let me know if there's anything I can do for you, Nancy. And don't worry about having to get out of the house. It's yours for as long as you care to stay."

Mom gave him a grateful smile. "Thank you, Liam, but you'll need the house for the new man. I'll have somewhere else to stay in a couple of weeks. I'm thinking of moving into town."

"Don't rush things," he advised.

"I won't. I just . . . well, I think it might be easier for

me to be in a new place, a place that doesn't have so many memories."

He put his arm around my mother and gave her a brief hug. "Okay."

Mom said, "Thank you for the flowers. They're magnificent."

Wellington Farm had sent a stand of flowers that took up a tenth of the room.

"I'll miss him too," Liam said. "Not like you, I know, but I'll miss him."

"I know you will," Mom said softly.

Liam glanced over his shoulder. "There are people waiting to talk to you. Please remember, if you need anything at all, give me a call."

"I'll remember," my mother said.

I was talking to one of Mom's fellow teachers when a frisson of tension ran across the crowded room. I looked at the door and saw Andy Bartholomew come in. Involuntarily, I glanced toward Liam and so did everybody else in the room.

Liam totally ignored the man who was advancing into the room. Andy didn't look at anyone either as he crossed the carpet to us. He took Mom's hand in his and said how sorry he was. Then he took my hand as well.

It was a measure of the respect in which Daddy was held that Andy Bartholomew would come into a room where he must have known he would find Liam. He didn't stay and he only looked at Liam once. The bleakness on his face was chilling. Liam did not look back.

Toward the end of the evening I was standing alone when Senator Wellington came up to me. "How's the job going, Anne? Was it worth all those years in vet school? You could have become an M.D. more easily, I suspect."

I forced a smile and looked up into the face of Liam's father. Laurence Wellington was almost as tall as Liam, but where Liam was black-haired, his father's hair was grayish-blond. He was serving his second term in Washington as Virginia's U.S. Senator and had all the easy charm of the southern aristocrat. I hadn't seen any sign of his wife, so I supposed she was getting cured again at the Betty Ford Clinic.

"I like it a lot," I said. "It's what I always wanted to do."

"One of these days you'll have to come and work here in Midville."

Instead of responding to him, I said, "I hear Wellington's got a Derby horse this year."

"Someday Soon certainly won the Florida Derby in convincing fashion. But you know Liam—he doesn't want to jinx the colt by talking about him too much."

The senator sounded a little impatient. They had never gotten along very well. "It will be exciting if he makes it to the Derby," I said. "It would do the breeding industry in Virginia a world of good to have a Virginia-bred win the Derby. And it would be great for the farm."

"That it would be."

A voice said, "Senator, I'd like to talk to you when you get a chance."

I said, "Go ahead, Senator, I'm going to check on my mother."

I went to stand at Mom's side and the senator gave his attention to Herbie Lowther, who probably wanted to talk to him about farming subsidies or something like that.

The following morning, Daddy's funeral was even more crowded than his wake had been. Senator Wellington had insisted on having the post-funeral luncheon, so after we left the cemetery we all met at Wellington.

Wellington, or the big house as we Fosters had always called it, stood imposingly behind a stone wall and a sweeping, park-like lawn dotted with large old trees. Long side wings and tall white pillars gave the pale gold house a classic southern colonial look. Personally, I had always thought it was the prettiest house in the world.

I hadn't been inside Wellington since I had left Midville for boarding school ten years ago, but the front hall looked exactly the same: spacious and wide and furnished with a glass-fronted bookcase, a marble-topped table containing a vase of fresh flowers and two Sheraton chairs.

The food was laid out in the dining room, another lofty, spacious room with an eighteenth-century four-pedestal Hepplewhite dining table and a sideboard, which was loaded with antique silver. Porcelain jars that had once belonged to Marie Antoinette adorned the mantel. I looked into the modern kitchen to thank Mary, the Wellington cook and housekeeper who had orchestrated the lavish spread of food.

I took a plate but I couldn't eat. I didn't feel like socializing, but then I didn't want to be left alone to think, either.

I felt a hand close over my elbow. "Come along," Liam said. "We'll go out to the porch."

I dutifully followed him onto the huge front porch, the way I had followed after him for most of my early life. We set our plates on a table and sat down in two of the wicker chairs.

He said, "I thought that Nancy might want to move to Maryland to be near you."

I shook my head. "She says she wants to stay in Midville. This is where her job and all her friends are. I think she's right. If she moved to Maryland she wouldn't know anybody, and I work long hours."

"Well, if she won't move to Maryland, I think you should move back to Virginia. It isn't good for her to be alone."

"Liam, Mom is a grown-up person. She has tons of friends and she's perfectly capable of living by herself. And besides Maryland is not that far away. I can easily come down here for weekends to visit, or she can come up to see me. So stop trying to make me feel guilty because I'm not moving home."

He sighed. "I've missed you, Annie. I've missed my little sister. I guess I'm not just asking for Nancy, I'm asking for me too."

I felt pain slice through me. If only he hadn't used the words "little sister," how happy I would be. I said flatly, "Well, it isn't going to happen."

He scowled. "I never thought you'd turn into such a hard-hearted witch."

My mouth dropped open. "I can't believe you just said that! Here I am, at my father's funeral, and you call me a hard-hearted witch?"

Color stained his cheeks and his blue eyes glittered. "Christ, Annie, I'm sorry. I don't know what came over me." He inhaled deeply. "It's just—I'm really upset at losing Pete this way. He was more of a father to me than mine ever was. I should never have said that to you. I'm sorry."

Impulsively, I reached across the table and put my hand on his. The jolt of electricity was so powerful that my heart jumped. How could he not have felt it too?

I looked at him. He looked a little startled, that was all.

I snatched my hand away. "It's okay," I managed to get out. "I forgive you."

He smiled at me. Whenever Liam smiled all my insides turned to goo. He stood up. "We should go back inside. People will be looking for you."

At that moment Frank Michaelson, the owner of Pine Tree farm, came out. Next to Liam's splendid six foot three, he looked tiny. "There you are, Anne. I have to leave, but I wanted you to know that if there's anything I can do for your mother, please let me know."

"Thank you, Mr. Michaelson." I stood up to take his hand.

"Looks like you got yourself a Derby horse," he said to Liam.

"Oh God, Frank, you know how it is. A horse's route to the Derby is so treacherous that I'm afraid to even think about it," Liam replied.

"Ford's a good trainer. You have him in good hands."

"I know."

"All right. I'll stop talking about it. But I wish you luck."

"Thanks," Liam said.

As Frank went down the porch steps I said to Liam, "I'd better be getting back inside."

"All right."

As we passed through the door into the house, Liam put a brotherly hand on my shoulder and gave it a gentle squeeze. "Chin up, brat."

All I could manage in reply was a nod.

CHAPTER 2

The house that had been home to me from the time I was six had originally been built to house the farm's overseer. It had been renovated in 1890 and then again in 1950, when the kitchen addition was put on. It had a center hall opening to porches on both ends. On the ground floor the parlor was on the left of the center hallway and the dining room was on the right. The kitchen was in the back. Upstairs there were three bedrooms.

It was a small house, but Mom loved it. All of the furnishings, with the exception of a grandfather clock, a painting of a horse and a few tables and chairs, belonged to her, and she had lovingly chosen each piece to go with the house's original woodwork. Daddy used to say she should change professions and become an interior decorator.

I was sitting in the April sunshine on the front porch having a cup of coffee when a dusty Jeep Cherokee stopped in front. As I watched, a blond-haired man got out and walked up to the porch.

"Kevin," I said. "How good to see you."

He came up the stairs and stooped to kiss my cheek. "I

am so sorry, Anne. I wanted to get here for the funeral, but I got held up."

"Would you like a cup of coffee?"

"I'd love coffee."

"Wait here and I'll get it."

When I came back with his coffee he asked about Mom.

"She went back to school this morning. She said it was better than just sitting around and thinking."

He smiled at me. It was a powerful weapon, Kevin's smile. He had made a fortune out of it in the movies. "You look gorgeous. How long are you staying?"

"I've taken off for the month. I didn't want Mom to be alone." I smiled wryly. "To tell the truth, I didn't want to be alone either." I sipped my coffee. "Why are you here if you didn't come for Daddy's funeral?"

"I just finished a nonstop run of promoting my new movie—I had a spot on Jay Leno, which is why I couldn't get here for the funeral—and I thought I'd come home for a little break. I miss the peace of Wellington when I'm in L. A."

Kevin was Liam's cousin, the son of Senator Wellington's brother. He had been brought up at Wellington because his parents had split and neither one of them had wanted custody of him. He and Liam were the same age—twenty-eight. I had known him since I was six, just as long as I had known Liam.

"Will Nancy be moving up to Maryland with you?" he asked.

"No, she says she wants to stay here. She has a lot of friends, and then there's her job at the school."

He looked doubtful. "Will she be able to stay in this house?"

"No, she's talking about moving into town."

"That might be better. She'll be less isolated."

"Yes. There are too many memories of Daddy in this house. I think she'll be better off starting anew."

His azure eyes looked sympathetic and he nodded. "How is your practice going, Anne? Do you like it?"

"It's long hours but I love it."

"That's good. You look great. If you ever get tired of being a vet, I'm sure I could get you a job in the movies."

I laughed. "I love being a vet, but thanks anyway."

"You get that horse-whisperer thing from your father. He had a magic touch with them."

"That's true."

"It's going to be hard to replace him."

I nodded. It was going to be impossible to replace him. "Do you get to do any riding?" he asked.

"Very little. I work too long hours to have my own horse."

"I don't get much riding either. How about we go for a ride tomorrow morning? There are still a couple of hunters in the stable."

"Clear it with Liam and I'd love to."

He got to his feet and I followed. He was two inches shorter than Liam, but I still had to look up at him. With his blue eyes, blond hair and golden tan, he looked like a Viking. He was currently one of the hottest properties in Hollywood.

"I'll meet you at the barn at seven," he said.

"Great," I said.

He took my hand. "Give Nancy my condolences."

"I will."

He bent and this time he kissed my mouth. "I'll see you tomorrow."

"Goodbye, Kevin," I said, and took the coffee cups back into the empty house.

After I had washed the dishes, I decided to take a walk around the property and go to visit Thunderhead, Wellington Farm's premiere stallion, the sire of Derby hopeful, Someday Soon.

The graveled path took me through acres and acres of black oak–fenced grassy paddocks, populated mostly by horses.

It was one of the most beautiful sights on all the earth. There were the paddocks that belonged to the mares and their foals; the paddocks that were inhabited by the year-lings; those that held the two-year-olds; and finally the stallion paddocks. Close to the stallion paddocks was a large and airy shed which hosted "the most expensive thirty seconds in sports." It was the breeding shed.

Thunderhead was on the far side of his pasture, and I stood at the fence and watched as he assessed my arrival. He was a big boy, a grandson of Mr. Prospector, a per-fectly balanced animal with a lovely head, a giant stride, long-sloping shoulders and powerful hindquarters. At the moment his glossy gray coat was somewhat spoiled by the dirt he had rolled in.

I watched him watching me, then I called his name. His ears flicked. Who was this stranger that knew his name?

He trotted toward me, stopped when he was about forty feet away, and glared. "Thunderhead," I said. Liam had named him after the horse in Mary O'Hara's epony-mous novel. He came a little closer, nostrils flaring. He was a little put out with me. This was his paddock, after all, and his farm, and who was I to intrude where I wasn't invited?

As a two-year-old Thunderhead had won three stakes races before an injury had caused Liam to retire him to stud. Last year his first crop of foals had been two-year-olds and they had done well at the races. Now his son, Someday Soon, was one of the favorites for the Derby. If he won, Thunderhead's reputation as a sire would be made. The stallion would be worth a fortune.

I watched him approach me, careful to keep my hands outside the fence. Stallions have a nasty habit of biting.

"You're gorgeous," I told him in the soft, melodious voice I always used for horses.

His ears flicked back and forth.

I stood there talking to him and he listened. In the distance, a cloud of dust appeared on the road and both Thunderhead and I watched as the pickup truck went by the mare's pastures and headed in our direction. The truck pulled up and Liam got out, wearing jeans and a collared navy blue knit shirt.

"Visiting with Number-one Stud?" he asked.

"Yes. He looks marvelous, Liam."

"One of his won the Fountain of Youth last year. And now Someday Soon is having this terrific season."

"Storm Cat move over," I said. At the moment, Storm Cat was the most popular and most expensive stallion standing at stud.

Liam leaned against the fence next to me. My heart beat a little faster. "I'll never get the money Storm Cat commands, not in Virginia, but if I could get even half it would be a salvation."

I looked at Liam's profile and he turned and looked back at me. The sun shone on his black hair and his long black lashes made his eyes look deeply blue. "Salvation?" I said. "That's a strange word for you to use."

His eyes looked bleak. "Things have changed around here since you left, Annie. For one thing, the stock market has crashed. Dad had a lot of money in bad stocks. For its entire existence, almost a century, the horse operation here at Wellington never had to worry about running at a profit. It was a gentlemen's avocation, propped up by private money—a small farm standing a few stallions and keeping a smallish number of quality mares. Since I've taken over, the horses have carried themselves, but Dad has always paid for the insurance and the upkeep of the farm buildings. Now it seems the money isn't there anymore."

I blinked. "Is your father going to sell the farm, Liam?" I asked in a hushed voice.

A muscle twitched in his jaw. "It's not as bad as that. But he's told me that I'm going to have to lease the land from him to run my business. And I'm going to have to shoulder the entire expense of the horse business as well. So there's a lot riding on Someday Soon's success. If he wins the Derby, it should enable me to generate enough income in stud fees to pay Dad the lease money he needs. Otherwise, it's going to be tight."

In the pasture, Thunderhead lowered his head and began to graze, all the while keeping one eye turned in our direction.

Liam looked out over the rolling hills, the large green fields with their run-in sheds, the graceful old trees. He said fiercely, "One day this place will be mine, and I'm not giving up the horses. I've worked too hard to build what I've got here."

"You'll make it succeed, Liam. I know you will."

His mouth softened and he smiled. "I've missed you, Annie. Your visits home from school were always so short."

Liam's smile made Kevin's look dull. I didn't reply.

"How old are you now anyway?"

"I am twenty-six, Liam."

He looked surprised. "Twenty-six. You mean little Annie is twenty-six already?"

"Little Annie is twenty-six, and you are twenty-eight. We're not children anymore, Liam."

"Believe me, sweetie, I know that." He looked at me. "But you don't look twenty-six. You still have those big brown eyes and that shiny brown ponytail that makes a guy just yearn to pull it."

You look your age, I thought. He didn't from a distance, but close up I could see the fine lines at the corners of his eyes and his mouth. Well, Liam had known some hard times in his life, that was for sure.

I said, "I just saw Kevin."

His face didn't change. "He must have gotten in after I left the house. Is he staying long?"

"I don't know. He said he was taking a break from promoting his new film. If it does as well as the last, he'll be in clover."

"I wish I had some of his money."

Deciding that we were boring, Thunderhead turned his back on us and continued to graze.

Liam reached out to tug my ponytail gently. Then he grinned. "I couldn't resist it." He straightened away from the fence. "We have a breeding session in an hour. I have to go see if the lady is ready. Can I give you a lift?"

"No, I'll walk. I'm reacquainting myself with the farm."

"Okay."

He got in his truck and drove away down the gravel road in a cloud of dust. I turned to look back at Thunderhead. Had I made a mistake in taking a month off from work so I could be here for Mom? After so many years of avoiding Wellington, of avoiding Liam, why would I do something so drastically different?

I knew the answer before I even asked the question. I had been in love with Liam since I was six years old. For ten years I had stayed away from him, hoping my feelings would run their course, like a virus eventually did. But it hadn't happened. I had dated other men, I had even come close to an engagement once, but in the end my feelings for Liam had always won out.

Absence hadn't worked; perhaps propinquity would. I had hero-worshipped Liam when I was a child. As an adult I would see him more clearly and, I was hoping, more objectively. I wanted, finally, to break the hold he had over me. I wanted to be free.

Or so I told myself as I leaned on the fence and watched Thunderhead pull up the green grass with his strong thoroughbred teeth.

That afternoon I took the car into town to pick up some supplies. Midville is in the heart of Virginia hunt country—there are nine separate hunts in the vicinity—and horses are everywhere on the landscape: in pastures; in horse trailers on the highway and back roads; on roadside signs. There are the restaurants with horsey-sounding names like the Coach Stop, the Jockey Club and the Horse and Hound. There's the tack shop right smack in the middle of Washington Street, the main street in town. There is a statue of a horse at the post office and horseshoes on the bathroom doors in the two local bars. There's an auto repair place called Auto Jockey. If you couldn't tell that Midville was horse country, you had to be blind.

I was in the Safeway, trying to decide if I wanted Tide or Cheer when a voice from behind me said, "Anne—is that you?"

I turned to find myself facing a red-haired young man in a suit. It was the hair that clued me in. "Justin," I said. "How are you?"

Justin Summers smiled at me. "You look great. I heard you went to vet school."

"I did. I'm working in Maryland now, but I'm home because of my father."

"I was so sorry about your dad. Everyone in town loved him."

My throat felt tight. "He was a good guy."

"He was that."

I managed a smile. "What are you doing here?"

"I'm just picking up some food for Lauren—my wife."

"You're married. That's wonderful, Justin."

"I'm married and I'm an attorney, working here in town."

"Better and better," I said.

"God," he said. "Seeing you brings so much back."

We were silent for a moment, each of us contemplating his words. "Any children?" I asked brightly.

"Not yet."

We talked for a few more minutes, then Justin pushed his basket away and I decided to take the Cheer.

I drove home, put the groceries away, and went out to the front porch to wait for Mom. The April afternoon was warm and I could see the back part of the big house through the just-greening trees. My mind wandered back in time, and once again I was six years old and it was my first day at Wellington.

My father had been hired to break and train Wellington's yearlings, and I was trailing along after him as he walked to the farm's office building to report to Brady Fitzgerald, the farm manager.

We walked into a room filled with pictures of horses. The gray-haired man behind the desk was on the phone and he gestured my father to a seat and kept on talking. As my father sat down I looked at the black-haired boy who was sitting on an old sofa against the wall. He wore jeans and a T-shirt that said VIRGINIA IS FOR HORSE LOVERS.

"Hi," he said. "Who are you."

"I'm Anne. My Daddy is starting work here today."

"Then he must be Pete Foster."

I nodded.

"He's come to break and train our yearlings and two-year-olds."

I nodded again.

He looked me over from my long brown braids to my well-worn jeans and sneakers. "Do you ride?"

I stared at him with as much astonishment as if he had asked me if I breathed. "Yes."

"I don't mean can you sit on a horse. I mean can you *ride*? The kid who was here before you was afraid of horses." He curled his lip in scorn.

He was the most self-possessed child I had ever met and he was starting to annoy me. I stuck my chin in the air. "You can ask my father if you like. He's the one who taught me."

Mr. Fitzgerald had hung up the phone and now he and my dad were talking.

The black-haired boy said, "I own two ponies. Do you want to go for a ride with me?"

"Sure," I answered recklessly.

"Ask your father."

I waited until there was a break in the conversation before I said, "Daddy, can I go for a ride with this boy? He's got two ponies and he said I could ride one."

Mr. Fitzgerald said, "I don't know if that's such a good idea. Liam is a Cossack with that pony of his."

My father looked at the boy's proud face. "I don't believe we've met."

"This is Liam Wellington, Pete. Lawrence's son."

My father smiled at Liam. "He won't do anything that Anne can't do as well."

Liam curled his lip once more.

My father said peaceably, "You wouldn't do anything that would get Anne hurt?"

"Of course not," was the lofty response.

"All right, then, Anne. But don't be late for supper."

The men went back to their conversation and I trailed Liam out of the room.

We went to the broodmare barn, which was laid out around three sides of a center courtyard. There was a statue of a horse in the middle. "Who is that?" I asked, looking at the bronze statue.

"That's On Course. He was bred here then he went to England and won the Epsom Derby. He also won the French Arc de Triomphe. He's the most famous of all Wellington's horses."

"Have you ever won the Kentucky Derby?"

"No." He gave me a burning look. "But we will some-day."

Two ponies were stabled in adjoining twelve-by-twelve stalls bedded deeply with hay. "Jake is my old pony; I'm too big for him now. You can ride him. I'll ride Tucker."

I looked at Jake, a small roan pony, and he came over to the stall door to nicker at Liam.

Liam reached in his pocket for a horse treat and gave it to him. Jake inhaled it.

Liam said, "You can use my saddle. I'll ride bare-back."

I was only six but I knew this invitation to ride was a kind of a test. I knew it was important that I pass it if I ever wanted to ride with Liam again.

"I don't need a saddle," I said. "I'll ride bareback too."

He frowned and looked down on me from his superior height. "Are you sure? I promised your father you wouldn't get hurt."

"I can ride anything," I said recklessly. "Daddy says I'm a natural."

His nostrils quivered. "We'll see about that."

We went to the tack room for bridles, put them on the ponies and walked out into the sunshine. "I'll give you a leg up," Liam said.

Once I was aboard, I watched him nonchalantly vault onto Tucker's back.

"Wow," I said. "I'd like to learn that."

He gave me a haughty look. "We'll see."

I hated the words "we'll see."

"We'll go through the woods and along Martin's Creek," he said.

And so we did, coming out on a wide-open grassy field, where we had a gallop. Jake was a great little pony and did his level best to keep up with Tucker's longer stride.

When we reached the fence at the end of the field we pulled up, and Liam gave me a brilliant smile. "Hey. You really can ride."

Even at six, his smile dazzled me. "I told you so."

"You're okay, Annie. You're a peanut and a girl, but you're okay."

I was thrilled at these words of praise, so thrilled that I didn't tell him not to call me Annie.

"The last kid who was here didn't even like horses," Liam said. "Can you imagine?"

"No," I replied honestly.

"He played video games all day." This was said with scorn.

"I like video games," I said.

"Of course you do. They're neat. But they're not as neat as horses."

"Of course they're not."

"Did you have a pony before you came here?"

"I learned to ride on one of the horses that ponies the racing horses. He was a quarter horse."

"We have a few of those horses here. We train our own yearlings for the track right here on the farm, you know."

"I know. That's why my dad has come here to work."

"Are you going to go to school here in Midville?"

"Yes. I'm going to be in the first grade and my mom is going to teach at the high school. Do you go to school in Midville?"

"Yes. I'll go away to boarding school in another couple of years, but for now I'm in Midville. I'll be in the third grade."

This seemed like a very elevated status to me. I said, "Wow." The ponies were walking steadily, their heads hanging down in front of them. "What is the school like? Are the teachers nice?"

"Yeah. It's okay. If you get Mrs. Morton you'll be lucky. She's very nice."

"I hope I get her then."

"If anyone gives you a problem, just tell me." He sounded very lordly. "I'll take care of it for you."

I was impressed. "Okay."

A small smile curved my lips as I remembered that exchange, and it took me a moment to realize that my mother's car had pulled up to the porch.

"How did it go?" I asked as she came up the stairs with her arms full of books.

"All right. It was much better than just sitting home and thinking about how much I miss your father. Everyone at school has been very kind."

I said, "I ran into Justin Summers in the Safeway this afternoon. He told me he's a lawyer in town."

"Yes. He married Lauren Ames. Do you remember her?"

"Sure. She was in my class."

My mother put her books on the table and one of the dogs from the big house came up the porch steps and curled up next to me. Four dogs lived on the farm: two coonhounds, a Springer spaniel and a black lab. They were out all day long but went inside to sleep at night.

"How about a cup of tea?" she asked me.

"Sit, I'll get it."

I went into the kitchen, which had golden oak cabinets to the high ceiling and linoleum on the floor. I took two cups and saucers down from the cupboard over the sink and filled the kettle.

Daddy had loved a cup of tea in the afternoon.

I felt tears sting my eyes and a lump come into my throat. Guilt twisted in my heart. These last few years I had always managed to find a reason for not coming home. And now it was too late. Daddy was dead and I had last seen him six months ago.

"Oh Daddy," I said. Tears streamed down my face. "Oh Daddy, I'm so sorry."

I waited until I had regained my composure before I took the tea out to the porch to my mother.

CHAPTER 3

The following morning I met Kevin down at the barn and we saddled up the hunters and went for a ride. One of the coonhounds and the lab followed as we went along the barn roads between the paddocks and into a wooded area. There was a trail through the woods that led to Martin's Creek, which we could ford and go onto the trails that ran through the Stanley property next door.

There had been heavy rains in the area the previous week but this morning was bright with April sunshine and wildflowers. I inhaled deeply and smiled. It was grand to be out on a horse again.

I quizzed Kevin about his girlfriends as we rode along. "Haven't you and Julia Monroe been a big item for awhile?"

"Actually, Julia and I have just broken up, which is one of the reasons I've sought shelter here at Wellington," he said humorously. "The press wants to know all the lurid details and I want to be let alone."

"I understand perfectly," I said sympathetically. "It must be horrible, having people peering into your private life all the time."

"It's not fun, but it comes with the territory. Usually I

can handle it. But right now, I'm tired and I just don't have the energy to cope."

I said positively, "Wellington will heal you."

He nodded. "That's what I was hoping."

I changed the subject. "Do I look all grown up to you, Kevin?"

He replied emphatically, "You most certainly do."

"Liam still calls me 'brat'."

"Liam still sees you as his little sister—poor, blind fool that he is."

I was silent and all we heard was the birds calling in the trees and the steady thud of the horse's shod feet on the dirt path. I said, "Do you think of me as your little sister?"

"Definitely not."

We came out of the tree cover and into a patch of sunshine. I turned to look at Kevin. His blond hair was haloed by the sun and his azure eyes contrasted stunningly with his tan. He really was gorgeous. He said, "You were such a skinny little thing. If I'd known what a beauty you'd turn into, I would never have wasted my time with Leslie that summer."

Leslie. The name had been spoken—and so casually too.

"She's never been found," I said.

"She's dead," he said flatly. "We may not have a body, but she's dead. Andy may try to keep up the fiction that she's still alive, but I think in his heart he knows she's dead."

A hawk sailed across the sky in front of us and I said, "It's hard to have closure without a body."

"True."

"Were you in love with her, Kevin?"

He shrugged. "We all were, Liam, Justin and me. She was so absolutely gorgeous."

I looked straight ahead as I confessed, "I always felt like an ugly duckling next to her. She was so sophisticated. And spoiled."

We were walking quietly in the peaceful early sunlight and our voices were quiet. Kevin said, "When you're the adored only daughter of rich parents, and you look like Leslie did, it's very hard not to be spoiled."

I said somberly, "I hated her. I was glad when she disappeared. Isn't that horrible?"

"Horrible but understandable. She had Liam in her toils that summer, as well as Justin and me."

I remembered the scene in the funeral home. "Does Andy really still blame Liam?"

"Yes. Remember, the murder weapon—if there was a murder, that is—was Liam's baseball bat."

My voice grew slightly louder. "Anyone could have picked up that bat. It was lying around in the summer-house with a lot of other game equipment."

"Which is exactly why the police didn't arrest him."

"I think it's unfair of Andy to blame Liam."

There was a long silence as the horses walked quietly forward. Kevin said, "I have a suggestion, Anne."

I turned my head to look at him. "What?"

"While you're waiting for Liam to notice you, how about trying to notice me?"

I looked at him uncertainly. He wasn't smiling.

I said, "I've always noticed you, Kevin."

He shook his blond head. "No. The only male you ever really saw was Liam. But that was when you were a child, Anne. You're all grown up now. It's time to put aside childish things."

"I know," I returned truthfully. "It's one of the reasons I'm staying at Wellington for a month. I've decided that I need to exorcize Liam from my life, and I've come home to do it."

He smiled his famous smile. "Good girl. So how about dinner tonight?"

I shook my head. "I don't want to leave Mom alone."

"She can come too."

I thought that was very nice of him. "That would be lovely."

"Great. I'll pick you up at seven."

My horse switched his tail in annoyance. A fly was bothering him.

I said, "This is a good place to trot."

"Okay." He started off and my horse followed.

We said very little until we were back at the barn and had turned the horses over to grooms to be untacked and brushed. Then Kevin smiled at me. "I'll see you and Nancy at seven."

"Great," I returned. He left the barn to return to the house and I turned to help out with the grooming.

I was eating my lunch on the front porch when Liam appeared. "Mind if I join you?" he asked and sat down without waiting for a response.

"Would you like a turkey sandwich?" I asked.

"A turkey sandwich would be great. I haven't even had a second cup of coffee today."

"I can make coffee if you want some."

"Annie, you're a lifesaver."

I said lightly, "That's what I was trained to be."

When I returned to the porch he was scratching behind Freddy's ears, the coonhound's eyes closed in bliss. I stopped for a moment inside the screen and looked at Liam's unguarded face.

He wasn't a beautiful man, like Kevin was. For one thing, his nose was too arrogant. Except for the blue eyes, he looked like one of those haughty Spanish aristocrats that Velasquez painted. In repose, his mouth looked stern. All of this changed, however, the moment he smiled.

When he saw me in the doorway with my hands full, he got up to hold the screen open. I set his turkey sandwich in front of him and poured him a mugful of coffee.

He took a long drink, like an alcoholic after a dry spell. Then he put the mug down and said to me, "I came because I have a red-bag pregnancy. It's My Ebony. Do you think you could monitor her? We're going to have to administer oxygen to the foal."

A red-bag pregnancy occurred when the placenta separated from the foal before birth, leaving the baby open to asphyxiation.

"Did you have an ultrasound?" I asked.

"Yes and it showed the placenta beginning to separate. I don't want to lose this foal, Annie. Thunderhead is the sire and I think he'll make a very nice match for My Ebony."

"You haven't moved her to the clinic?"

"No. I think it's best for foals to be born at home. Their immune systems are already programmed for the farm where their mother lives."

"You have the oxygen?"

"Yes." He took a bite of his sandwich.

"Okay. I'll look in on her."

"Thanks." He looked at me speculatively.

"Is there something else?"

"I have twenty yearlings to get ready for the July Keeneland sale and nobody to break them."

"You're going to have to hire someone to replace Daddy."

"I know that, but their training should begin now. Do you think you might help out? You have your father's gift with horses."

I replied immediately. "Of course I'll help out, Liam."

He gave me the smile that I found far more devastating than Kevin's. "Thanks, Annie."

I cleared my throat. "So tell me about Someday Soon."

"God, Annie. I'm so scared. He looks so good and I'm afraid to hope."

"I saw the Florida Derby on TV."

"I was there and my heart was in my throat. Did you see the finish he put on?"

"Yes, he was magnificent. What was he, nine horses back?"

"He was ten back and twenty lengths off the pace. He put in a stupendous finish. He made the other horses look like they were standing still."

I had brought out a carafe filled with coffee and he poured himself another cup. "John is going to run him in the Wood Memorial in New York next week. That will be his prep race for the Derby."

"Who are his chief competitors?"

"Bob Baffert has a horse in the Wood, Honor Bright. He's owned by the Dubai sheikhs and I think he'll be our main competition."

"Are you going to New York for the Wood?"

"No. I went to Florida for the Derby, but there's too much going on here right now. I have mares booked to

Thunderhead almost every day from now through the beginning of May."

"Wow. That's great."

"Yeah. We got a rush of bookings after Someday Soon won the Florida Derby. People are trying to get in early on his daddy before the price goes up."

We sat for another half an hour, talking about the farm, about my practice, about my experiences in vet school. It had always been easy to talk to Liam. He really listened.

When he got to his feet to go, I stood up as well. He said suddenly, "My mother is coming home."

"That's nice," I said neutrally. Liam had been his mother's champion against his father his entire life.

"She's been at that rehab center in New Canaan."

So I hadn't been too far wrong.

"I hope to God Dad gets rid of his latest bimbo," Liam said savagely. "That's what drives her to drink like she does—his constant infidelities."

I thought that the senator's infidelities were certainly a part of the drinking, but there had to be something more. I mean, Mrs. Wellington always had the option to leave him if his infidelities were so destructive to her psyche.

Prudently, I did not share my thoughts with Liam.

We talked for a little bit longer and then Liam pushed his chair into the table. "It was great talking to you again," he said. "I've missed my Annie." He bent and kissed my cheek. "Thanks for the lunch, brat." And he was on his way.

After I had washed and put away the lunch dishes, I decided to take a drive over to the cemetery to visit Daddy's grave. No tombstone had been put in place as yet; it was just a hole in the ground filled in with dirt.

I cried and when I had pulled myself together I drove into town to get an ice cream. There was a line and I noticed Justin Summers standing in front of me. He got his ice cream and went to sit at a picnic bench under the trees. When I got my ice cream, I joined him.

"Where'd you get your law degree?" I asked him as we licked our cones.

"Same place where I went to college: UVA. I got a partial scholarship and took a loan out for the rest of it. I didn't have any loans from college thanks to my football scholarship."

Justin had been the star quarterback of Midville's state-winning team ten years ago.

"Did you have any offers to go pro?"

"I have a bum knee, Anne. I wouldn't last a week in the NFL."

"You're better off as a lawyer. I read an article that said football players have abbreviated life spans."

"I've never regretted my career choice. When I got out of law school, Mr. Benson took me into his practice. He said he'd make me a partner when I turn thirty."

"That's great."

"I think so. I'm happy."

"Did you know that Kevin is home?"

"No. Kevin and I don't exactly correspond."

"Do you keep in touch with Liam?"

"No. After the case was over, we didn't really want to spend much time together."

"Is the case over? Was it officially closed?"

"No. Technically it's still open, but it's been put in the cold case category. The only thing that might make the police open it is if someone found Leslie's body. Which is unlikely after all this time."

"You're sure she was killed, then?"

He licked a drop from the side of his cone. "They found a baseball bat with her blood on it. Yes, I think she was killed."

"I think so too. I just can't imagine you or Kevin or Liam doing it." I took a bite of my own cone. "Someone else must have killed her and disposed of the body."

Justin raised his eyebrows. "Why are we talking about this?"

I sighed. "I don't know. Coming home like this, with time on my hands, it just keeps coming back to me. My mother and father hustled me off to boarding school right after it happened, so I missed the investigation."

"It was pretty awful. The police practically said that it was Liam or Kevin or me. They just didn't have any proof. So now the three of us have to go through life wondering if people think we are killers."

I nibbled on the edge of my cone. "If you feel like that I would have thought you'd leave town and not come back to practice."

He wiped some ice cream off his mouth with a napkin. "Mr. Benson made me such a good offer, and then there was Lauren. All of her friends are in this area. She didn't want to move."

"I imagine it's pretty well forgotten by now."

"It is. But every time I see Kevin or Liam, I think about it. Someone killed her, Anne. She didn't run away—not Leslie."

A little drip of ice cream fell onto my hand and I licked it off. Justin finished his cone, smiled and said, "It was nice talking to you, Anne."

"It was nice talking to you too." I watched as Justin went off to his car.

*   *   *

I drove back home, still thinking about Justin. He really had had a fantastic high-school career. What Bruce Springsteen would call the "glory days." I bet a lot of my contemporaries used him as their lawyer. They'd figure he had to be good at the law, he was so good at everything else.

I had been a lowly sophomore when Justin was a senior, and the only reason he knew me was because I had sometimes been included in the circle that had formed around Leslie the summer after her graduation. I remembered how Liam and Kevin had come home from their boarding school, full of excitement from graduation and anticipation at entering the University of Virginia in the fall. It hadn't taken long for them to meet Leslie.

My mind was preoccupied with the past the whole drive home, and after I parked the car and sat on the porch, I shut my eyes and let the past engulf me. Once again I was sixteen years old and asking my parents if I could go to a barbeque at Leslie's house.

My mother wasn't keen on my going. "That's the fast crowd from school," she worried. "I'm sure there'll be drinking. I wouldn't put it past Andy to get a keg. He lets Leslie have everything she wants."

We were in the kitchen and my mother was making dinner. "I promise I won't drink any beer," I said. "And Liam is going. He'll take care of me."

My mother was chopping an onion. "From what I hear, Liam is going to be too busy with Leslie to have much time for you, Anne."

"Leslie has a boyfriend. She's with Justin Summers."

My mother sniffed and blinked her eyes. "She was with Justin when Justin was the best pickings around.

Now that Liam and Kevin are home, her horizon has expanded."

"Kevin is better looking than Liam."

"Yes, he is."

"If she drops Justin maybe she'll take up with Kevin."

My mother put down her knife. "Honey, I wish you would get over this crush you have on Liam. He's too old for you."

"He's only two years older. Lots of senior boys have sophomore girlfriends. Anyway, I'm a junior now, not a sophomore."

"In sophistication Liam is at least ten years older than you, Anne. He comes from a family where you have to grow up fast. You've had a more sheltered life."

"Don't you like Liam, Mom? I thought you liked him!"

"Of course I like Liam. Both your father and I are very fond of him."

"Then why isn't it okay for me to like him?"

"It's okay for you to like him, but not as a boyfriend, Anne. As I said before, he's too old for you."

I said stubbornly, "I want to go to this party. Leslie invited me and I want to go."

"We'll compromise. Your father will drive you and pick you up at eleven."

"Mom!"

"Take it or leave it, Anne."

"Oh, all right." I stomped out of the kitchen and threw some sticks for the dogs to relieve my frustration.

Daddy took me to the party and came in with me to make certain that Leslie's parents were going to be there.

"If they're not here you're going home," he told me.

I was mortified to be escorted by my father and when

he went up to Mr. Bartholomew and spoke to him I wanted to cringe.

The two men spoke together for a few minutes, then Mr. Bartholomew put a hand on my father's shoulder. Daddy said something, then he turned and walked back to me. "It's okay, Leslie's father is going to be here. I'll pick you up at eleven."

"Okay," I said sullenly.

My father left and I moved shyly to join the gathering of young people on the back patio. Unfortunately, the crowd did not include Liam.

Andy Bartholomew built the family farm, Thornton Hill, ten years before. It had white clapboard siding and was as big as a hotel, with windows everywhere. I had never been inside, but all of those windows must have made it very bright.

The back patio was brick and very large. Hamburger and hotdog rolls were piled on a big gas grill, and there was a keg. A crowd of seniors, dressed in khaki or jean shorts and T-shirts, had broken up into small groups and were drinking beer and laughing and talking with the comfortable ease of people who knew each other very well. I knew most of them by sight, but I was quite sure that none of them knew me.

I felt like I was the only girl present who didn't have blonde hair.

Mom was right, I thought dismally. *I shouldn't have come.*

Then salvation arrived. Liam came around the corner of the house and advanced out on to the patio. I went to him the way a steel shaving flies to a magnet.

"What are you doing here, Annie?" he asked.

"Leslie invited me."

His blue eyes narrowed slightly. "She did? When?"

"She called me yesterday."

"Ah."

"What's 'ah'? Is there something wrong in her inviting me?"

"I'm surprised your parents let you come."

"Daddy is picking me up at eleven."

"Liam." It was Leslie herself. She wore jean shorts and a white shirt, which she had tied to expose her perfect midriff. Her golden hair hung loose around her shoulders and her eyes were a brilliant green. She was stunning.

Liam gave her a long, silent look. Then he said, "How's it going, Leslie?"

She linked her arm in his. "Come along with me. There's something I want to show you."

I watched them walk away feeling like the little match girl with her nose pressed up against the windows of the rich. I wished I hadn't come.

"How about a soda?" I turned and it was Andy Bartholomew. "Your father doesn't approve of beer, but I can offer you a Coke, or a Sprite."

I blushed. "I don't want to be a trouble, Mr. Bartholomew."

"Not at all. Come with me and we'll fix you up."

Andy Bartholomew had been a halfback for the New York Giants and a few years after retirement, he had bought this property in Virginia and built a home and a stable. He was a very large man and whenever I had met him he had always been genial. My dad had once said he was the perfect conversational partner; his two topics were horses and football.

I accepted a Sprite from the table where the soda was

being kept and he said, "If you want to go home early, Anne, just let me know. I'll be happy to take you."

Did I look that out of place?

"Thank you," I said dismally.

I was standing there feeling very lonely when Kevin came in. I was about to go over to him when Leslie appeared out of nowhere and went to his side. In an almost exact replica of her greeting Liam, she put her hand on Kevin's arm.

"There you are, Annie." It was Liam, coming up behind me. "What are you doing, trying to get some pointers from Leslie?"

"I thought that Justin was her boyfriend."

"That's right. He was."

"They broke up?"

"That's what I heard. He's not here tonight, if you notice."

He was holding a glass in his hand that wasn't beer. "What's that?" I asked.

"Scotch."

"Where did you get it?" I asked suspiciously. "There's only beer and soda out here."

He smiled. "Leslie has a secret stash."

Leslie was leading Kevin in our direction. "Liam, Anne," she said. "Are you hungry? My dad is going to grill hamburgers."

Everyone gathered around the grill and Mr. Bartholomew joked with the crowd of boys. When he had finished grilling and gone inside, Leslie rolled a couple of joints and passed them around.

They went from hand to hand and finally one came to me.

My parents would kill me if they ever found out that I

had smoked marijuana. I lifted the joint to my lips, then someone snatched it out of my hand.

It was Liam. "Your father would murder me if he found out that I allowed you to smoke pot," he said. "Stick to the soda, Annie."

"Oh, don't be such a spoilsport," Leslie said.

I was secretly relieved, but I made a token protest. "I'm not a baby, Liam."

"Don't smoke pot, Annie."

"You do."

"Yes, but you're better than me. Come on, I'm going to take you home."

"Are you serious?" Leslie asked.

"Yes. Why did you invite her? She's too young."

"She's always hanging around you. I thought she'd like to come to the party if you were here."

I felt like I was two years old, being talked about like this.

Liam said, "Come on, Annie." He turned to go.

"Liam," Leslie said sharply, "Are you coming back?"

I waited, hoping that he would say no.

He said over his shoulder, "I'll be back." Then, to me, "Now let's get going, brat."

I had come because I had wanted to be near Liam, but I couldn't have been happier to leave. "I'm sorry to be such a nuisance," I said when I was inside his new BMW convertible, a graduation present from his parents.

"Leslie shouldn't have invited you. That's not your kind of crowd, Annie."

"Is it your kind of crowd?"

"I fit in a lot better than you do."

"Are you in love with Leslie?"

He laughed. "Not yet, but I'm working on it."

We pulled up outside my house.

"I don't like Leslie," I said.

"Then why did you go to her party?"

Because you were going to be there. But what I said was, "I thought it would be rude to refuse."

"Come on," he said. "Out of the car. Your father will be glad I saved him a trip."

Reluctantly, I climbed out of the car and began to walk toward my front door. He stayed until I was safely into the house.

Thinking back now, from the vantage point of age twenty-six, I could see that that barbeque was the start of the rivalry between Liam and Kevin over Leslie. It was a rivalry that went on all summer and culminated in Leslie's disappearance on August 15. The only clue to her vanishing was the bloody baseball bat that had been found in the summerhouse that stood at the far end of the lawn at Wellington.

I leaned back in my wicker chair, stared over the porch rail, and let my mind return to the day when I had heard the news of her disappearance.

I had been out at the training track watching my father work with a pair of yearlings in the starting gate when my mother came up to me.

"Lesley's gone missing," she said. "Do you have any idea where she could be?"

I looked at her blankly. "Missing? What do you mean missing?"

"She didn't come home last night and no one can find her."

"You mean she didn't come home after the Hunt Ball?"

"That's right. Apparently, she told her parents that either Liam or Kevin would take her home, so they left without her. They didn't miss her until this morning, when her mother looked in her room and found the bed unslept in."

"Oh my God. Did either Kevin or Liam take her home?"

"No. She went missing from the ball itself."

"Have the Bartholomews called the police?"

"Yes. Technically they're supposed to wait twenty-four hours before they start searching, but Andy persuaded them to start immediately. It isn't like Leslie not to come home."

The police found the baseball bat in the summerhouse when they searched it late in the afternoon. It had been stained with blood and DNA tests showed that the blood belonged to Leslie. But they had never found a body.

I was still thinking about all of this when my mother pulled into the driveway. She came up on the porch, put down her books, sat in the second wicker chair, and began to sob.

"Oh Mom," I said helplessly. "Oh Mom."

"I've been crying all the way home in the car. I can't seem to stop. I just miss him so much, Anne. There's this great chasm in my life where he used to be."

"I know," I said. I put my hand over hers where it rested on the table.

She continued to cry. I kept my hand where it was until her sobs began to abate. "Can you get me another tissue?" she asked.

I went into the house and came out with a box of Kleenex. She blew her nose. "I'm sorry, honey."

"There's nothing to be sorry about. And there's noth-

ing I can say to make it better. You're just going to have
to go through the grieving, Mom. There's no way around
it."

"I know."

"How about a cup of tea?"

"Okay."

We both went into the kitchen and I set the kettle on
the stove to heat up. We had just sat down at the table to
wait when someone knocked on the front door.

It was Liam's father.

"Hello, Senator," I said.

He gave me a warm smile. "Hello Anne. Is your
mother around?"

"Yes, come in, please."

"Who is it?" my mother called from the kitchen.

The senator walked through the short hall and stepped
into the kitchen. "It's just me, Nancy. I came to see how
you were doing."

"Senator Wellington. How nice of you to come."
Mom's eyes were still red.

"I wish there was something I could do to help you."

"Thank you, but there's nothing."

"Don't worry about the house. You can stay for as long
as you like."

"Thank you. Liam said that as well. But I'm going to
look for a house in town."

"Would you like a cup of tea, Senator?" I asked.

"That would be very nice."

"Sit down then, and you sit down as well, Mom. I'll
make the tea."

I listened to the two of them talking as I put three
teabags in the teapot and waited for the water to boil.

Lawrence Wellington was in his mid-fifties and looked

younger. He was tall and lean and tan and fit, with blond, gray-streaked hair and gray eyes. He had Liam's arrogant nose. He had been born to wealth and position and both of those things hung about him like an aura. You knew you were in the presence of someone very high up in the world when you were with Lawrence Wellington.

The kettle whistled and I filled the teapot and put it on the table, then I put out cups and saucers, foregoing our usual mugs. Mom poured the tea while I unearthed some cookies from the pantry and laid them on a plate.

When I sat down, the senator was talking about Daddy. "He was one of the most highly respected men in Midville," he told my mother. "His word was like gold."

I felt tears sting my own eyes. It was true. Diogenes would have found his honest man if he had found my father.

"And you, Anne," he said, turning to me. "You've grown into a beauty."

"Thank you."

"It's hard to believe that you were once that skinny little girl who followed Liam around like a puppy."

I winced at his description of me. It matched everyone else's.

"Anne is a veterinarian now, Senator," my mother said proudly.

"So I have heard. That's quite an accomplishment." He smiled. "I understand vet school is just as hard, if not harder, than medical school."

"It was hard enough," I said.

"Are you practicing yet?"

"Yes, I'm in an equine practice in Maryland. I took the month off to help Mom find a new place and to move."

He increased the wattage of his smile. When Lawrence

Wellington turned the full force of his magnetic personality on you, you felt it. "How thoughtful of you," he said. "Your dad was terribly proud of you, you know."

"I was proud of him too."

"He was a good man. There aren't many men I can say that about as wholeheartedly as I can say it about your father."

My mother said, "Thank you, Senator. The flowers you sent were just beautiful."

He finished his tea and stood up. "I must be off. Remember, if you have any needs don't hesitate to ask. Pete was like family to us."

"Thank you," my mother said again.

The senator went out.

My mother said, "How sweet of him to stop by that way."

"That's two votes he just put in his pocket," I returned.

"Anne! What a mean-spirited thing to say."

"Sorry, Mom."

"Don't you like the senator?"

In fact, I did not like the senator. Liam didn't like him either. I said, "Did Liam get a chance to tell you about that house he saw for rent in town?"

"Yes. I was just going to tell you about it, as a matter of fact."

I said, "Do you want to take a look at it?"

"Yes. Yes, I do. Perhaps I can go after school tomorrow."

I said, "We'll ring Liam later and find out the details. I have to talk to him anyway about the yearlings he wants me to break."

"I didn't know you were going to help with the yearlings, " Mom said.

"He asked me to. Daddy's absence leaves a big hole in the farm operation. The yearlings have to be prepped for the July sale and Daddy had just started working with them."

"That's kind of you, honey."

I shrugged.

"Well, I have some papers to grade. I think I'll put an hour in on them before dinner."

I looked at her. She was a pretty woman, my mother, with soft blond hair and large brown eyes. I had inherited her eyes, but my hair was brown, like my dad's. I went over to her, put my arms around her and held her tight. "I love you, Mommy," I said.

"I love you too, honey."

We both sniffled a little, then she went out to the porch to gather up her books and I looked in the refrigerator for something to make for dinner.

CHAPTER 4

There are a number of ways to break a young thoroughbred. The aim of breaking is to teach the horse to carry weight on its back, to steer with bridle and bit, and to travel in the company of other horses. Daddy always took his time with this, and as a result he turned out calm, self-confident horses who were a pleasure for the next trainer to deal with.

Liam told me that Daddy had already started the horses long reining, which entailed putting a light harness with a bit on the young horse and attaching long reins. The trainer then walked behind the youngster, holding the reins and teaching the colt or filly to go left when pressure was put on the left rein and right when pressure was put on the right rein.

There were twenty-five yearlings to be broken this spring. Jacko Scott had helped my father for years and he took me around too, commenting on each horse's progress and temperament.

"They've been long-reining for almost three weeks," he told me. "Your Dad was going to start to pony them for conditioning." Ponying involved leading the youngster while riding another horse, preferably one who was bombproof.

"Okay," I said. "Let's get to work."

I had Jacko and two other exercise riders to work with, and while Jacko and I worked with half of the youngsters with long reins, the exercise riders ponied the other half. Then we switched groups and did the same thing again.

By the time we finished, it was three o'clock. I went back to the house, showered and was sitting on the porch with a cup of tea when Mom drove up. She had a strange look on her face as she came up the stairs.

"What's wrong?" I asked. "Didn't you like the house?"

"Oh, the house is fine. I told the agent I'd rent it."

"Then why are you looking so anxious?"

She put her books on the table and sat down. "There's a rumor going around town that a body was found in the Stanley woods."

My heart jumped. "What?"

"John Kelleher was at the police station when Frank Stanley came in to say his dog had found a body. It had been buried but evidently the heavy rain we've been having washed away a lot of the dirt."

My hand went to my mouth. "Oh my God. Do you think it could be Leslie?"

Mom sat down and stared at me somberly. "I think it probably is. Who else has disappeared around here?"

"Jesus, Mary and Joseph," I said.

"Amen."

"Has Liam heard this news?"

She shook her head. "I don't know."

"It was found on the Stanley property? I thought the police searched there!"

"They did, but she'd been buried. She was only found now because the grave became uncovered with the rain."

"Oh my God," I said. "This is going to open up the whole thing all over again."

"If it's Leslie, it will."

"It has to be Leslie. Who else can it be?"

"I hope it is her," my mother said. "Perhaps the Bartholomews will have some kind of closure now. It must be dreadful, the not knowing for sure what happened."

"I suppose that's true," I said. Selfishly, I had been thinking about what it would mean for Liam. But for Leslie's parents . . . and for Leslie herself . . .

I remembered the way she had looked the night of the Hunt Ball, the night she disappeared. She had been wearing a gold dress that matched her gold hair. Kevin had called her the Golden Girl.

Now she was just something a dog had found.

I shivered. It was terrible. Poor Leslie.

My mother went into the house and I remained on the porch, staring at a pot of flowers standing on the stairs and thinking back to that night she had disappeared.

There had been a party at Wellington for the members of the Wellington Hunt that night and I had gone with my mother and father.

The house had looked beautiful. All of the furniture had been pushed back in the salon and a three-piece orchestra played music for dancing. The dining-room table was spread with a sumptuous array of food. All of the guests were in formal evening attire and even I wore a long dress and high-heeled sandals, my hair done in a French twist instead of my usual ponytail.

Senator and Mrs. Wellington were standing in the

front hall to greet their guests. Liam's mother looked lovely and her eyes clear as she spoke to me. "How grown up you look, Anne. That's a very pretty dress."

"Thank you, Mrs. Wellington."

My parents and I moved first into the library, where a number of people were gathered. I looked around for Liam.

Leslie was in the corner standing in front of the Federal breakfront that held a writing desk and a collection of rare books. Kevin was with her. She saw me and signaled for me to join them.

"I'm going to talk to Leslie and Kevin," I told my parents and they nodded and let me move away.

Leslie and Kevin were drinking champagne and as a waiter went by with a tray full of glasses, Kevin snagged a glass for me. I took a sip and said, "Where's Liam?"

Leslie gave me an amused look. "He's around here somewhere."

Kevin grinned at me. "You look great, Anne."

"Thank you. So do you."

And it was true. Kevin in a tuxedo was something to behold. My eyes went to Leslie. She was wearing a gold dress and her hair was loose around her shoulders. She looked absolutely gorgeous.

"You look beautiful, Leslie," I said.

"Thank you." She was so accustomed to compliments that she merely accepted them as her due.

As I took another swallow of champagne, Kevin signaled the waiter, who came over with his tray of drinks. Both Kevin and Leslie took another glass.

"Alyssa is sober tonight," Leslie commented.

Kevin said, "Yes. Uncle Lawrence read her the riot act. I heard him."

"I wonder that they stay together; they certainly don't seem happy."

"Aunt Alyssa is Catholic and doesn't believe in divorce."

Leslie laughed. "How uncomfortable for her."

I took another sip of my champagne. "This is good."

Leslie smiled at me. "It's delicious. I always like to start a party with champagne."

She was always nice to me, which only made me hate her more. I didn't want her to be nice. I wanted her to be a bitch. If she were mean to me, Liam would get mad at her.

Leslie and Kevin had each finished their second glass of champagne.

"If you've had enough of the bubbly, the bar is set up in the family room," Kevin said.

"Sounds good to me," Leslie replied.

"Come on, Anne, and I'll get you another glass of champagne," Kevin said.

I looked with a little surprise at my empty glass. "Okay."

The three of us crossed the hall and went into the salon where people were dancing. We passed through and went into the room just beyond it. This was a less formal room, with comfortable furniture, a television set and a sound system. It was where the family usually hung out. A bar had been set up here and Leslie and Kevin went up to it and got glasses of Scotch on the rocks.

I wondered that nobody monitored their underage drinking.

"Leslie. How nice to see you here." It was Randal Johnson, a member of the hunt. He was twenty-six and had that look on his face that men seemed to get when they beheld Leslie.

"My dad is a member, so I got to come," she said.

Kevin said, "I got to come because I live here."

"Oh sorry, don't you know each other?" Leslie said. She made introductions.

"Would you care to dance with me?" Randal said.

"Sure," Leslie replied. She put her half-drunk scotch down on a table and went with Randal into the next room where the music was playing.

Kevin looked at me. "What will it be, Anne? Do you want to dance or do you want to go and get some food?"

"You don't have to take care of me, Kevin. You can wait here for Leslie if you want."

"I don't want," he said shortly. "So which will it be?"

"Food, then."

"Good choice. Come along." I followed him back through the salon, into the hallway, then behind the stairs where an addition had been put on the house for the dining room and kitchen.

Liam was in the dining room, talking to Maisie Fullerton, one of the hunt members. I approved. Maisie was thirty, at least.

"There you are," Kevin said to him. "Anne was looking for you."

He gave me a mechanical smile. "You look very nice in that dress."

Nice, I thought. *I bet you've never told Leslie she looked nice.*

"Thank you," I said.

"What are you drinking?" Liam said to Kevin.

"Scotch."

"I think I'll get some."

"Leslie is there. She's dancing with Randal Johnson."

Liam's face darkened. "I don't care where Leslie is."

My heart leaped. It sounded as if Liam was mad at her.

Kevin said lightly, "Come on, Liam. Don't be sore. What does it matter that Leslie gave a little of her time to me?"

Liam looked grim. "Time? She gave you something more than time."

Kevin's golden eyebrows shot up. "You can't know that."

"I saw how the two of you looked when you came back to the party last night. I don't think you were just talking."

"What does it matter what we were doing? No one would have noticed if you hadn't made a big deal of it."

Liam said through his teeth, "I don't share. Leslie can have me or she can have you, but she can't have us both."

The two of them had forgotten that I was there and I stood very still and quiet so they wouldn't notice me.

Kevin's blue eyes glittered. He said, "We were all drunk."

"I know."

Kevin shrugged. "Have you tried the food?"

"Not yet. First I'm going to try the Scotch."

"Okay. See you later."

I put some food on a plate and let Liam walk away.

I had taken a few bites of ham when someone said my name. I turned and saw one of the boys from school. He was a senior but we had worked together on the school newspaper. "Hi, Michael," I said. "What are you doing here?"

"I came with Kim Malone."

I nodded. Kim was a senior also, but she was not part of Leslie's crowd. She was a horse person, like me.

"You look very pretty," he said.

"Thank you." Pretty was better than nice.

We stood talking for a few minutes and then Michael asked if I wanted to dance. I was anxious to get back to the salon so I could find out what Liam was doing, so I agreed.

The next few hours passed uneventfully. I danced with Michael, with my father, with Kevin and with Liam. I spent some time with Justin Summers, who had come as someone's date. I tried to keep an eye on Leslie, but she disappeared for a while. At least she didn't disappear with Liam, because I was watching him too. I also drank two more glasses of champagne.

It was after midnight when I went out to the back patio to cool off. I was flushed from all of the champagne, and it wasn't until the door had closed behind me that I realized I wasn't alone. Liam and Leslie were standing in front of the fountain that was the centerpiece for the backyard garden. They were too far away for me to hear what they were saying, but they appeared to be having a fight.

I should have left. I had no business spying on Liam's private moments, but I couldn't tear myself away. All summer I had been miserable watching Liam and Leslie together. If they were going to break up, I wanted to know about it.

Suddenly, Leslie reached up and pulled Liam's head down to her. For a long moment, while my heart silently cracked, they kissed. Then Liam pushed her away. He said something and her face blazed with anger. She shouted at him. I could hear her voice although I couldn't make out what she was saying. Liam said something back. He looked furious.

I don't want to be caught here if one of them comes back to the house. Slowly and carefully I opened he back door and let myself back inside. I waited by the door, pretending I was just coming out when they came back.

Liam came first. His eyes were blazing with anger as he almost bumped into me. "Get out of the way, Annie," he said grimly and went on by.

Instead of pursuing him, I waited for Leslie. Her color was higher than usual as she came in the door, but she looked more composed than Liam had. She went into the dining room and I saw her begin to talk to Justin Summers.

Shortly after that, my parents left to go home and I had to leave with them.

The next day we found out that Leslie had never come home. Her father had driven her to the party and stayed for a while, but had left when Leslie promised that either Kevin or Liam would drive her home. Kevin said he looked for her but, when he didn't find her, he assumed Liam had driven her home. Liam said he had a headache and had gone upstairs to bed. He said he hadn't spoken to Leslie during the party.

The police talked to me as well. I said I had spoken to Leslie at the start of the party, but that was all. I said I had no idea where she could have gone. I never said a word about the argument I had witnessed between Leslie and Liam. If Liam wanted it to be known, he could volunteer the information. I would die before I would give him away.

The pot of flowers I had been looking at began to blur, and I blinked and came back to the present.

There was going to be another murder investigation. Leslie hadn't buried herself. Someone had hit her with a baseball bat and then buried her in the Stanley woods.

If the police began making inquiries again, Liam might be in danger. After all, it was his baseball bat, even if his fingerprints had not been on it. Someone had wiped the bat clean and, now that there was a body, the police would be looking for more evidence.

And I was more determined than ever not to tell anyone what I had seen.

Midville was shaken by the discovery of Leslie's body. Andy and Gloria were well known and well-liked by everyone in town. The undeniable confirmation that their daughter was indeed dead was hard on them, and the town sympathized.

I found out about the police investigation from an impeccable source. Michael Bates was a policeman in town and he called to ask me out to dinner after we met in the Safeway in town. Wait long enough and you would eventually meet all of Midville in the Safeway.

We went to see Kevin's new movie and then out for drinks and a burger afterward. We sat in a booth in the Coach Stop and I quizzed him about the investigation.

"Her skull was caved in," he told me soberly. "It will be in the papers tomorrow. Someone used that bat with great efficiency."

I shuddered, as if I felt that blow upon my own skull. "Poor Leslie," I said. "What a terrible way to end."

"At least her parents will have something to bury now."

We were both quiet for a minute as we thought about

that. Then I said, "Is the inquiry into her death going to be reopened?"

"It will have to be. Although, now that ten years have passed, I don't know how we're going to gather new evidence."

I sipped my wine. "There was that Skakel trial. The jury convicted him after twenty years."

"Yeah, but he confessed a number of times. No one has obliged us by confessing that he killed Leslie."

"True."

"Who's in charge of the investigation?"

Michael took a swallow of his beer. "The chief is taking charge. He'll be questioning all the old witnesses, and looking for new ones, I expect."

"Will they think it's Liam?"

He shrugged. Michael was a very nice-looking man, with smooth brown hair and hazel eyes. "I don't know, Anne. It was common knowledge that Liam and Leslie had a falling out. Leslie punished him by going off with Kevin. The night of the Hunt Ball the two weren't speaking to each other. Did Liam kill her in a jealous rage? Maybe, but we have no proof. Justin Summers was at the party also, and everyone knows he was angry at being jilted."

"What about Kevin?" The more suspects the police had, the better, I thought.

"Kevin looks to be in the clear, although he certainly had access to the bat. It seems as if Leslie was in the process of changing from Liam to Kevin, which leaves Kevin with no discernible motive."

"What if it was a stranger?"

He shook his head. "I don't think so, Anne. Why

would Leslie go out to the summerhouse with a stranger? And why would a stranger want to kill her?"

"I don't know. There are these serial killers who just go around killing people indiscriminately."

"I don't think that's the case here. Leslie was killed by someone she knew."

I sighed.

"Hey!" he said. "We're on a date. Let's talk about ourselves."

"Okay," I said. "You go first."

"What do you want to know?"

"How long have you been in police work?"

"I went to college and got my degree in law enforcement. When I graduated I was lucky enough to find an opening on the Midville force. I've been on the job for six years now."

"And you like it?"

"Very much."

"That's good. And what about your love life?"

He took another swallow of beer. "I married Kim Malone after I graduated from college. We divorced last year."

"Oh, I'm sorry."

He shrugged. "Don't be. It was just one of those things. We had gone together for so long that I think we got married because we were expected to. Anyway, it didn't work out."

I swallowed a piece of my hamburger.

He said, "How about you? Any serious boyfriends?"

"One. We almost got engaged, but then I realized that I liked him but I didn't love him."

"You were lucky to find that out before you got married."

"I know."

"Is there anybody special in your life right now?"

There was always someone special in my life, only he didn't know it.

"No," I said. "No one special."

He smiled at me. "That's good."

It occurred to me—actually it had occurred to me when I accepted his invitation—that keeping in touch with Michael would be a good way for me to keep in touch with what was going on in the murder investigation. I gave him my best smile in return.

CHAPTER 5

The Bartholomews held a private service and burial for Leslie, and life went on in a seemingly normal way in Midville. It wasn't normal, though. There was an undercurrent of anxiety in the town as the police conducted their questioning of all the people who had attended the Wellington Hunt Ball.

Chief Murphy came out to the house one day after school and questioned Mom and me about the ball. Mom had nothing to tell him. "What about you, Anne?" the chief inquired. "You were a part of Leslie's crowd. Do you know anything about this fight between Leslie and Liam?"

My heart sank. He knew about the fight. Had someone else seen Liam and Leslie together that night?

"I . . . I don't know what you mean," I said weakly.

"I've been told that Liam and Leslie had a falling out the night before the ball. Do you know anything about that?"

Relief flooded me. He didn't know about the fight I had witnessed. I said, "No. I really wasn't part of that crowd, Chief Murphy. I was only a sophomore and they were seniors. I hung with them sometimes because I'm a friend of Liam's. That's all. I really don't know anything about a fight between Liam and Leslie."

After a few more questions, the chief left and Mom said to me, "I hope you're not hiding something from the police, honey."

I gave her a blank look. "What would I be hiding?"

"I don't know, but you kept saying 'really' and you usually do that when you're hiding something."

"I do? I never knew that."

"Are you hiding something?"

I looked her straight in the eye. "No, Mom. I am not hiding anything."

Satisfied, she nodded.

Mom had gone inside and I was still sitting on the porch when Liam pulled up in the farm pickup. He got out, followed by a dog, and came up to the porch. I watched him, my heart increasing its beat as it always did whenever I saw him.

One lock of curly black hair fell over his forehead, as usual, and his deep blue eyes were set like gems in his tanned face. He exuded magnetism. He didn't have Kevin's looks (who did?) but even Kevin did not have Liam's sexual force.

"Do you have time to go over the horses with me?" he asked.

"Sure," I said over the beat of my heart.

He sat down. "I appreciate your helping me out like this, Annie. Having you in charge is as good as having Pete."

"What a lovely compliment."

"You have a special way with horses. You always have. I respect that in you."

In fact, it was the reason Liam had always been so tolerant of my tagging along after him. He thought I was great with horses and that gave me a special place in his heart. It's too bad it wasn't the place I wanted.

We spent almost an hour going over all of the yearlings I had been dealing with, discussing their aptitudes and their progress in training. "The Going West colt is very good," I said. "He's curious but trusting. He's got personality. You might have something there."

"He wasn't one of the ones I was thinking of keeping." Most of the yearlings were sent to the big Keeneland sale in July. Wellington kept only a few to race under its own colors.

"I would. I just have a feeling about him."

"Okay, I'll think about it."

We finished discussing the horses and I said, "Would you like something to drink, Liam?"

"I'd love a cup of coffee, if you have it."

"Come on into the kitchen with me and I'll put a pot on."

We went through the house to the kitchen, and Liam sat at the maple table while I put the coffee on. Mom was upstairs.

He looked around. "How many hours did I spend in this kitchen when I was a kid?"

"A lot," I replied.

"I think I spent more time with your parents than I did with my own." He didn't sound bitter, just matter-of-fact.

"I think you did," I agreed. "You were the son Daddy never had."

He sighed. "He was a wonderful man, your father. I learned a lot by watching him—and I don't just mean about horses. I miss him very much."

I brought the coffee to the table. "We all do." I set a

mug in front of him and one at my own place. Then I sat down. "Have you spoken to the police?" I asked.

"Yes." He sounded grim. "They think I did it, Annie. It was my bat and Leslie and I had had a falling out. They think I did it."

"They have no proof of anything," I said earnestly. "Just be careful of what you say to them."

He looked into my eyes. "Do you think I did it?"

I looked directly back. "No."

He laughed a little shakily. "Faithful little Annie. I can always count on you."

I forced a smile. "I've been seeing Michael Bates. He's on the police force, you know, and from what he says the police don't have enough evidence to indict anyone. So just be careful."

He stopped in the act of raising his mug to his lips. "Seeing as in dating?"

"We've gone out once."

He stared at me. "I didn't know that."

"Sorry I didn't ask for your permission," I said.

He looked uncomfortable. "I'm sorry, I didn't mean to jump all over you. I'm just not used to thinking of you with anyone but me."

I let that statement sink into my brain as he went on to something else.

Later, when he'd left, I thought about it some more.

Could I possibly get Liam's attention by going out with someone else? I'd never dated anyone when we were young, and when I finally did start to date, I'd been away at school.

I'm not used to thinking of you with anyone but me.

They were the most encouraging words I'd ever heard

from him. Perhaps, if I continued to see Michael Bates, Liam would see me with new eyes.

After awhile, I went upstairs to my bedroom to change my clothes. I went into the bathroom to wash my face and stood there staring at myself. Maybe I had to make a few changes to force Liam to see me with new eyes.

First there was my hair. I wore it as I had always worn it, shoulder length so I could easily put it up in a ponytail. It was thick and shiny and brown, with a scintilla of curl.

Maybe I should get it cut. Mom's hair is short and it looks great.

I looked at the rest of my face, taking in my mother's large, brown eyes and my grandmother's nice, straight nose. I was a pretty young woman, and men usually liked me. So what could I do to make Liam look at me as a woman and not as his little sister?

I'll get rid of the ponytail, I thought. *That'll do for starters. I'll make an appointment at the beauty parlor in town as soon as I get a chance.*

I made a note to ask my mother for the name of her hairdresser, then went to the closet to get out my clothes.

The following day, we started getting the young horses ready to wear saddles. We began in a stall, where they felt safe, with someone just half laying across the youngster's back while a helper maintained control with a lead shank. Getting a horse accustomed to weight on its back is trickier than one might think. Nature programmed the horse to fear weight on its back; in earlier times, it would mean that a predator, such as a lion, had leaped down upon it. Every instinct the young horse has goes on alarm when he feels the weight of a person leaning on his back.

For some horses this training is truly traumatic and for

others it is easy as pie. You never know what the reaction is going to be until you do it. Some horses let you put a saddle on almost right away, and others make you wait a month.

Daddy's program was always the same, though his timetable was tailored to fit the individual horse. The youngsters went from feeling weight on their back, to a rider getting on them bareback, to a saddle just resting on their back, to a saddle being girthed, to a rider actually getting in the saddle. Once they had experienced all of these things successfully in the stall, they were ready to leave the stable for the track.

I had finished for the day and was walking back toward the house when a Mercedes pulled up beside me and Senator Wellington said, "Can I give you a lift, young lady?"

I said, "I'm dirty. You don't want me in that nice car."

"Sure I do," he said and leaned over to open the door. "Come on. You must be tired."

"I'm never tired," I said truthfully.

"Ah. How wonderful to be young."

We chatted casually as he drove along the farm roads, leaving a trail of dust in our wake. When we got to the front of my house, he turned off the engine and said to me, "I'm worried about Liam."

My heart jumped. "Because they've found Leslie's body?"

"Yes. I don't like the kind of questions Murphy has been asking. And I don't like Liam's hostile way of answering. It makes him seem guilty."

"You know Liam," I said. "He always goes on the offensive."

"Yes, but it isn't smart just now. Will you talk to him, Anne? He won't listen to me."

"Me?"

"Yes. He values you. If you talk to him, he'll listen."

"Well, I'll try," I said doubtfully.

He gave me a warm smile. "Thank you. You've grown into a beautiful young woman—but I suppose everyone tells you that."

I was a little embarrassed to be receiving such a compliment from Lawrence Wellington. "Th . . . thank you," I stuttered.

He reached over and patted my hand. "How charming you are. Don't change, Anne."

"I'll try not to," I mumbled.

When he had driven away I climbed up the steps of my house, confused. Had Lawrence Wellington been coming on to me?

No, it couldn't be, I decided. He was just being nice to a girl he had known almost all her life.

I thought that he must be really worried about Liam if he had felt the need to come to me.

The second week in April, the investigation into Leslie's death was pushed off the front page as everyone's thoughts focused on the upcoming Wood Memorial race, which would be held at Aqueduct in New York City on April 14. Someday Soon would be running; it was his last prep race before the Derby, and it would give everyone an idea of how he would perform.

For Liam and the Wellington farm's breeding business, the outcome of the Triple Crown races was vital. If Liam could stand a Kentucky Derby winner (as well as the Derby winner's sire) at the farm, he would be able to cash in on stud fees—at least for the first few years when everyone would be wanting to breed to the hot new stallions. There was usually a lull then, while people waited to see how the stud's offspring did on the track. That was the key. If they did well, then the mares would continue to come. The big money in racing wasn't at the track; it was in the breeding shed.

Liam wasn't going to New York for the race; there was too much happening on the farm for him to leave. He was kind enough to call Daddy and me horse whisperers, but Liam was a whisperer in his own right. He particularly loved his mares. It wasn't smart to get too attached to the young horses; so many of them had to be sold. But the mares stayed and Liam loved them. He was there when they conceived their babies, he was there while they carried their babies and he was there when their babies were born. I remember Daddy teasing him that he was like a surrogate husband.

On April 14, a crowd of us gathered in the family room at Wellington to watch the running of the Wood. CBS had a half-hour show leading up to the race, and most of it was devoted to Bob Baffert's horse, Honor Bright. In a brief interview with John Ford, Someday Soon's trainer, the reporter commented on how much faster Honor Bright had been training than Someday Soon. "We're training for stamina," Ford replied. "This is a horse that comes from off the pace. We want to see how he'll do in the Wood as a prep for the Derby."

"How good is the Baffert horse?" I asked Liam as we stood together behind the sofa and watched the TV.

"He's a good horse. Baffert has a big mouth, but he knows his horses. Honor Bright is legit."

"Do you think Someday Soon can catch him?"

He looked at me. "We'll see very soon, won't we? John's instructions to Miles Santos were not to join Honor Bright in a battle for the lead. He was to ride as he had in the Florida Derby and come from off the pace."

My mother said, "How I wish Pete could have been here."

I looked at her. Everything reminded her of Daddy's absence. I was grieving too, but my life had not greatly changed. Mom's had.

Someday Soon was the second favorite, after Honor Bright. We stood tensely watching as the horses were loaded into the starting gate.

"He doesn't have to win," Liam said. "He just needs to finish well. The Derby is a longer race."

The announcer said, "Someday Soon is going in quietly." I watched as the bright royal blue and white of Wellington's silks went into the box.

"Come on, baby," Liam muttered. "You can do it."

And they're off! the announcer said.

Tango With Me, a speed horse, went right to the lead with Honor Bright at his hip. Someday Soon was in the middle of the field, in fifth position, about nine lengths behind. The field held position as they went around the first turn. They galloped along the backside, Someday Soon maintaining his spot off the pace. When they reached the three quarters of a mile mark, the timer said "One-ten," and on the lead Tango With Me began to falter.

Liam said, "Come on, Buster, come on!" Buster had been the Wellington stable nickname for Someday Soon.

Miles Santos found a spot on the rail and gunned Someday Soon through it. He accelerated.

"Here he comes!" my mother cried.

Someday Soon kept coming, passing horses as he thundered down the track.

I felt Liam grab my hand and squeeze it.

Two tiring horses stood between our boy and Honor Bright on the lead, and Someday Soon rocketed by them as if they were standing still. But Honor Bright was not tiring and when his jockey hit him with the whip, he responded.

"Buster's too late to catch him," I cried despairingly.

I was right. Even though Someday Soon was making up ground with every stride, the wire came too soon. Buster was still three lengths behind when Honor Bright crossed the finish line.

A great sigh went around the room, as if everyone had let out their collective breath.

"He did very well," Senator Wellington said. "You have nothing to be ashamed of, Liam."

I felt Liam's hand tighten on mine. He didn't reply.

Mom said, "If it was the Derby, and we had an extra eighth of a mile to run, he would have won."

"Yes, he would have," I agreed. "He was closing at the end."

"That big bay horse had no quit in him, though," Liam said soberly.

I said, "The good thing about all of this is that Buster will no longer be a favorite and that will be less stressful on everyone."

"Get the racing channel and we'll find out how the rest of the Derby preps went," Liam said.

Someone clicked the remote and the station came up. Eventually we got reports from all of the tracks where three-year-olds had run that day. The favorite, Mileaminute, trained by D Wayne Lukas of California, had won the Bluegrass, and in the Arkansas Derby another frontrunner had won. It had not been a good day for come-from-behinders.

"That's okay," Liam said when we turned the TV off. "The California trainers won today; we'll see who wins in the big race."

"Who owns Mileaminute?" my mother asked.

"Prince Salman of Arabia."

"Are there any Coolmore horses entered in the Derby?" I named the single, most powerful force in the racing industry today, the Irish stud run by John Magnier.

"I'm sure they'll have an entry that they're training in Ireland."

Mom said, "Well, our horse is being trained in Kentucky and I hope he wins."

Liam laughed.

We stayed around talking for a while then Liam said, "Who wants to go out to eat? Dinner's on me. I think Buster distinguished himself."

"Sounds good to me," Kevin said. "How about it, Anne? Can you come?"

"It depends on my mother," I said. I had no intention of letting her go back to the house alone.

"Come on, Nancy," Liam said. "We'd love to have you."

At first Mom demurred, but then she gave way. Liam called around for a reservation and the four of us all ended up going to the Horse Shoe Inn for dinner.

The Horse Shoe was not one of the premier restaurants in town. It was a steak and fish place, with a salad bar. Mom and I ordered shrimp and the men ordered steaks. As we sat eating our salads Kevin said, "I hear you went out with Michael Bates, Anne."

My mouth dropped open. "How did you hear that?"

"The old Midville grapevine. He's a cop now, isn't he?"

"Yes. How do you know Michael, Kevin? He wasn't part of Leslie's crowd all those years ago."

"I know about him because you went out with him," Kevin returned. "I've been keeping my eye on you, Anne."

His response startled me and I gave him a look.

"How can someone who looks like you be so unassuming?" Kevin asked with amusement.

I said, "I thought going out with Michael would be a good way to find out about how the investigation is going."

"My God. The poor man. He probably has no idea that you had an ulterior motive."

He was making me sound underhanded. "I like Michael," I said. "He's funny."

Liam said, "Did you have *another* date with him?"

He was frowning. This made me very happy. "Why not?" I asked breezily. "He's nice and he's handsome and he asked me."

Mom said, "You don't want to hurt him, Anne."

I didn't want to do that at all. I had hurt John, the man I had almost been engaged to, and it had not been a pleasant experience.

"All I did was go to a movie with the guy," I protested. "I'm not going to marry him."

"Well I should hope not," Liam said.

"I almost did get married once, or at least I almost got engaged," I said to him.

He said peremptorily, "When was this?"

"A year ago."

His brows furrowed.

I said deliberately, "I'm twenty-six, Liam. I'm not a child anymore."

Kevin said, "So did your boyfriend tell you anything about the investigation?"

"He's not my boyfriend . . ." I began in annoyance. I looked at Liam. "At least not yet," I amended.

"Do you know he's divorced?" Liam asked me.

"Yes, he told me."

"You're Catholic. You can't marry a divorced man."

"For God's sake," I said. "I went out with the man twice and Kevin says he's my boyfriend and Liam thinks I want to marry him. Are they crazy or what, Mom?"

"I think they're a little ahead of themselves," she replied with a smile.

"They certainly are."

"My question still remains," Kevin said. "Did you find out anything new?"

I shrugged. "Nothing that isn't already common knowledge. Leslie was hit with the baseball bat. Apparently the attack took place in the summerhouse and the body was transported to the Stanley woods and buried."

"And I'm the police's favorite candidate for being the murderer," Liam said bitterly.

"You always were," I pointed out. "But they don't have any more evidence now than they had ten years ago. Michael said they didn't have enough to make an arrest."

Liam said intensely, "Well I wish they would find out who did it. I don't relish people thinking I was the one and that I got away with it."

Kevin put down his empty glass. "You avoided each other at the party. That's what I told the police."

Liam said, "I never spoke to Leslie that night, and I

most certainly didn't club her over the head with a base-ball bat."

An alarm bell rang in my brain. I looked at Liam. He seemed perfectly sober, perfectly truthful. Yet he had just told a lie.

Of course he's lying, I thought defensively. *He'd have to be crazy to come out and say he and Leslie had an argument just before she disappeared. The police would be all over him.*

I said, "Andy is really pushing the police. If he wasn't such a high-profile person, I don't think they would have reopened the case."

"Andy thinks I did it." Liam's voice became even more bitter than before. "He acts like I'm unclean. I feel sorry for him and all that, but it isn't fair to me."

My mother said, "To lose a child is a terrible thing. To lose an only child is even worse. And to lose her the way the Bartholomews lost Leslie is unspeakable."

We were all quiet after that. Then dessert was served and we all got into Liam's BMW and went home.

CHAPTER 6

At two in the morning, Liam called me at the house. "Pennyroyal is having problems, Annie. Can you come?"

"I'll be right over," I said.

I put on my jeans, pulled a warm Virginia Tech sweatshirt over my head and ran out the door.

The light over the foaling stall was on in the mare's barn when I arrived and found Liam and Jacko in the stall with a groaning, heaving Pennyroyal.

"The baby is twisted," Liam told me. He looked very pale in the stable light. "One foot is coming out but not the other."

The correct way for a foal to be born was to come out with both front feet first, then the head which was tucked between the front legs, then the rest of the body. One of Pennyroyal's foal's legs was out of position and caught in the birth canal. It would have to be straightened out for her to be able to push out the baby.

Pennyroyal was lying in the straw with one of her foal's forelegs poking out of her vagina. "Do you have gloves?" I asked Liam.

Silently, he handed me a pair of long latex gloves. I

knelt beside Pennyroyal and reached in around the foal, feeling for the other leg.

You have to be strong to turn a foal in the birth canal, which was one of the reasons I worked out with weights. Finally I managed to get the baby righted and the second leg came out of the mare. I reached in, hoping to find the nose between its legs. It was there.

"I think we're out of the woods," I said. "Now it's up to her."

The rest of the birth was a textbook delivery. About ten minutes later, the foal was almost completely out of its mother's womb and a few minutes after that, the baby slid out onto the bed of straw. She was dark bay in color, with a star on her forehead and two white anklets on her hind legs.

"A filly," Liam said with pleasure. He toweled the foal dry of the birthing fluid, to keep her from getting cold in the night air, then placed her in the straw next to her mother so that Pennyroyal could finish the job with her tongue. The licking would encourage the filly to stand.

Usually foals stand for the first time between a half hour and an hour after birth. Pennyroyal continued to lick her baby's haunches and the foal made an effort to get her thin spindly legs under her and stand up. It took a few tries, but she eventually got to her feet.

There are few things more awesome than the way these newborn babies get to their feet in such a short time. Human babies don't walk until almost a year after birth, but foals stand, and nurse, and within a few days Pennyroyal's daughter would be running at her side out in the sunny pasture with the other babies and their mothers.

We left the mother and baby in peace to continue their bonding. "Like a cup of coffee or tea?" Liam asked me as we walked out the barn door.

"Sure," I said. "Your place or mine?"

"We're closer to your place."

"Okay."

We both washed our hands at the sink and I put the kettle on the stove to heat and sat at the table across from him.

"I'm glad you were here, Annie," he said.

"I'm glad I could help."

"I thought of trying to straighten her myself, but I thought a vet would do a better job." He gave me a measuring look. "You're stronger than you look."

"You have to be strong to work with horses. I work out at the gym three days a week."

"Do you have muscles?"

"You bet I do."

"Let's feel." He reached across the table and cupped his hand around my upper arm.

Once again that bolt of electricity shot through me. He dropped his hand and gave me a startled look. Had he felt it too?

"That *is* a muscle," he said.

Maybe he was just surprised that I had a real muscle.

"I know."

The kettle whistled and I went to fill the teacups.

He was looking down at his hands as I brought one of the mugs to the table for him. The usual unruly lock of hair was falling over his forehead and he needed a shave. I put the cup in front of him and he flashed me a quick smile. "Thanks."

I always felt his smile in my heart.

I brought my own mug to the table and took my usual seat. "Mom says she liked the house. Lucky for us you saw that ad."

"Yeah."

I thought he was looking tired. And worried.

"Has anything happened?" I asked.

"Yesterday an auditor showed up to look at the farm books."

I frowned. "What does that mean?"

"I'm not sure, but the farm and the horses belong to my father. They are part of his assets. If he's really in financial trouble, I suppose his creditors could come after the whole shebang."

"Oh Liam, no."

"It's not a happy scenario."

"You don't own any of the horses?"

"Actually, I own Buster. I saved the money to buy Pennyroyal and two other mares, and I paid the stud fees on them when I bred them. So Buster is mine."

"And the rest of the horses are your father's?"

"They belong to the farm, which belongs to my father."

"What made you buy Pennyroyal for yourself?"

"It dawned on me one day that, after years of hard work, I had no financial stake in the farm. I was completely dependent on my father. He paid me a salary and I ran the farm. I decided that I would be better off financially if I bought some horses on my own."

"It sounds as if you made a wise decision."

"Still, I don't know what I'd do if the farm was lost. It's been in my family for almost two hundred years!"

"It would be a terrible shame," I agreed. "But I doubt

things will come to that point, Liam. Your father won't want to sell it. It won't look good for him."

"That's true." He sipped his tea. "It's nice having you home, Annie. I've missed you."

"You've missed my sympathetic ear, you mean."

He smiled. "No matter what happened, I always knew that you'd be on my side."

"That hasn't changed, Liam." I hesitated. Should I say this? But I had never had any secrets from Liam. I said quickly, "I saw you and Leslie together the night of the Hunt Ball, you know. You were out by the fountain and I came out onto the back patio to get some air. You were yelling at each other."

He went perfectly still. His blue gaze got hard. "You never told me this."

"I know I didn't. And I didn't tell anyone else, either."

"Why?"

"Because it would make you even more of a suspect than you already are."

"And that's precisely why I've said nothing about it." His voice was bitter. "Leslie was trying to make me jealous, and she succeeded admirably. I was furious with her, but I didn't kill her, Annie. I promise you, I didn't kill her."

"I never thought you did. That's why I didn't say anything."

"Why are you telling me this now?"

"I don't know. Habit, I guess. We don't keep secrets from each other."

He said, "Are you going to tell the police now?"

I gave him an affronted stare. "How can you ask me such a question? Of course not."

"You must be pretty sure that I didn't do it."

My stare became even more affronted. "Of course you didn't do it."

He put his teacup down. "The thing is, Annie, someone did. And it had to be someone who was at the party. Leslie went out to the summerhouse with someone; I'm sure she didn't just wander out there by herself."

I shivered a little. "I know."

He sighed. "I've thought and thought and I just cannot imagine anyone I know doing such a terrible thing."

I said again, "I know."

We were quiet for a while. Then Liam said, "Enough of such depressing conversation. We should be happy. Pennyroyal has once again given birth to a beautiful baby."

I lifted my teacup. "To Pennyroyal."

Liam touched my cup with his. "To Pennyroyal."

We drank.

He said, "So tell me about this guy you almost got engaged to."

"There's nothing to tell. He was a very nice man and I liked him a lot. I just didn't love him like he loved me. It wouldn't have been fair of me to marry him, feeling the way I did."

"I almost got engaged once myself," Liam offered.

My heart plummeted. "You did? To whom?"

"A girl I met at the University of Virginia. She was a cheerleader."

I immediately pictured a beauty with blue eyes and long straight hair, like Jennifer Aniston's. "What stopped you from getting engaged?" I asked.

"Same thing that stopped you. It just didn't feel right."

I nodded.

There came a step at the door and my mother, wearing pajamas and slippers, peered into the kitchen. "I thought I heard voices down here."

"We didn't mean to wake you, Mom," I said.

"I woke up on my own, and then I heard the voices. Hello, Liam. How are you?"

"Fine, Nancy. Annie just delivered a foal for me, that's why we're up so late."

My mother came further into the kitchen. "Was there trouble?"

"A little. Pennyroyal's foal was coming out with only one foot. Annie turned the baby so that both feet could come out at once. Both mother and daughter are doing well, I'm happy to report."

"Would you like a cup of tea, Mom?"

"No thank you, honey. I'm going back to bed."

"I'll be up in a few minutes."

She nodded and disappeared into the hallway. Liam got to his feet. "I should be getting back home. You need your beauty rest."

I smiled at him in reply.

He came over to where I was sitting, bent and kissed me on the cheek. He was so near that I could feel the warmth from his skin. "Thank you for helping out tonight."

"You're welcome," I returned a little breathlessly.

"By the way, tell your mother if she wants to move herself, I'll be happy to help out with one of the horse vans."

"Thanks, I'll tell her."

"Well . . . I'll see you tomorrow."

He seemed strangely reluctant to leave.

"Oh, Liam. Can you tell Kevin that I'm not going to ride with him tomorrow morning—actually this morning. I think I'll try to catch an extra hour of sleep."

"Are you and Kevin riding out in the mornings?"

"Yes, didn't he tell you?"

He scowled. "He didn't say a word."

"Oh. Well, we're just exercising the hunters. It's good for them."

His scowl didn't lift. "I like to be informed of these things."

"Sorry. I thought Kevin had told you."

"Kevin doesn't tell me anything."

He sounded very stiff.

"Do you want us to stop riding?"

He said through his teeth, "I didn't say that. I just said I like to know when my horses are being ridden."

"Fine," I replied. "So now you know. But I don't want to ride this morning. Will you tell Kevin, please?"

"Yes."

"Goodnight, Liam."

"Goodnight." He paused. "Thanks for helping with Pennyroyal."

"I was happy to be of assistance."

He nodded. "Well . . . goodnight."

"Goodnight."

He went.

I sat back down at the kitchen table and stared into my empty teacup. Well, this looked promising, I thought. Clearly Liam was annoyed that Kevin and I were riding together, and I didn't think it was because we were taking the horses without his permission. I thought about this for a little while and then I yawned, fatigue flooding through me. I gave up thinking and went to bed.

I was working with one of the yearlings in his stall when one of Senator Wellington's assistants came to the stall door. "I'm Brent Walker, Dr. Foster," he said. "Would you mind terribly if I watched? I've always liked horses."

"You can watch as long as you stay quiet and don't get in the way," I said.

"Okay. Thanks."

I turned my attention back to the Going West colt. I was having Jacko get on his back for the first time; always a tricky situation. I gave Jacko a leg up and when the colt felt the man's full weight for the first time, his ears went back.

"It's okay, little boy," I crooned. "You're just fine."

The colt went forward, trying to walk out from under the weight. I let him walk, still holding him by the lead shank. Jacko patted his neck and spoke to him. We kept this up for perhaps five minutes and then Jacko dismounted.

I rubbed the colt's forehead and gave him a piece of sugar. "What a good boy. What a good boy."

"That was fascinating."

I startled at the voice. I had forgotten that Brent Walker was still there.

He smiled at me. "It's a far cry from those old Westerns, where they got on a horse and rode out the bucks."

I smiled back. "The goal is not to scare or alarm the horse. By the time we finish with these exercises, the horse will tolerate a person on his back with relative calmness."

"What are you going to do now?"

"More of the same. We have twenty-five yearlings to break and each one of them gets the same treatment you just witnessed."

"Wow. You sure must have a lot of patience."

A strand of hair had come loose from my ponytail and I took off the rubber band and re-did it. I hadn't yet gotten around to getting my hair cut. I said, "Every good animal person has patience."

"Do you mind if I stay around and watch some more?"

"Of course not."

Brent stayed for the rest of the morning and he walked with me back to the house when I went home for lunch. We parted at my front door and he said, "The senator and Mrs. Wellington are dining with friends tonight and I'm on my own. Would you like to have dinner with me at a restaurant in town?"

My first impulse was to say no, but then I remembered my plan to show Liam that other men thought I was grown-up enough to take out. I smiled. "That would be lovely."

He gave me a boyish grin. He was a nice-looking man of about thirty, with a short haircut and blue-gray eyes. "Great. I'll pick you up at seven?"

"Sounds good."

A front had come in the previous night and the weather had turned cooler. I wore my ever-serviceable black slacks with a lavender sweater set. Brent picked me up at seven and we drove into town to the Jockey Club, parked the car and went inside.

The Jockey Club was one of Midville's finest restaurants. This was the first time I had been in it, and I

looked around curiously. The walls were all richly pan-
eled in dark wood and pictures of famous racehorses
hung on the walls. The tables all wore fresh white tablecloths and fresh flowers.

I smiled at Brent and when we were seated I confided
that I had never been in the restaurant before. He looked
surprised. "How can that be?" he asked.

"If I had lived in Midville all the time I'm sure I
would have come, but I was away at school and I work
in Maryland now."

"Are you at a hospital or do you work in a private
practice?"

I picked up the menu. "A private practice that spe-
cializes in horses."

"You look awfully small to be working with such
large animals."

I had heard this comment before. "I'm stronger than
I look," I said evenly.

We both looked at the menus for a minute, then,
when he looked up from his, I asked, "What about you?
What do you do in your job?"

He folded his menu. "I'm sort of the middleman between the senator and the rest of the world. I make sure
things get done properly."

"That sounds like a big job."

"It's big in scope. That's why I like it. It's not boring."

"Do you handle the press? I know the *Post* had two
articles on Leslie being found."

"Yes, I handled the press on that one. The senator is
usually very good about meeting with the press, but he
didn't want to say anything officially in regard to that
particular story."

The waiter came to take our drink order and I ordered a glass of White Zinfandel. Brent had a Scotch and soda.

"Do you like working for Senator Wellington?" I asked.

"Sure," he said.

"Is he sincere, do you think?"

He shrugged. "He's as sincere as anyone in Washington ever is."

"That's a cynical remark."

"I suppose it is. Why did you ask me that question?"

"I was curious. I've known the senator almost all my life, but I don't really know him at all. And I've heard things about him."

"What have you heard?"

"I've heard he's not faithful to his wife."

He gave a harsh laugh. "If fidelity to one's wife was a prerequisite to being in Congress, there'd be a lot of men weeded out."

"That's a depressing thought."

Our drinks came and I took a sip of my wine. When the waiter came back I ordered the salmon. So did Brent.

"Don't judge the senator too harshly, Anne," Brent said when we were alone again. "It can't be easy being married to a drunk."

"Ah, but does Mrs. Wellington drink because he's unfaithful or is he unfaithful because she drinks?"

"Which came first, the chicken or the egg?"

I smiled. "I guess it is a lot like that."

"Let's talk about something more interesting," he said.

"What?"

"Let's talk about you. What kind of schooling do you need to become a vet?"

I obliged and let him change the subject. We talked of other things for the rest of the evening.

Brent took me home, and when I went in, my mother was sitting in the living room watching television. I looked to see if there were signs of tears but she looked okay.

"What are you watching?" I asked.

"Law and Order."

"That's what we need in Midville," I said. "Someone like the *Law and Order* detectives to find out who killed Leslie."

"If they arrest anyone, honey, it will be Liam. I don't think you want that."

"Liam didn't do it and I want them to find out who really did. It's horrible for him to have to live with people thinking he's guilty."

"It's hard to believe that *anyone* we know could be guilty of such a vicious thing."

"Maybe it wasn't anyone we know. Maybe it was someone from the outside. I don't think the police should rule that out, Mom. Who knows? Maybe some vagrant was making his home in the summerhouse and he panicked when Leslie found him. That could have happened, couldn't it?"

My mother looked at me pityingly. "I suppose so, honey."

"Don't look at me that way," I said with annoyance. "People are murdered by strangers all the time."

"They are," my mother said.

Law and Order had finished and the news was coming on.

"I'm going to bed," I said.

"I'm going to watch the news."

I hesitated, then I leaned over and kissed my mother on the cheek. "Goodnight, Mom."

"Goodnight, honey."

I left the room, went upstairs and got into bed.

CHAPTER 7

Mom wanted to move as soon as the paint dried on the walls of her new house, so Thursday morning Liam came over to the house with an empty horse trailer, which he parked in front. We had already moved a collection of cartons out onto the porch.

I was surprised, and pleased, to see Kevin get out of the van after him. Two moving men were definitely better than one.

Both of the men were dressed for the job in jeans and sweatshirts. I wore the same outfit myself, and so did Mom. "We were all on the same wavelength when it came to clothes," I said with a laugh.

"Don't worry, Anne," Kevin teased. "Nothing can mar your beauty—not even a bulky Virginia Tech sweatshirt."

"You're much more gorgeous than I am," I shot back. And it was the truth. His jeans were molded to his body and his blond hair shone golden in the morning sun. His azure eyes regarded me with a smile of approval.

Liam said in annoyance, "We're here to work, not to participate in a mutual admiration society."

My mother said, "What do you want to load first, boys? The furniture or the boxes?"

"Let's put the furniture on first," Liam said.

Kevin agreed and the two of them went into the house and took out the sofa.

"Mom and I will continue to bring out the boxes," I said.

"Just don't clutter up the doorway," Liam warned. "We need to be able to get in and out of the house."

"Thank you for pointing that out," I said tartly. Did he think I was an idiot?

He shot me a look, but didn't reply.

Kevin said, "How are we going to get the bureaus down that narrow staircase?"

Liam said, "Someone got them up. We have to be able to get them down."

After they had worked for an hour, both men shed their sweatshirts and worked in the T-shirts they had on underneath. Kevin was surprisingly muscular. He looked as if he worked out pretty regularly. I guess he had to keep in good shape for his job. A Hollywood star could not get flabby. Liam's muscles were less obvious than Kevin's. He looked as if he had got them from work, not from working out. He was strong, though. The two men actually did manage to get my mother's triple dresser through the bedroom doorway and down the stairs and into the truck.

We made three runs with the truck to get the furniture and most of the boxes over to the new house. Then my mother said, "Dinner is on me tonight. Why don't you boys go home and get cleaned up and meet us at the Horse and Hound for dinner at six-thirty?"

"You don't have to take us out to dinner, Nancy," Liam said. "We were happy to be able to help you."

"Liam's right," Kevin backed his cousin up. "You must be tired."

"I am tired but I have to eat and I would like you boys to join us. Please let me do this. You saved me a fortune by moving me; a moving van would have cost far more than a mere dinner."

There was a pause. I sent a silent message to Liam, *Say yes.*

"All right," he said. "We'll accept your gracious invitation."

I nodded my approval. "Can I borrow your car, Mom? I want to run out to the farm to see how the day's training went."

"Of course. The keys are in my bag."

I located her purse and took out the keys.

Liam said, "I'd better get the truck out of the street."

Kevin said, "I'll catch a ride back home with Anne."

Liam scowled. Kevin gave him a kind smile. I said, "I can drop you at the house on my way to the barn, Kevin."

"Thank you," Kevin replied.

Liam gave me a searching look. I looked back innocently. Then, "Oh, all right," he said.

I said to my mother, "Don't wear yourself out unpacking. I'll be home in an hour to help you."

"Yes, ma'am," my mother said.

Liam had already gone out to the truck when I left the house with Kevin. We got into my Mom's Honda, and I pulled out of the parking space and turned onto Washington Avenue. We started back toward Wellington.

Kevin said, "I haven't worked that hard in years."

"Don't be funny," I said. "You probably work out harder every day in the gym."

"I'm flattered."

"Seriously, thank you for helping out. I don't think Mom is very flush in the pocket at the moment."

"Does she need a loan? I could . . ."

"No. It's nothing like that. She has her teacher's salary, after all. It's just that she had the funeral bills to pay and she had to put two months' security down on the house."

"This is so hard for her," Kevin said sympathetically.

"It is. They were very close. She told me she feels as if she's had an amputation."

"You must miss him too."

"I do, but my life wasn't entwined with Daddy's the way Mom's life was. I guess that's the price you pay for having a good marriage."

"Your parents had about the only good marriage that I know of," Kevin remarked.

I looked at him in surprise. He was looking straight ahead, affording me a view of his perfect profile.

It was true, I thought. His own parents had not only ditched their marriage, they had ditched their son as well. And nobody in their right mind would call the Wellington marriage a good one. For both Kevin and Liam, my mom and dad were unusual.

"I was lucky," I said softly and returned my eyes to the road.

"If your parents were so great, why did you stay away so much?" Kevin asked.

I sighed. "I was very upset after Leslie disappeared. I was so afraid the police were going to arrest Liam. Mom and Daddy thought I'd be better off if they sent me away to school. They just wanted to get me away from the whole poisonous atmosphere. Then I went to Virginia Tech, which is a haul from here. Then I was in vet school;

then I was doing a residency. There just wasn't time for me to be home very often."

He nodded. "I haven't been home all that much myself. It's ironic that I chose this particular time to come for a vacation."

"You mean because of Leslie being found?"

"Yes."

"It's a terrible thing," I said somberly. "To think of someone taking that bat and bashing out Leslie's brains."

"Yes, it is."

"I hope the police find the bastard who did it."

"Do you really hope that, Anne?" There was the faintest touch of pity in his voice.

I lifted my chin. "Yes, I do. Everyone thinks Liam did it and it's not fair to him."

Kevin said reasonably, "What if he did do it? Do you want him caught?"

"He didn't do it," I said fiercely.

"All right, have it your way."

We were silent as I drove down the Wellington driveway. Kevin got out. "See you for dinner," he said cheerfully.

I nodded and drove off to the yearling barn.

It wasn't until I was home again that I realized I had promised Michael I would go out to dinner with him. "Damn," I said, and explained my problem to my mother.

"Why don't you invite Michael to join us?" Mom said.

I didn't want to miss having dinner with Liam, so I said, "I'll call him right away."

I tried his work number first, but it was his day off, so I looked up his home number and called him there. There was no answer but I got his answering machine and left a message for him to meet us at the Horse and Hound at seven o'clock.

Kevin and Liam came in separate cars and consequently made separate entrances to the restaurant. Kevin's entrance was an event. All the diners looked up from their meals to stare at the famous movie star as he made his way across the room. When he reached our table and bent down to kiss my cheek I murmured, "I feel as if I should curtsy to you."

He laughed, showing his perfect teeth. They were natural. Kevin had never had to have braces.

Michael came next. He did not look happy to see he was part of a large party, but he politely greeted my mother and Kevin.

Finally, Liam arrived.

I looked at him as he stood in the doorway scanning the room for us. I knew him by heart, from his tumbled black hair to the tips of his brown loafers, but I still got that thrill of recognition whenever I saw him.

My mother shook her head slightly and I tried to dim the radiance that always came to my face whenever Liam was near me.

He came across the room, stopping to speak to two separate parties before he reached us.

I smiled at him and said, "Have a seat. Do you know Michael Bates?"

Liam gave poor Michael an evil look. "Sure," he said. "How are you, Michael?"

"Fine, thank you, Liam."

"Has your divorce been finalized?"

Michael looked surprised, as well he might at being questioned so rudely. He narrowed his eyes. "As a matter of fact, it has."

At any moment I expected one of them to growl at the other.

My mother said, "I believe the waiter wants to take our drink order."

Liam and Michael left off glaring at each other and told the waiter what they wanted to drink. Then Kevin said, "Is there anything new in the police investigation, Michael?"

Michael took a quick glance at Liam. "Not really," he said.

I didn't like that glance at all, but I didn't want to discuss the case in such a public place. So I smiled and said, "How is Someday Soon's training coming along, Liam?"

"John is pleased with him. He's not looking to put up the fast training-run numbers that Baffert is; he's building stamina into Buster. He's a good trainer; he knows what he's doing."

"Only a little more than a week till the Derby," I said.

Liam said, "I know. Part of me is frantically excited and part of me is scared to death."

Michael asked, "You're going to Kentucky to see the race?"

Liam looked at him as if he had seven heads. "Of course."

"Can I come too?" I asked. "I've never been to the Derby."

"Sure you can come," he said. "Nancy, why don't you come too? After all, Buster was one of Pete's babies."

My mother shook her head. "I have too much to do here, what with unpacking and everything, but thank you anyway Liam."

"Maybe I'd better stay home too," I said. "I can help you move the furniture, Mom."

My mother frowned at me. "It will really annoy me if you stay home for my sake, Anne. Go to the Derby."

I hesitated. I really wanted to go to the Derby, but I felt guilty about leaving her.

"I mean it, Anne."

I didn't put up much of a fight. "Well, all right . . . if you're sure?"

"I'm sure."

"Great!" Liam said. "I'll call the hotel about getting you a room."

"Okay."

Outwardly I was composed; inwardly I felt like a kid with Christmas coming.

After everyone had gone home, and I had my mother alone in the new house, I asked her if she had really meant what she said about my going to the Derby with Liam.

"Absolutely," she replied.

"But why, Mom? You and Daddy spent years helping me to stay away from him. Why this change of heart?"

"We thought Liam would be a case of out of sight, out of mind," she replied. "And our strategy seemed to be working. You went out with some nice young men, and we thought you were going to become engaged to John Elliott."

I had been helping her to make up the bed in her bedroom, and now I tucked the blanket under the corners and said, "What's different now?"

"What's different is that you broke up with John and, after years of avoiding Liam, you came home here for a month, where you would be sure to come into contact with him. And maybe it's a good idea. Maybe you can exorcise Liam from your heart by seeing him as he really is, and not as the idol you always thought him."

I smoothed down the blanket. "That's exactly why I came back," I agreed. "That, and I wanted some time with you."

The two of us tucked the sides of the blanket in.

"All my life I have compared the men I met to Liam," I said soberly. "I don't want to do that anymore. I need to see him clearly, not with the eyes of an adolescent admirer."

"I'm glad you see that, honey."

We put pillowcases on the pillows.

"I wonder how long Kevin will be staying," Mom said.

I said, "I think he's hiding out from the press. He broke up with the actress he was going with—Julia Monroe—and all the gossip press was after him. He told me he was going to stay until things quieted down."

"I read about that split," Mom said.

I stared at her in astonishment. "Since when have you been a reader of the tabloid press?"

"I read about it while I was standing in line in the Safeway. It was the headline in the *Enquirer*."

We collected the rest of our sheets and blankets and moved into what would be my room. The men had set up the bed this afternoon as well and it stood solitary amidst a floorful of boxes. We began to put the bottom sheet on.

"Why don't you change your mind and come?" I asked.

She shook her head. "It would be too hard, honey. I don't feel like partying. I'll watch the race on television."

"All right."

We picked up the top sheet and finished making the bed.

CHAPTER 8

Liam and I left for Louisville very early Friday morning. The Virginia newspapers, like the papers around the country, had been full of Derby news all week. During the drive, Liam and I discussed and dismissed almost everything that had been written.

In the last week the press had reported that Someday Soon had a knee injury; that he had peaked in the Florida Derby and was on a downhill slide; that there was little hope for him to beat Honor Bright, the horse he had finished second to in the Wood.

"No matter what anyone says about speed, the Derby is an endurance race," Liam said. "As long as Buster doesn't get caught behind a line of horses, I think we'll be okay. The Derby is such a melee, though. You need some racing luck if you're going to win."

The first glitch in our Derby plans came when we got to the hotel and discovered that I didn't have a room.

Liam was furious. "I called two days ago and was assured there would be a room for Dr. Foster."

"I'm so sorry, Mr. Wellington, but your reservation never got entered into the computer."

"Damn." Liam turned to me. "We're never going to get into another hotel. Everything will be booked solid."

"Why don't I just share your room? It's only for two nights."

Liam turned back to the hotel clerk. "Does my room have one or two beds?"

"It has one king-sized bed."

"King-sized beds are humongous," I said. "We can keep out of each other's way."

Liam glowered. I said, "Most of the men I know would be thrilled to be sharing a room with me. What's the matter? Do you think I'll bite you?"

His black brows drew even closer. "Don't be silly."

I said to the hotel clerk, "We'll take the one room."

Once Liam had given his credit card imprint, a bellboy put our luggage on a cart and took us to our room. He opened the door and brought the two suitcases in.

As Liam tipped the bellboy, I went to the window and looked out. The first things I saw were the twin towers of Churchill Downs, the racetrack. I felt a chill run up and down my spine.

Liam came over to stand beside me. "There it is," he said. "One more day and we'll know."

"Can we go and see him?" I asked.

"Sure. He is my horse, after all."

I hugged myself as if I were trying to keep my exuberance under wraps. "This is so exciting," I said.

He grinned. "It is, isn't it? Do you want to change before we go to the track?"

I looked down at my jeans and pink knit shirt. "This will do."

Liam, who was dressed almost identically except that his shirt was blue, said, "Great. Let's go."

"Do you have the key?" I asked as we left the room.

He felt in his pocket. "Yep."

Even though it was late afternoon, the stable area at Churchill Downs was filled with people. I kept close beside Liam as he pushed through the crowd. A photographer caught sight of him and called, "Mr. Wellington, look this way." Involuntarily, Liam and I looked toward the man who had yelled and a flash went off.

The photographer came up to us. "Who is the girl?" he asked Liam.

"She's my vet," he said shortly.

The photographer gave me a skeptical look.

"It's perfectly true," I said. "I am Dr. Anne Foster."

"Come along, Annie," Liam said, taking me by the hand. "I want to see Buster."

I let him lead me down a shedrow and we stopped in front of the Dutch door of the stall at the far end. We looked inside and had a wonderful view of a bright chestnut rear end.

"Buster," Liam called. "How are you, boy?"

The horse turned at the sound of his voice and came toward the door, ears pricked forward.

Someday Soon was a beautiful horse, with a glowing chestnut coat, the sloping shoulders and muscular haunches of his father, and his mother's lovely head. Liam reached in his pocket and produced a lump of sugar, which he tossed into Someday Soon's feed dish.

The colt immediately stuck his nose in the dish and ate the sugar.

"He looks fabulous, Liam," I said.

Liam nodded. "He looks great, healthy and ready."

A thin young man dressed in jeans came over to us. "Don't git too close to the horse," he said.

Liam smiled. "It's all right. I'm Liam Wellington, the owner."

"Oh." The young man nodded. "Well, just be careful of where you a stick your fingers. Red is okay but there's one or two of 'em here that would take your hand off if they got a chance."

"I presume 'Red' is Someday Soon," Liam said.

"Yessir. That's our name for him. Red."

"He looks wonderful," I said. "Are you his groom?"

"Yes, ma'am. I'm Henry."

Someday Soon returned to the front of his box and nickered. I have always thought that a horse's nicker is the sweetest sound in the world.

"Hello darling," I said softly. "How handsome you are."

Someday Soon graciously allowed me to scratch his forehead.

I said to Liam, "Well, if looks could win, he'd be a shoo-in."

"He's a credit to John—and to Henry," Liam said.

We stayed around the barn for about an hour, then we went back to the hotel. There was a message on our voice-mail to call John Ford, Someday Soon's trainer.

While the two men talked, I opened up my suitcase and hung up the suit I was going to wear to the Derby tomorrow. I hadn't had time to buy a hat, something which all women wore on Derby Day, but my shell pink suit was dressy enough. I had also brought a non-crushable black dress, the kind that you can dress up with jewelry and heels.

Liam hung up and said, "John wants us to go to a bash someone is having in our hotel tonight. I think I ought to go. There will be lots of owners and trainers there and I might have a chance to talk up Thunderhead as a sire."

"Great. What time does it start and will there be food?"

"It starts at seven. There's probably going to be hors d'oeuvres, but not dinner."

"Do you want to get something to eat first?"

"I do. There was a coffee shop downstairs, or we can order from room service."

"Let's order in."

"Okay. There must be a menu around here someplace." He picked up a folder from the dresser. "Here it is."

We called room service and Liam ordered a hamburger while I got a turkey sandwich. We were both hungry so it was pretty quiet as we wolfed the food down. Then Liam put on the TV to watch the news.

The local channel was full of Derby news. There was a lot of footage of Bob Baffert, who had two runners: Honor Bright, which belonged to Sheikh Mohammed of Dubai, and Kerry's Way, a come-from-behinder like Someday Soon.

Liam was not a Bob Baffert fan. Liam belonged to the old thoroughbred aristocracy, who bred and raced relatively small, quality stables. Such a stable would be lucky to have a Derby runner every five years; Baffert, on the other hand, trained hundreds of horses every season and had one or two to enter every year.

"I wonder if he wears those sunglasses in the dark?" Liam said.

Baffert was famous for his shock of white hair and his small black sunglasses.

"You have to hand it to him, though," I said. "The man knows a good horse when he sees one."

Liam scowled. He seriously did not like Bob Baffert.

We were sitting side by side on the bed facing the television. He was only inches away from me and my body was so attuned to him that I swear I knew when he blinked.

The station interview person had a short interchange with John Ford, Someday Soon's trainer. Ford was brief. "I have him where I want him. I think he'll run his best race tomorrow."

"Do you think he has the kick to come from off the pace?"

Not a muscle moved in Ford's face. "I wouldn't be running him if I didn't think that we could win."

The interview reporter laughed cheerfully. "Well, that's true." The camera cut to someone else.

Liam smiled. "John will never make it as a television personality."

"He's much too taciturn," I agreed. "But you're pleased with him as a trainer?"

"Yes. He prepares his horses in the classic style. He doesn't run his two-year-olds until the autumn and he believes in long slow gallops. I couldn't have chosen anyone better for Buster."

I nodded and reached up to pull the rubber band off my ponytail. My hair fell around my shoulders.

"You have such beautiful hair, Annie." He picked up a lock between his thumb and his forefinger and smoothed it. "Why do you always wear it in a ponytail?"

My breath quickened at the touch of his hand. "It's out of my way in a ponytail. Actually, I'm going to get it cut short."

He looked appalled. "What? You can't be serious."

"I'm very serious. I just haven't found the time yet to go into town to the beauty parlor."

He swung around so he was sitting sideways on the bed, facing me. "You've always worn your hair this way. Why change it now?"

"I think the short hair will make me look older. You're always going on about how young I am."

He scowled. "Please don't get your hair cut because of some stupid thing that I said."

I looked at him steadily. "You just asked me why I wanted to change a style that I've worn all my life. I'll tell you why. I want you to notice that I'm not little Annie any more. I'm all grown up, Liam. I'm even a full-fledged veterinarian."

His blue eyes were trained on my face. Without taking my eyes away from his, I reached out, picked up his lean sinewy hand and laid it on my breast. "That is the breast of a woman, not a child," I said.

He pulled his hand away as if it had been scalded. "Christ, Annie," he said. He was breathing hard, as if he had been running.

I gave him my nicest smile. "I trust I've made my point."

He said forcefully, "You've made it all right."

"Then I don't have to get my hair cut?"

"No. You do not have to get your hair cut to prove to me that you're no longer a child."

"Okay, I'll leave it be then."

The national news came on and we both turned our attention to the television, pretending to watch.

We each changed in the bathroom and went down to the party in the Regency Room.

The place was packed with owners and trainers and other "connections," such as breeders. Someday Soon was the only horse whose breeder was also his owner. In one corner of the room Bob Baffert was holding court, while D Wayne Lukas occupied another. Both of them had two horses running in the Derby, and in the early betting two of their colts were co-favorites: Honor Bright for Baffert and Mileaminute for Lukas. Someday Soon was rated fourth on the morning line at eight-to-one.

I didn't know a soul and I stuck close to Liam as we made our way to the bar. A number of people knew him, and he introduced me as we went along. I met the Canadian couple who owned Tango With Me. They had made their money in gold exploration. I met a seventy-seven-year-old oil, banking and lumber tycoon. I met a partnership which was made up of four former turf reporters. When finally we reached the bar, I had my usual, a glass of White Zinfandel. Liam had a scotch.

Everyone in the room was talking about the Derby.

How can they find so much to say? I thought as I trailed Liam to the food table. An elderly couple was standing in our way, and Liam said to them, "Are you the Winslows? Do you own Armageddon?"

The two of them beamed, obviously relieved to have someone to talk to beside themselves. "You bet we do," Mr. Winslow said.

Liam held out his hand. "I'm Liam Wellington. I own Someday Soon."

"Pleased to meet you." Mr. and Mrs. Winslow both smiled.

We stood and talked for a while, then we resumed our trip to the buffet table. Liam, who had just eaten a hamburger and a load of French fries, filled a plate.

"Aren't you going to eat, Annie?"

"No thanks," I said.

Near the doorway, we encountered John Ford and his wife. He and Liam shook hands, and I was introduced.

John had brown hair salted with gray. There was a fine network of wrinkles at the corners of his eyes, testifying to the time he spent outdoors.

"Horrible crush, isn't it?" Mrs. Ford said.

"It certainly is," I agreed.

"How does our boy look, John?" Liam asked.

"He looks good. I think he's ready."

"Great."

"The suspense is killing me," I said humorously. "I feel like I'm a little girl again, waiting for Christmas so that Santa Claus can come."

John Ford grinned. "You've hit the nail right on the head there, Dr. Foster."

We stayed until ten, with Liam making it a point to talk to as many owners and trainers as he possibly could; then at last he said in a low voice, "What do you say we get out of here?"

"Sounds good to me," I said. "If I drink one more glass of wine, I'll be drunk."

"Actually, I think you're a little drunk already."

I glared at him. "I am not. I can handle three glasses of wine."

He shook his head. "I think you can handle two glasses of wine. The third put you over your limit."

"How do you know that?"

"Your eyes are glazed over. Trust me, Annie. If there's anyone who knows the signs of too much to drink, it's me."

I thought of his mother. "Maybe you're right," I conceded. "Maybe I didn't need to take that third glass. But it was such a ghastly party that I had to do something."

He laughed. "It wasn't a ghastly party."

"It was all right for you. You knew people. I didn't know a soul."

"I introduced you to a ton of people."

"I don't like parties with a ton of people. I like small parties with people that I know."

"I like them best, too."

The elevator had reached our floor and Liam guided me out. "I just hope you don't have a headache tomorrow for the Derby," he said.

"I'll take a couple of aspirin before I go to bed."

"Good idea."

We reached our hotel room and went in. Liam said, "Do you want to use the bathroom first?"

"Yes, thank you." I washed my face and hands at the sink, brushed my teeth, put on a moisturizing cream, and got into my blue pajamas with a men's cut. I ran a brush through my hair and left it loose. Then, carrying my clothes, I went back into the bedroom.

Liam looked at me. "I don't usually sleep in pajamas and, since I thought I would be alone, I didn't bring any."

"Wear your shorts. I don't care." I brought my clothes over to my suitcase and began to fold them.

He stood there for a long, silent moment, watching me. Then he went into the bathroom and I could hear the shower running. I finished folding my clothes into the suitcase and went over to the bed. In truth, that third glass of wine had knocked me for a loop. All I wanted to do was lie down and close my eyes.

I was almost asleep when Liam came out of the bathroom. I was too tired to open my eyes to get a glimpse of him in his shorts. I felt him getting into the big bed on the other side. *This is nice,* I thought sleepily. The next thing I knew, it was morning.

I sat up, pushed the hair out of my face, and looked around for Liam. He was nowhere in sight but the bathroom door was closed. I looked at my watch, which I had forgotten to take off the previous evening. It was eight-thirty.

I went to the bathroom door and called, "Do you want to order breakfast from room service or do you want to go downstairs?"

"Let's go downstairs," he called back.

It was a little early for my pink suit, so I picked up a pair of khaki pants and a clean, yellow knit shirt. Then I waited for Liam to come out of the bathroom.

He was wearing a pair of blue striped shorts and nothing else. I thought he looked as beautiful as a Michelangelo statue. He pushed a lock of hair away from his forehead and said, "The bathroom is all yours."

"Thanks." I picked up my makeup case and went inside.

After I had showered, I put on some blush and lipstick and put my wet hair in a ponytail. Liam was waiting for me outside.

"That's great timing, Annie," he said amiably. "Every other woman I know would have taken at least twice as long."

"Thanks," I said expressionlessly, and wondered how many other women he had shared a hotel room with.

I put my pajamas back in my suitcase and Liam and I left the room to go downstairs.

CHAPTER 9

After breakfast, Liam and I went to Churchill Downs to check on Buster and we walked into what looked like a giant picnic. Tents were erected everywhere on the backstretch while owners and trainers glad-handed their guests. I caught a glimpse of the Crown Prince of Dubai in front of Bob Baffert's barn.

There wasn't any of the circus-like atmosphere at John Ford's barn, however, and when we got there Buster was being walked up and down the shedrow.

"How is he?" I asked Henry.

"Busting out," Henry said. "He's ready to bust out."

Liam smiled at me. "That's how he got his nickname."

John Ford came up to us. "He's as good as he was for Florida," he said. There was a fraction of a pause before he added, "Maybe better." He patted Liam on his shoulder. "Don't worry, he's going to be a credit to his mom and pop and the farm he came from."

"Thanks, John," Liam said.

"I need to go shopping for a hat," I told Liam.

"You don't need a hat. Just do something fancy with your hair. Believe me, the hair will look better than a hat."

"It's a tradition that women wear hats to the Derby," I said.

"The hell with the tradition. I am staying here for the races, not traipsing all around town looking for a silly hat for you."

The Derby was the last race of the day; there would be a full card of races before it was run. I said, "Give me your car keys. When Buster wins I want to be properly attired."

"Oh, all right, I'll drive you. I have to go home anyway to change my clothes. But you have to be fast."

"I'll be a whiz." I didn't care what kind of hat I got, I was just determined not to be the only bareheaded woman in the paddock enclosure.

Liam double-parked outside a department store. "I'll wait here for you."

"Okay." I dashed inside and found the hats almost straight away. I figured the store would have a bunch of them but it looked as if a lot of the stock had already been bought. I picked a yellow straw with a rolled brim and a pink ribbon, which would match my suit. I didn't even try it on; it was going to have to do.

I was back at the car within five minutes. "Good job," Liam commented.

Both of us were too nervous to eat lunch, so we went back to the hotel, where I got into my pink suit and arranged my hair in a French twist, over which I put the hat. Liam was wearing a blue blazer, white shirt, red tie and gray slacks.

I could feel the tension bubble in my stomach. "This is so exciting."

He gave me a wry grin. "I feel sick to my stomach," he admitted.

"He'll do great; I have a good feeling about this race."

"I hope you're right, brat. A lot is riding on one horse's back today."

Properly attired, we left the hotel and went to pick up Liam's car.

The weather was perfect; eighty degrees with low humidity. It hadn't rained for a week, so the track was fast. In fact, as the day went by, it became very clear that the speed of the track favored front runners. Horses like Mileaminute and Honor Bright would be able to lay off the pace set by such speedsters as Tango With Me, and when the time came to make their move, they'd be rested and ready. The late closers, such as Buster, would have a hard time passing the second tier.

Three track records were set in the course of the afternoon. It was looking more and more difficult for Buster.

"Buster will have the stamina for a mile and a quarter. I think he can do it." This was Liam's refrain all afternoon as we watched the races from seats in our owner's box.

Half an hour before the eighth race—the Derby—was to be run, Liam and I made our way out to the backside. We stood with Buster as he was saddled up and taken to the paddock.

"He looks marvelous," I said to Liam.

And he did, but he wasn't getting any attention. All of the crowd's attention was on Baffert's big bay horse, Honor Bright. "Hah," Liam said. "All of these people are in for a big surprise."

Buster tossed his head as if he agreed. Then the call went out: "Riders up!"

All around the paddock, trainers began to give their jockeys a leg up. There was Jerry Bailey in crimson and gold on Honor Bright, then Gary Stevens on Epic Challenge and Kent Desormeaux on River Rush. Jorge Chavez blessed himself before vaulting into the saddle of Tango With Me. John gave Miles a leg up, and the line of splendid horseflesh began to move toward the paddock exit.

The owners, trainers and grooms followed the horses, and Liam and I joined the crowd as we moved out of the paddock and into the tunnel that would take us to the track. As we passed through the darkness of the tunnel I sent up a prayer, *I know I shouldn't pray about such an unimportant thing as a horse race when people are suffering and dying, but please, Dear God, let Buster win!*

We came out into the sunlight at the end of the tunnel and the horses moved onto the track where each was picked up by an outrider. They began to trot down the track in front of the grandstand. The University of Kentucky marching band struck up "My Old Kentucky Home."

I got goose bumps. All around me people were singing, "*Weep no more my lady, Oh weep no more today. I will sing a song of my old Kentucky Home, of my old Kentucky home far away.*"

Liam said to me as we pushed through the crowd to get to our box, "There were 36,152 thoroughbred foals registered with the Jockey Club the year that Buster was born."

"Wow," I said. "What are the odds of any one of them getting to the Derby?"

"Very low."

I bit my lip. "I can't stand this. I think I'm going to be sick."

"Don't you dare desert me now."

I clutched Liam's arm. "I can't bear to watch."

He gave me a hug. "We'll know soon." John Ford and his wife arrived in the box but, aside from a quick smile, none of us spoke. All of our attention was on the glossy chestnut colt wearing the number nine.

The horses had finished their parade up the track and now they turned and headed back toward the starting gate. I watched Buster cantering down the track, his face pulled over the withers of the sensible quarter horse that was leading him. He seemed perfectly calm. Much calmer than I.

My whole body felt frozen with tension. I could tell Liam was the same. They started loading the horses into the gate and we looked at each other. I moved a fraction of an inch closer to him, then we both returned our focus to Buster, who was waiting patiently to be loaded. My dad had taught him well.

One of the assistant starters took hold of his bridle and another assistant got his flank and he walked quietly into the gate. The door closed behind him.

For one moment that seemed frozen in time, all of the horses were in their stalls, poised to erupt into full flight. Then the bell went off, the gate sprang open and the horses surged forward. The Kentucky Derby had begun.

I lifted my field glasses and tried to pick Buster out from the pack of horses crowding the field.

"Shit," Liam said. "He got bumped on his way out of the gate."

"He has plenty of time to make it up," John Ford said.

We watched amidst the noise of the crowd as the field sorted itself out. Tango With Me ran to the front, as expected, followed by Enzo and Kerry's Way. The three set a scorching pace. A few lengths behind were Honor

Bright, Point Taken and Mileaminute. Behind them came the rest of the field, including Buster.

"Christ, they're going fast," Liam muttered as the front runners passed the first quarter pole.

The early speed on the front could be a good thing for the horses in the second tier, like Honor Bright. It simply wasn't possible for the horses on the lead to maintain that pace over a mile and a quarter; they were sure to fade and leave the track open for the horses that had been lying just off the pace.

A few moments later, the announcer informed us that the third tier of horses, in which Buster was running, was fourteen lengths behind the leaders.

I said, "Damn. He's too far back. And he's in the middle!"

"Miles is going to get caught in traffic if he doesn't watch himself," Liam said tensely.

As if he had heard Liam's words, Miles angled forward, slid between two horses in front of him, and got himself open on the outside part of the track.

"He's free," I cried.

Buster began to pass the horses in the third group that were in front of him.

The horses headed into the second turn and Tango With Me, who had set a blistering pace on the lead, began to tire. He dropped back, as did the horses that had been running with him, and the horses in the second tier, Honor Bright, Point Taken and Mileaminute, caught and passed them and moved into the lead.

For a fraction of a mile, the three horses raced together. Then Honor Bright pulled away to the front, running on the rail. The crowd was screaming for the favorite as he began to pull away from the field.

The original front running horses were fading fast, and Buster caught and passed them on the turn. When he came off the turn there were three horses in front of him: Honor Bright, Point Taken, and the fading Mileaminute.

"Here it is," Liam shouted to me. "Miles has done his job. Now it's up to Buster."

My eyes were glued to the bright chestnut colt on the outside who now was thundering down the stretch, his long stride eating up the ground. Buster caught and passed Mileaminute as if he wasn't even moving.

I was jumping up and down and screaming, "Go Buster! Go!"

"Honor Bright's still running hard," Liam said.

"Honor Bright is toast," I said.

As I spoke, Buster caught Point Taken and passed him.

"Come on Buster!" I shrieked.

"Go, go, go!" Liam was yelling.

Honor Bright was not giving up, but Buster was closing in on him fast. There was a very long moment when Buster caught him and for a few seconds the two horses ran head to head, eye to eye.

"Come on, fella!" Liam shouted. "Come on!"

As if he had heard his owner, Buster began to pull away. One-hundred-and-twenty-five-thousand voices screamed as, all by himself, Buster crossed the finish line, the winner of the Kentucky Derby.

Pandemonium erupted in our box. I threw my arms around Liam's waist and hugged him. "We won," I kept saying. "We won."

He bent his head and kissed me. His eyes looked as blue as the sky in his suntanned face. "Oh Annie," he said. "Oh Annie."

I grinned up at him.

"Congratulations," John Ford said to Liam, extending his hand. Liam ignored the hand and gave John a hug.

"You did a great job, Johnnie. A great job."

Mrs. Ford and I were hugging each other and doing a jig at the same time. My hat had fallen off.

Several security men came into the box and told John that they were there to escort him and the rest of Buster's connections to the winner's circle. Liam and I held hands as we fought our way through the crowd to the horseshoe-shaped enclosure that was used only once a year.

I tried to catch my breath and calm down before we entered the winner's circle, but it was impossible. Liam looked at me and laughed. "Your hat is crooked."

I straightened it. "Okay now?"

"Okay."

It was chaos in the winner's box. The television cameras and mics and reporters took up half the space. "Mr. Wellington." It was a local news reporter. "How does it feel, having the Kentucky Derby winner?"

It was a stupid question, but I guess he had to ask it.

"It feels great," Liam said. "I bred that horse myself, and I'm very proud of him."

"Why isn't your father, the senator, here today?"

"He had other commitments," Liam said evenly.

A roar went up from the crowd as the winning time was posted. It was under two minutes; Buster had just run the third fastest Derby in history.

"Wow," I said.

"Pennyroyal's baby did us proud," Liam said. His eyes were very bright.

A television reporter put an arm around Liam and pulled him in front of the camera. "How does it feel to win the Kentucky Derby?"

"It feels great," Liam said.

"When did you know you had it won?"

"When he made his move and started passing horses. It was the same move he made in the Florida Derby. I thought we had it won then."

Someone called "Sandy! We're ready to present the trophy."

"Come on," the TV person told us and we followed him over to the stand that had been set up. Buster was wearing the blanket of red roses that signified the winner. The governor of Kentucky was standing ready to present the trophy. We all went to take our places and the silver trophy, topped with a horse draped in a ruby-studded shawl, was placed in Liam's hands.

"This couldn't have happened without the work of John Ford," Liam said into the microphone. "Wellington Farm bred this horse and raised him but he wouldn't be a Kentucky Derby winner if it wasn't for John."

A cheer went up from all the Kentuckians, many of whom had bet on Buster because he was the only Kentucky-trained horse in the race.

"Will you be going to the Preakness?" the TV man asked. The Preakness was the second race in the Triple Crown.

"If he's healthy."

My God, I thought. *This craziness isn't over. Buster is now a potential Triple Crown winner. He has to run in the Preakness in two weeks.*

The television cameras were turned off, Buster was led back to his stall for a well-deserved bath and feed, and the rest of us prepared to troop off to the press conference that had been arranged for the Derby winner's connections.

"How about dinner afterward?" Liam asked John Ford.

"We'd love to," the trainer answered.

So that was what we did. After the press conference we went back to the hotel to freshen up, and to leave my hat behind, and then we met the Fords at a restaurant John knew.

We were all high before we even had a drink. "You did a perfect job with him," Liam said. "You did exactly right."

John tried not to look too pleased. "I know that everyone is in love with speed right now, but speed asked for too early in training can burn a horse out. As I've said a million times before, the Derby is an endurance race. So is the Belmont. The Preakness is another story."

"Do you think he'll be ready for the Preakness?"

"I hope so. I'll be able to tell you more in a week."

"Let's not worry about the future," I said. "Let's just celebrate the present. Out of the thirty odd thousand foals registered the year Buster was born, he was the one who won the Kentucky Derby."

"That calls for a drink of champagne," Liam said. He had ordered a bottle for the table.

We all raised our glasses. "To Buster," Liam said. "To Buster," we all echoed.

We had a nice dinner; the Fords were very pleasant people and the men got drunk on several bottles of champagne.

"It's a good thing we can walk to our hotel," I told Liam.

"What would you have done if we couldn't?" he asked.

"I would have driven."

"My guardian angel," he said.

"What?"

"That's what you've always been," he said. "And my good luck charm too."

There were many things I wanted to be to Liam, and an angel and a charm were not included in the list.

"Come on," I said. "A walk will do us good. Help to clear our heads before we go to bed."

"Okay."

He was walking perfectly straight, but he had drunk three quarters of a bottle of champagne and I didn't think he was really sober.

We said goodbye to the Fords, who were driving back to their farm. I noticed it was Lorraine Ford who got behind the wheel. John had been celebrating as much as Liam.

The fresh air felt good and we walked in silence along the streets of Louisville.

The first thing we saw as we came into our hotel room was the message light blinking on the telephone. Liam pushed the button and the first of twenty-three messages came over the wire.

We listened for a while. Then, "Good grief," I said. "Every person you've ever met must have sent you congratulations."

"It does seem that way."

There was one notable absence. There was no word from Liam's father.

"He'll be furious he missed it," Liam said. "What an opportunity to have his picture taken."

"Why didn't he come?"

Liam shrugged. "Who knows? He probably didn't want to be associated with a loser."

I was silent. Liam's indifference was even more damning than bitterness would have been. Liam truly didn't care what his father did. As if he was reading my mind he said, " I miss your dad, Annie. He was more of a father to me than my own father ever was."

I thought of the many hours Liam had spent in my house, doing his homework, watching my mom bake a cake, or playing cards with Mom, Daddy and me. His only exposure to normal family life was with my family. His own was almost classically dysfunctional.

"Too bad your mom didn't come," he said now, as if he had been following my thinking. "She would have had a good time."

"I think she's avoiding things that remind her too vividly of Daddy. That's why she was anxious to move. The house has too many memories."

"You can't run away from grief, Annie. I know that for a fact."

He was very grave.

I kicked off my high heels and wiggled my feet. "Ah. My poor feet. I haven't worn heels in years."

"They look very nice," he said. "You have great legs, Annie."

His tone was fraternal. *At least he noticed,* I thought.

I went into the bathroom to change and came out in my pajamas. *I should have worn a sexy nightgown,* I thought. But then, I didn't own a sexy nightgown.

I went over to the bed and got in, plumping up my pillow so I could sit up against it. He smiled at me, his eyes as blue as sapphires.

"I'm glad you were with me, Annie. There isn't anyone I'd rather share this day with than you."

My throat ached. I wanted him to get into bed next to

me, and hold me, and make love to me. I said, "I'm not your sister, Liam. It wouldn't be incest for you to kiss me."

The blue eyes became troubled. "I know that, but that's not how I feel. We grew up together. Your family was my family. We're not related by birth, I know, but I can't help the way I feel, Annie. It just wouldn't feel right to have anything sexual between us."

I took a deep breath and said calmly, "I don't feel that way about you."

"You hero-worship me. You always have. It's not a grown-up emotion, Annie. You need to open your eyes and start to notice other men."

"I've done that. I almost married one. But there's no one like you, Liam. That just the way I feel."

He looked even more troubled. "I'm sorry."

"I'm sorry too. So what you're saying is, I'll have to look for another man."

"I'm afraid so."

I sighed. "Okay."

I stayed awake a long time, with Liam sleeping quietly beside me.

You hero-worship me, he had said. I suppose that was true, but that was only a small part of my feelings for him. Quite simply, I loved him. I always had; I always would. And he loved me, but not in the way that I wanted.

Could I change that? I wondered. *What would happen if he thought he was losing me to another man?* And the perfect man was right at hand. Kevin was staying at Wellington for another week and I didn't think he'd object to a little flirtation.

I had had this idea before, but now I took it seriously.

I'll start tomorrow, I thought. *Should I tell Kevin what I'm trying to do?*

I don't think so. He might not want to go along with it. Kevin's ego would object to being used to make Liam jealous.

I had no fears that Kevin would be hurt by my using him this way. He was a superstar; he could have any woman he wanted. I doubted very much that he wanted me. But he wouldn't be averse to a flirtation, especially if the flirtation bothered Liam.

I'll start tomorrow, I thought again as I settled myself to sleep. I glanced over to the far side of the bed and saw Liam's bare shoulder peeking from underneath the blanket he had pulled up over him.

I love him so much. This is a rotten plan I have, to make him jealous, but I'm desperate. If I don't do something soon, he might marry someone else.

On that frightening note, I settled myself to go to sleep.

CHAPTER 10

L iam and I went down to breakfast early because we were planning to drive back to Virginia. Unbelievably, there was a reporter in the restaurant waiting for us.

John Ford had warned us last night. "You don't just have a horse anymore, you have a Kentucky Derby winner. Life isn't going to be the same."

"It won't bother me so much," Liam had said. "I'm going back to my farm. You're the one who's going to be in the fishbowl."

Now Liam answered the questions the reporter asked with great courtesy and then we went to our table and ordered breakfast.

"How long will Buster stay at Churchill Downs?" I asked.

"John said he'd keep him in Kentucky for a week and then send him to Maryland so he can have a couple of gallops over the Pimlico track."

The waiter came with our coffee and I fell on mine. Once I had had a bracing drink, I asked, "Do you think the Preakness will be too short for him?" The Preakness was a sixteenth of a mile shorter than the Derby. If the

Derby had been the length of the Preakness, Buster would not have won.

"It's John's job to make sure that it's not," Liam replied.

"Can you imagine if Buster won the Triple Crown?"

He shivered. "Don't say it out loud, Annie. It's too scary."

"It would be crazy."

The waitress came with our orders. I had French toast and Liam had scrambled eggs and bacon.

Liam said, "There's a five-million-dollar bonus to a horse that wins the Triple Crown. A few million dollars would go a long way if I have to get myself another farm."

"Another farm? Surely it won't come to that."

"I don't know, Annie. I don't like it that auditors are looking at the farm books out of season. There's nothing wrong with the books; I don't mean that. But the farm is part of Dad's assets. If he's really in over his head, it may have to be sold."

I poured syrup over my French toast. "I don't think your father would ever sell the farm. It's his heritage!"

"He may have to; or he may just sell off all of the horses."

"He owns Thunderhead, doesn't he?"

He lifted a forkful of eggs. "Unfortunately, yes. Thunderhead belongs to the farm, not to me."

"Well, at least you'd have Buster. And Pennyroyal too."

"I also own two of the other mares, My Holiday and Crescent Moon. I bought them both last year at the Keeneland auction. I own their foals as well."

"Buster is already worth a lot of money, Liam. You can charge a huge stud fee for a Kentucky Derby winner."

"I know, but I keep thinking about how much I could charge if he was a Triple Crown winner."

We both were silent for a while as we contemplated this awesome possibility.

I said, "Even if the horses aren't sold, it might not be a bad idea for you to think of going out on your own."

"I have been thinking of it; that's why I bought Pennyroyal and bred her to Thunderhead. I just hate to think of leaving Wellington, Annie. It's my heritage as well as Dad's."

We finished eating in silence, then Liam said, "I just want to go over to the barn to see Buster before we leave."

"Okay."

We drove over to Churchill Downs and found a ring of reporters hanging around Buster's stall. "Hey there, fella," Liam said and went up to the stall door.

Buster recognized his voice and came to the door. Liam scratched behind his ears and Buster moved his head so Liam could get to the good spots.

The press all wanted to know about Liam's plans for the Preakness.

"We'll see how he recovers from the Derby before we decide about the Preakness," Liam said.

"What kind of a horse is he?" one of the reporters asked. "Is he friendly?"

"He's friendly with people he knows. He actually has a very pleasant temperament. He gets it from his mother."

We stayed answering questions for about fifteen minutes and then we departed to make the drive back to Virginia.

*   *   *

There was a sign posted on Washington Avenue as we drove into Midville. It read MIDVILLE, HOME OF KENTUCKY DERBY WINNER SOMEDAY SOON.

"Isn't that nice?" I said.

"Yes. I wonder whose idea that was."

Liam drove me to my mother's new house and, as he was getting my suitcase out of the trunk, my mother came running out.

"You won!" She gave Liam a giant hug. "You did it! The whole town is bursting at the seams with pride."

"We noticed the sign on the way in."

"That was the Horse Council's idea."

My mother gave me a hug too. "Pete would have been so proud of you, Liam. I'm sorry he isn't here to see this."

"Who says he isn't here?" Liam said. "I can certainly feel him looking over my shoulder."

Mom stood on her tiptoes and kissed his cheek. "You're a good boy, Liam. You deserve this."

"Thanks, Nancy," Liam said softly.

He carried my suitcase inside for me and then he left to drive out to the farm.

"Well," my mother said. "Tell me all about it."

We settled down in the kitchen with a pot of tea and I filled her in on what had happened.

"I saw you on television," Mom said. "You were wearing a hat."

"Women wear hats to the Derby. I made Liam take me to a department store so I could get one. And it looks like I'm going to be stuck with it. Liam wants me to wear it to the Preakness. It could be a lucky charm, he says."

My mother laughed.

"Did it look too silly?"

"Not at all. It looked charming."

I looked at her suspiciously but her face was serious.

"There's been a break of sorts in the case since you left," Mom said.

"A break? What happened?"

"Apparently Justin and Leslie had a fight the day before the party. Someone came forward who saw them shouting at each other, or at least, Justin was shouting."

"Who saw them?"

"One of the Nathan daughters. She was only ten when she witnessed it and at the time she didn't comprehend the significance of what she saw. She came forward now because she's old enough to understand how important such information could be."

"Did she overhear what they were saying?"

"No. But she said that Justin had his hands closed in fists."

"So Liam wasn't the only one to have a fight with Leslie."

"Apparently not. And no one actually saw any confrontation between Leslie and Liam. This evidence against Justin is more damning."

I felt a pang of guilt, but not enough to allow me to give up the evidence that I was harboring.

"Did the police question Justin?"

"Yes. But he hasn't been charged."

I took a sip of tea and thought about Justin. "He was such a hero in high school, Mom. I don't think adults can fully comprehend how awesome Justin was to us common mortals. He could have had any girl he wanted. It had to have been humiliating to see Leslie transfer her affections to Liam. And she did it so quickly. One week

Leslie and Justin were a couple, and the next week they weren't."

Mom poured herself a little more tea. "I don't know. It's hard to imagine anyone doing such a terrible thing because his ego was hurt."

"It could have been more than his ego. Perhaps Justin truly loved her."

"You don't kill the person you truly love."

"Well then, maybe Justin didn't do it."

Mom said, "But if Justin didn't do it, and Liam didn't do it, then who did?"

"Maybe it was a serial killer. You seem to read about one every time you open the newspaper these days."

"I don't think the police are leaning that way," Mom said.

"It's depressing. Here we had such a wonderful time at the Derby, and we come home to be faced with this again."

The front doorbell rang. "I'll get it," I said and went to open the door. Michael Bates was standing outside. He was in uniform.

"Good," he said. "You're home."

"Come on in. Mom and I are having tea. Would you care to join us?"

"Tea sounds wonderful."

I brought Michael into the kitchen where he and Mom exchanged greetings. I got another mug out of the cabinet and poured him the last of the tea. I put the kettle on to make more.

"I know you're interested in the Bartholomew case," Michael said to me. "I just came by to give you a heads-up. The *Washington Post* was on the line to us today.

They were asking about Liam's connection to Leslie's murder."

I felt my heart sink. "Oh no."

"I'm sorry, Anne. I know you're close to Liam. But he's in the limelight now that he has a potential Triple Crown winner and someone evidently tipped the *Post* off about Leslie's body being found."

"Did you tell them Liam is a suspect?" I asked through my teeth.

"We said he was one of several suspects."

"Damn!" I was really upset.

Mom said, "Do you know who tipped the paper off?"

"No, Mrs. Foster. The paper wouldn't say."

"When did this happen?"

"We got the call today. It should be in tomorrow's *Post.*"

I said, "Does Liam know yet?"

"No, I just stopped by here on the off chance that you'd be back."

"I'd better tell him."

"It might be a good idea to prepare him."

"Thanks, Michael, for stopping by."

He pushed his chair back and stood up. "No problem. The whole town is so proud of Liam. It's a shame this had to happen at the same time."

"I know." I walked Michael to the door. He said, "How about dinner tomorrow night?"

I was going to say no, but then I thought I should keep my link to the investigation. "Sure," I said.

"I'll pick you up at seven?"

"Great."

Michael left and I went back to Mom.

"This is terrible," I said.

"I know."

"Do you have Liam's cell phone number, Mom?"

"Your father had it. Let me look in his phone book."

The number was in the book but when I called it there was no answer. "I'm going to take a run up the house and see if I can find him," I said.

"All right, honey."

I pulled out of the driveway and took Washington Street through town and onto the main road until I got to Lewiston Road where I turned right and went to Wellington Road. Wellington was the third farm in and I turned into the driveway and parked in front of the house. It was the dinner hour and I knocked on the front door. No one answered, so I went around to the back patio and knocked on the kitchen door. Liam answered. He was sitting at the kitchen table eating a plate of what looked like stew.

"Annie! What are you doing here?"

"Are you by yourself?"

"Yes. Dad went back to Washington for a few days."

"Where's Kevin?"

"I don't know. I haven't seen him since I got home."

"I have some bad news, Liam. The *Washington Post* is going to print a story tomorrow about finding Leslie's body."

His mouth tightened. "Shit."

"I know. Michael Bates stopped by to tell me. I thought you should know so you can be prepared if the press comes calling."

We had been standing at the door and now he said, "Come on in. Do you want some stew?"

I shook my head. I didn't want any food.

"Sit." Liam gestured to the chair across from him. We both sat down.

"It'll make a great story," Liam said bitterly. "Owner of Kentucky Derby winner is suspected of murder."

"I know. What are you going to do?"

"Nothing. If the press shows up here I'll just say 'no comment'."

"That's probably the best thing."

"I certainly am not going to try to defend myself from a crime I didn't commit."

We were sitting in silence, both of us contemplating the ramifications of a *Post* article when Kevin walked in from the dining room.

"Welcome back, Anne," he said. And to Liam, "Congratulations."

"Thanks."

"You looked adorable in your hat," Kevin said to me.

That made me smile. "Thank you."

"What's going on here? You both look as if you'd lost your last friend."

"The *Washington Post* is printing an article about Leslie's body being found."

Kevin, more than anybody, understood the importance of bad publicity. "Damn," he said. He looked at Liam. "And they're connecting it to you?"

"I just had a Kentucky Derby winner. For this brief moment in time, I'm more newsworthy than you are."

"Well this girl has come forward about seeing Leslie arguing with Justin Summers. No one actually saw you argue with Leslie, did they?"

I kept my eyes on Kevin's face. "No," Liam said. He did not look at me.

"Do you think Liam should get a lawyer?" I asked Kevin.

He shook his head. "Get a lawyer and you'll look guilty. Just refuse to answer questions."

"That's what I was going to do," Liam said.

I said, "I still think a lawyer might be a good idea."

Kevin's "No," clashed with Liam's, "I'm not hiding anything. I don't need a lawyer."

"Okay," I said mildly.

Liam said to Kevin, "There's more stew on the stove, if you're interested."

"Mary's stew?"

"Yes."

"I think I'll have some." He took a plate out of the high wooden cabinet that was over the sink and dished out some stew. He took his plate back to the table and began to eat.

I said to Kevin, "Do you want to ride tomorrow morning?"

"With you?"

"With me."

Kevin bathed me in the radiance of his smile. "I would love to go riding with you, darlin'."

I smiled back at him.

Liam frowned.

My spirit lifted.

I stood up. "I have to be getting home. I just wanted to give you a heads-up on this newspaper story, Liam. I'm surprised no one has tried to interview you yet."

"We were in transit for most of yesterday."

"That's true."

Kevin said to me, "If anyone questions you, just say no comment."

"Are you sure? Maybe we should be friendly to the press. Get them to like us."

"The press never likes anyone, darling," Kevin assured me. "All they're interested in is a nice juicy story."

Liam said, "I'm not defending myself to the press. I didn't do anything wrong."

"Okay," I said. "I'll see you tomorrow morning, Kevin."

He smiled at me again. "Have a good night, Anne."

"You too."

"See you later, Liam."

He grunted something in response and I left.

CHAPTER 11

The *Washington Post* article rehashed Leslie s disappearance and then recounted how her body had been found. It named Liam and Justin as the major suspects and made a big deal of Leslie being the daughter of Andy Bartholomew, former star of the football Giants.

"The coroner will have to look at the body," Michael told me as we were driving to the restaurant for dinner.

"Is there much left to look at?" I asked.

"You don't want me to describe it to you."

I said hastily, "You're right, I don't."

"Doc Marshal is away on vacation, but one of the other state forensic specialists will check it out. I expect they will verify our belief that she was killed by a blow to the head."

"I don't expect there will be any DNA left that might give you a clue."

"It would be nice if that happened, but ten years is a long time to be buried in the woods."

I thought of Leslie and shivered. *"Golden lads and girls all must/Like chimney sweepers come to dust,"* I quoted softly.

"I'm afraid so."

We drove in silence for a minute, then he said, "Cheer up. We're on a date. Let's talk about something positive. How about that Someday Soon?"

I followed his lead and told him what it had felt like to watch our colt come home first.

"I saw you on television," he said. "You were wearing a hat."

"Good grief. Everyone has commented on my hat. Didn't you notice that practically every other woman at the track that day was wearing a hat?"

"I wasn't looking at the other women. I was looking at you."

We pulled into the restaurant driveway and the valet came to open the door for me. Michael surrendered his key and we both walked into the Spinning Wheel Inn.

The Spinning Wheel was a tourist restaurant with the kind of olde English atmosphere the AAA likes to recommend. Michael had made a reservation and we were shown to a table in a crowded dining room. We had been served drinks when there was a stir around the room and I looked up to see that Kevin had come in.

For a moment I saw him as the other people in the room must see him, the beautifully sculpted face, the helmet of golden hair, the tall slim body that moved as easily as a cat's.

"Wow," I said to Michael. "Is he gorgeous or is he gorgeous?"

"I know. I was always a little surprised that Leslie chose Liam over Kevin."

I wasn't but I didn't say so. At this moment, Kevin saw me, and his face broke into its famous smile. He came over to my table to say hello and to introduce the man who was with him as his agent.

We all exchanged greetings.

"Are you two here to talk business or would you like to join us?" I said.

Kevin said; "I can talk business anytime, but I don't get many opportunities to dine with you, darling. Thank you for the invitation."

There were two empty chairs at our table and Kevin sat down and waved his agent, Alan Keyes, to the other.

The agent did not look happy, but he sat.

Michael did not look happy, but he said nothing.

Kevin smiled at me and said, "Have you ordered yet?"

"Just drinks."

The waiter appeared immediately with our drinks on a tray. Kevin ordered a Martini and his agent ordered a diet Coke.

The rest of the room watched us, some openly, some surreptitiously. I said, "Do you ever get used to having people stare at you?"

"Just ignore them," he said.

Alan said, "It's the price of fame, Dr. Foster."

Kevin said, "It's when they stop staring that I'm in trouble."

I said, "Michael and I saw your new movie the other night. It was very good." I turned to include Michael in the conversation. "Wasn't it, Michael?"

Kevin lifted an eyebrow. "Are we horning in on a date, Anne?" He looked at Michael. "I'm so sorry."

Michael looked as if he didn't believe him. "That's okay," he said.

I felt a pang of guilt. The Spinning Wheel was expensive and here poor Michael had asked me out and I had landed him with this extra baggage.

I said to Kevin, "We'll let you pick up the check to atone."

Michael began to protest. Kevin waved his hand. "Please, Bates. It's worth it for me to have dinner with Anne."

Michael looked at me. I gave him an innocent smile.

It was not an entirely comfortable dinner. Kevin and I did almost all of the talking. Alan Keyes was clearly annoyed that he had lost his opportunity to talk privately with his client, and Michael was annoyed that he had lost his opportunity to be alone with me.

But Kevin would find a way to tell Liam that he had had dinner with me. I knew I could count on that. It had always been clear among the three of us that I belonged to Liam. If Kevin won my allegiance, he could claim a major victory in the private contest the two of them had waged for as long as I could remember.

I was counting on two things in my plan involving Kevin. One, Liam's natural possessiveness wouldn't like seeing me with any other man; and two, seeing me with Kevin, more than anyone else, would drive Liam crazy.

"I'm sorry, Michael," I said as we got into his car to go home. "I really didn't think they'd join us; I just invited Kevin to be polite."

"It certainly wasn't the evening I had planned," he said a little sulkily.

"I know and I'm sorry."

A frown still furrowed his brow.

I reached out to lay my hand on his sleeve. "Are you going to sulk the whole way home?"

He sighed. "No. I won't be as adolescent as that."

"Thank you."

"I have the day off tomorrow. Are you free?"

"Actually, I've taken over my father's job and I'm helping to break Liam's young horses. I'm pretty busy during the day."

"Convenient for him, I imagine, your being a vet."

"Yes. Having Daddy die so suddenly was difficult. He has to find a new man and, until he does, I'm it."

"When do you go back to your own job?"

"The beginning of June."

He turned his head to glance at me. "Would you like to stop somewhere for a drink before I take you home?"

"No thanks. I don't like to leave Mom alone for too long."

He nodded. "Home it is, then. How is she settling into the new house?"

"Physically, she's settling in well. Emotionally is another story. She wanted to get away from everything that reminded her of my father, but I don't think it's as easy as she had hoped."

"You can't avoid grief," Michael said. "You have to go through it."

He sounded as if he spoke from experience.

I sighed. "You're right."

"You have to grieve too, Anne. Right now, you're focused on your mother, but you can't ignore your own feelings."

I was quiet for a while. Then I said, "Thank you, Michael."

"You're welcome."

"Did you lose a parent?"

"My mom died last year."

"I'm sorry."

"It was especially hard because I was going through the divorce at the same time."

"Do you have children?"

"No. That was one of the problems with Kim and me. I wanted children and she didn't."

"She had her horses."

"Exactly."

"I've seen a lot of women like that in my practice."

We pulled up in front of Mom's new house. "Well, goodnight," I said brightly. "Sorry I blew our evening."

"Every time I go out with you, I end up in a crowd," he said half-jokingly. "If I invite you out again will you promise it will be just you and me?"

I laughed. "It's a deal."

"I'll call you, then."

"Okay."

He got out of the car and came around to open the door for me. Then he walked me up to the door of the house. When we reached the door, I looked up at him. He bent his head to kiss me on the lips. "Goodnight, Anne. I'll talk to you soon."

"Goodnight," I replied.

Mom was reading a book in the living room when I went in. The furniture was all in place although there were still boxes stacked against the wall to be unpacked. She looked up from her book. "How was your dinner, honey?"

"Very nice." I decided not to tell her about Kevin joining us. She had warned me off Kevin before and I didn't want to worry her unnecessarily.

We sat talking until the news came on. We usually watched the news out of Washington and, after all the political news had been reported, the station did a piece on Leslie.

"Damn," I cried. "Now it's on television."

The camera showed the place in the woods where Leslie's body had been found. They showed an excerpt from the press conference Andy had held shortly after his daughter had been found. And they showed a clip of Liam accepting the Kentucky Derby trophy.

"Shit," I said. "The police have no case against Liam. This kind of thing shouldn't be allowed."

"They only said that he was one of the people questioned in regard to the murder," my mother pointed out. "They didn't say he did it."

"They didn't show any of the other people who were questioned."

"The other people aren't the son of a U.S. senator and didn't just win the Kentucky Derby."

"There's Kevin. He's bigger news than Liam. They only mentioned him in passing."

"True."

"This case is horrible, Mom. It's like a curse that you can't get rid of."

"I don't think they're ever going to solve it, Anne. It was too long ago."

I sighed.

My mother stood up. "I'm tired; I'm going to bed."

I got up to kiss her goodnight. "I won't be long after you," I said. "I just want to get the weather."

"Goodnight, honey."

"Goodnight, Mom."

She stopped at the staircase and looked at me. "You know, this is the worst, knowing that I have to get into that empty bed and sleep alone."

"I know."

Tears filled my eyes as I watched her go up the stairs.

She was still young and pretty, my mother. I wondered if someday she might marry again.

"Everything just stinks," I said out loud.

Then I thought of the Kentucky Derby and the upcoming Preakness Stakes. *Well, perhaps not everything,* I corrected myself.

The weather was over and I stood up, turned off the television and went upstairs to bed.

On Saturday and Sunday Midville held its annual Hunt Country Stable Tour. A selection of local stables opened their doors from 10 to 5 for those who had bought a ticket to benefit Trinity Episcopal Church's outreach programs. Newstead Farm, which belonged to Bertram and Diana Firestone, would be shown, as well as the Mellon barn, Rokeby; Pine Tree, which was owned by the Michaelsons; and Andy Bartholomew's barn, Blue Ridges. Wellington always took part in this charitable endeavor and this year was no exception.

All the hotels and B&Bs in Midville were booked for the weekend. Midville itself was a tourist attraction, with its quality shops, art galleries, fine restaurants, and legendary inns. The village had been named for its location as the midpoint stagecoach stop of the Alexandria-Winchester Turnpike; today it was the midpoint of the Virginia horse industry.

Wellington did not open all of its barns to the tour; it opened the broodmare barn, which was built around a courtyard with the statue of On Course in the center. The visitors could also view the acres of rolling fields and horse paddocks populated with mares and their babies.

When I drove up to the barn at nine o'clock I had to pass a girl standing in the driveway checking tickets.

There were already some tourists walking along the stalls, reading the names on the brass plates and standing in front of the monument to On Course, Wellington's biggest star until Someday Soon had come along.

I stayed for an hour, answering questions and trying to project an air of welcome. At ten o'clock I was surprised to see Senator Wellington appear. He was dressed in chinos and a blue knit shirt, with brown loafers on his bare feet, and he carried a cup of coffee in one hand.

"Good morning, Senator," I said. My voice must have given away my surprise because he gave me a charming grin and said, "We politicians never miss an opportunity to press the flesh, Anne."

He was a very good-looking man, almost as slim as Liam, with a minimum of gray in his thick blond hair. He exuded charisma. I don't know why I was so uncomfortable around him, but I was. I responded to his smile with a forced one of my own and said, "It's starting to get crowded now. You'll have a better audience."

"Senator Wellington!" A woman came up to us. "How wonderful to meet you. Your office helped me out with an immigration problem last year. They were wonderful."

"I'm glad to hear that," Senator Wellington replied. He began to talk to the woman and I turned away.

A young girl came up to me and asked, "Where is the mother of Someday Soon?"

"She's out in the paddock with her new baby," I said.

"Can you point out which paddock?"

"Sure. Come along with me."

I took the girl out to the paddock and pointed out Pennyroyal, with baby by her side.

"She's beautiful," the girl said. "It must be so exciting having a Kentucky Derby winner."

"It certainly is."

The girl was about fifteen, and I stood talking to her for a few minutes. We then walked back to the barn and the girl said, "OhmyGod, it's Kevin Wellington."

It was indeed Kevin, who had come down to the barn to look for me. "Oh there you are, Anne."

"Yes."

The girl next to me sounded as if she were hyperventilating. I suppressed a smile and said to her, "I'm so sorry but I don't know your name."

"Sarah," she breathed.

"Sarah, this is Kevin Wellington."

"I love your movies," Sarah said. "I've seen them all."

Kevin gave her his professional smile. "Thank you. That's always nice to hear."

"Do you . . . would you . . ." She held up her Stable Tour program. "Would you mind signing this for me?"

"Not at all." Kevin took the program and scribbled his name.

"Thank you!"

"You're welcome." He looked at me. "I'm going to the driving range to hit some golf balls. Do you want to come?"

"Thanks, but I can't. I promised Liam I would sort of monitor the stable tour for him."

"Why can't he do that himself?"

"He has a breeding appointment for Thunderhead this morning."

Kevin lifted an eyebrow. "Don't you think you're getting old to be Liam's little errand girl?"

I smiled. "Old habits die hard."

A group of people had formed next to us, obviously

waiting to ask Kevin for his autograph. "I'll leave you to your fans," I said.

He nodded at me, his blue eyes chilly, and his fans moved in. I went to get a bottle of water from the cooler I had in my car. Kevin signed for all the autograph-seekers, then left, and I took another group of people out to see Pennyroyal.

CHAPTER 12

At noon, Liam put in an appearance at the broodmare barn. "How are things going?" he asked me.

"Very well. I've answered a ton of questions and pointed out Someday Soon's mother to an assortment of people."

"Thanks a million, Annie. I don't like to leave the barn unattended on days like this. Some idiot might just decide to light up a cigarette."

"Everyone has been very well behaved."

A woman came up to us. "Excuse me, but is it possible for us to see Someday Soon?"

"He's at the racetrack, ma'am," Liam said. "He won't be coming back here until the season is over."

The lady moved away and Liam said to me, "Do you want to come back to the house for some lunch? Chip promised me he'd keep an eye on things here."

Chip Owens was Liam's farm manager, the one who saw to the maintenance of the farm: the mowing, fencing, trucks, tractors, and manure spreaders. He arrived at the barn within fifteen minutes and Liam and I were free to go to lunch.

There were two dogs in the truck with Liam, and I had

to sit in the middle of the seat so the dogs could look out the window. "How did the breeding go?" I asked as he drove along the farm road in the direction of the house.

"Very well. The mare was a good girl. We got it on the first try."

"What are you charging for Thunderhead's stud fee?"

"Fifteen thousand dollars. If Buster wins the Triple Crown I can quadruple that."

"And think of the price Buster himself will command."

"I know. As long as the farm stays intact, I'll be sitting pretty. I don't need Dad's money to keep going; the farm will be able to pay for itself."

We reached the house and the dogs piled out of the truck and went to lie down on the front porch. We went into the house, through the hallway and the dining room and into the kitchen. It was empty. Liam went to the refrigerator and opened it to look inside.

"It looks pretty bare," he said.

"Maybe Mary hasn't gotten around to shopping this week."

"There are eggs. Do you want scrambled eggs?"

"Not really. How about tunafish? Is there any tunafish?"

He opened a tall cupboard and looked inside. "Not that I can see."

"Do you feel like going into the Coach Stop?"

"Good idea."

We got back into the truck. I watched his hands on the steering wheel as we turned onto Wellington Road. They were slim and long-fingered. I imagined one of those hands touching my breast and my breath quickened.

He said, "I hear you had dinner with Kevin last night."

I decided not to mention the presence of Michael and Kevin's agent. "Yes. We went to the Spinning Wheel. I haven't been there in ages."

"What is this anyway, going out with Kevin? Was it a date?"

"It was a man and a woman who like each other having dinner. Is that so surprising?"

He scowled. "I hope you're not going to start dating Kevin, Annie. That would be a big mistake."

"Why?"

"Kevin's not your type."

"And pray tell then, who is my type? Michael Bates?"

"Bates is a divorced man. You should stay away from him."

"Is there anyone you would approve of my going out with?"

A muscle twitched in his cheek. This was looking promising. "Not Kevin," he said. "Kevin is like your brother."

"Please don't start that stuff again. You choose to think of me as a sister, and I can't help that, but I can assure you that Kevin has no such hang-ups. Nor do I."

"I thought you were interested in me!"

"I was, but you squashed that pretty fast. I'm not going to become a nun because of your phobia."

"All right. Go out with whomever you want. But stay away from Kevin."

"Why?"

"He really isn't your type."

"You have no idea of what my type is."

"It's someone like me."

I said soberly, "There is no one else like you."

We pulled up in front of the Coach Stop and, miracle of miracles, there was a parking space. We got out and went into the restaurant.

I saw Brent Walker in the corner with another man. He waved to me and I waved back.

"Isn't that my father's flunky?" Liam demanded.

"He is your father's aide," I corrected.

"Have you gone out with him?"

"We had dinner one night."

"Jeez, Annie, do you ever stay home with your mother?"

"Yes, I do," I said hotly. "What a rotten thing to say."

"I'm sorry, but it seems to me you're dating every eligible guy who comes your way."

"And if I am, it's none of your business, Liam. Do I ask you who you're dating?"

"I just broke up with Dotty Carmichael," he said stiffly.

"Lucky Dotty," I said.

"There's no need to get nasty."

"Do you know something, Liam? You're a real dog in the manger. You don't want the bone but you don't want anyone else to have it either."

His splendid arrogant nose quivered.

Good, I thought. *That one got him.*

I stared into his cobalt blue eyes and I liked what I saw there. There was anger, but there was also confusion.

Excellent. Clearly I had to keep on dating Kevin. Kevin was the one who had exacted the biggest response.

The waitress came to our table and I ordered a tunafish sandwich. We spent the rest of lunch talking about the upcoming Preakness and how Buster was training for it.

I went back to the farm with Liam because I had left my car there. He had another breeding session that afternoon and I asked him if I could watch. He was agreeable, so I tagged along with him.

The breeding shed was a large square building with a high steel roof. Because the walls were unpadded, mare and stallion mated in the middle of the floor, instead of pressed against the wall the way they did it in Kentucky.

The breeding team had assembled in the shed and the men were talking about last night's baseball game when we came in. The mare was brought in first, after she finished her session with the teaser stallion. The teaser is a gentle horse, usually a quarter horse, whose job it is to stroke the mare's libido by his own interest. He gets the mare ready for the stud, in other words.

Quickly the men prepared the mare. First her genital area was scrubbed with disinfectant. Then one of them wrapped her tail in gauze, a precaution that prevented a long, sharp, stray hair from working its way into the act, getting stuck and causing lacerations to the stallion. A leather strap was attached to one of her forelegs. This would be used to hold her leg off the ground so she couldn't kick the stallion. For the safety of the stallion, she was also fitted out in padded booties on her hind feet. Finally, a leather mantle was placed over her shoulders, for protection in case the stallion tried to bite her.

Thunderhead came in on two legs, roaring loudly enough to shake the roof. The mare moved a little uneasily and the man at her head murmured reassuringly.

Thunderhead roared again and began pawing at the ground, arching his neck and flailing his tail. He knew what he was here for and he was ready for action. The man holding his chain lead shank brought him closer to the mare.

The four men in the barn prepared to facilitate the action. One of the men put a twitch on the mare's nose, to keep her standing quiet. The leg strap man lifted her foreleg off the ground. The tail man held her tail out of the way, and the fourth man guided Thunderhead to the place he was looking for.

The thirty most expensive seconds in sports took place.

Before he dismounted, Thunderhead made a little nickering sound and pressed his face to the mare's covered shoulder.

"How sweet," I said.

The much quieter Thunderhead was led away and the mare was taken back to her stall. "Where is she from?" I asked Liam.

He gave me a triumphant look. "She's from Kentucky."

"Wow. Her owner is getting in on the bargain basement price."

"I have five more Kentucky mares booked this month. I booked them the day after Buster won the Derby."

"Did you boost your price?"

"I doubled it."

"That's great."

He nodded.

I said, "Thunderhead seems to enjoy his work."

"He does. Which is why I'm giving him the time off when breeding season is over and not shipping him to

South America." He was referring to the practice pio-
neered by the Irish stud Coolmore, of sending stallions
to the Southern Hemisphere, where the seasons were
turned around, so that they could double their bookings.

"Good for you," I said.

We were walking back to his truck. "Where did you
leave your car?"

"Over by the broodmare barn."

"Okay."

We both got into the truck and Liam began to drive. A
Jeep Cherokee was coming up the road in our direction
and I recognized Kevin at the wheel of his rental. I
waved. "Look, it's Kevin."

"Yeah, I can see that."

Kevin held up his hand indicating that we should stop.
Liam did and Kevin got out of the Jeep and came over to
my window. "There's a concert in Washington tomorrow
night at the Kennedy Center and I've been invited.
Would you like to come with me? The president is going
to be there."

"Wow," I said. "How fun."

"It's formal. Do you have a gown with you?"

"I don't, but it's not too late for me to nip into Tyson's
Corner and buy something."

"I'll drive you if you like. I'm very good at judging
evening gowns."

"That would be wonderful. Thanks a million, Kevin.
I'll take my car home right away. Can you pick me up?"

"Certainly. I'll see you at your house in a half an
hour."

"Great."

Kevin drove off and Liam, who had listened to our

exchange with a stony countenance, said, "Didn't I just tell you to stay away from Kevin?"

"You did and, as you can see, I have absolutely no intention of listening to you."

"He bribed you and you fell for it."

"Liam, he asked me out and I accepted. Get over it."

He stopped driving and turned to look at me. "Why are you doing this to me? I was so happy to see you, and we were getting along just fine, and then you started this business with Kevin."

"How on earth can my going out with Kevin hurt you?"

"I worry about you with him."

"What do you think he's going to do? Rape me?"

"No. But Kevin has his own agenda, Annie. And that agenda might not coincide with yours."

"All I know is that I was just invited to a great concert by the most handsome man in Hollywood, and I'm looking forward to going. So please don't say another word."

"Okay, okay. But I think you're making a mistake."

"Fine. That's your prerogative. Just don't tell me about it."

He pulled into the parking area for the broodmare's barn, stopped the truck and waited for me to get out.

I flipped my hand in farewell and climbed down.

"If you get hurt, don't say I didn't tell you so."

"Stop being such a doom-sayer. I'll see you tomorrow."

I collected my car and drove home. I had changed my clothes and was just coming down the stairs when my mother came in from school.

I felt a pang of guilt. Liam was right. I never seemed to stay home with her.

I'll be here with her tonight, I thought. I went to kiss her. "How was your day?"

"Okay. What about yours?" She put her bookbag down on a hall chair.

"I watched Thunderhead cover a mare this afternoon."

She gave me an amused smile. "How nice."

"And Kevin invited me to a concert at the Kennedy Center tomorrow night. The president is going to be there. I said I'd go. Is that all right with you?"

"What kind of a question is that? Of course it's all right. It's more than all right. It's great."

"I'm going into Tyson's Corner to look for a dress. It's formal. Do you want to come along and help me pick one out?"

"To be truthful, honey, I'm tired."

"That's okay. You stay home and rest."

I wasn't thinking of dresses when I got into Kevin's Jeep. "What's wrong?" he asked. "You look as if you've got the weight of the world on your shoulders."

"I'm worried about Mom," I said. "She always seems to be tired. I'm afraid she's getting depressed."

He threw me a quick, azure glance. "She just lost her husband. It would be strange if she wasn't depressed."

"I suppose that's true. But she always used to be so filled with energy."

"Your dad's only been dead for a few weeks."

"I know. Maybe she should try going to one of those bereavement groups."

"Is there one in Midville?"

"I don't know. I think I'll call the funeral parlor. They should know about things like that."

"Good idea."

"Where do you think I should look for a dress?"

"Let's try Neiman Marcus first."

Shopping with Kevin was an experience. He was recognized everywhere we went. I was sort of used to his good looks, but seeing the dazzled expression in women's eyes as they looked at him reminded me of how spectacular he was.

I told him, "I keep forgetting you're a big Hollywood star; I just treat you like Kevin, the boy I grew up with."

He smiled at me. "That's why I like being with you. You're comfortable."

I beamed at him. "Exactly. We're comfortable with each other."

I tried on dresses in Neiman Marcus and Lord & Taylor and finally settled on one from Nordstrom. It was a bronze taffeta, strapless, with a tight waist and a full, graceful skirt.

"Maybe I should buy a necklace to go with it," I said.

We went to the jewelry counter and I looked at the costume jewelry to see if I could find something amber. There was nothing that took my fancy.

Kevin said, "You know what, Anne. That diamond pendant you're wearing will be fine."

I looked down at the single diamond drop that had been a graduation present from my parents. "Do you think it's enough?"

"Yes, I do."

"Fine. No one will be looking at me anyway. Not if I'm with you."

"Oh, you more than hold up your end, darling."

"That nice of you to say."

"How about dinner? Shopping always makes me hungry."

"I think I'd better get home, if you don't mind Kevin. I've been leaving Mom alone too much, I think."

"Okay. Home it is."

We chatted easily during the drive back to Midville and Kevin dropped me off at my house where I went inside to spend a quiet evening with my mother.

CHAPTER 13

The concert was a combination of Billy Joel and Elton John and it was terrific. The TV cameras were out in force, and Kevin was photographed from the time he stepped out of his car until we went into the Kennedy Center building.

I was surprised to see that Senator Wellington was there with Mrs. Wellington. We met briefly in the lobby and stopped to exchange greetings. The senator looked at me and said, "You look lovely, Anne. You complement Kevin perfectly."

There was something in the way he looked at me that made me uncomfortable. I forced a smile. "Thank you."

Mrs. Wellington said, "Lawrence is a good judge of female beauty. Of *young* female beauty, that is."

I had no idea what I should reply to that.

Kevin gave a comfortable laugh. "All the Wellington men are good judges of beauty, Aunt Alyssa. That's why Uncle Lawrence chose you." He glanced at his watch. "I think we should take our seats."

We moved apart and as we were shown to our seats I said to Kevin, "Thanks for getting me out of that. He was hitting on me, right in front of his wife!"

"He's incorrigible." Kevin didn't sound too concerned. "And he has a lot of success with women. He's charming and good looking and he has a ton of money."

We had excellent seats, toward the front part of the orchestra in the center. After we had been seated I said, "Liam said his father took quite a hit in the stock market."

"So did everyone else."

"He told Liam that he wasn't going to put any more money into the horse business."

"The horse business is Liam's baby, not Uncle Lawrence's. If he needs money he'll pull it out of the horses first."

"But he could put Liam out of business!"

"That's too bad, but Uncle Lawrence is going to take care of Number One."

"What kind of a father is that?"

"You know Liam and his father have never been close. I've always gotten along with Uncle Lawrence better than Liam does. He blames his father for Aunt Alyssa's drinking."

"It can't be good for your self esteem, to be married to an unfaithful man."

"Probably not. At least he confines his philandering to Washington. He's always been a model husband when he was at Wellington. Aunt Alyssa is able to hold up her head at home."

"He's never at Wellington for very long."

Kevin laughed.

I said, "What if he hit on Leslie and she threatened to tell Mrs. Wellington?"

"Don't tell me that you think that the *senator* did it?"

"It's a possibility," I argued. "She went missing from his party."

"That's true. But there's nothing that connects Uncle Lawrence to Leslie."

"That doesn't mean there wasn't anything."

"I think you're reaching a little bit here," he said.

"Maybe. Maybe not."

"And maybe Liam did it. Leslie slept with me, Anne, and Liam knew it. You know he has a temper. Maybe he picked up that bat and clobbered her with it."

"He didn't. I know Liam, and he would never do such a thing."

" 'Hell hath no fury like a woman scorned'," he said. "But that quote can apply to a man as well as a woman."

"It could more easily apply to Justin Summers than Liam."

He raised a skeptical eyebrow.

"Stop it, Kevin! You know Liam would never do such a thing. Stop trying to get a rise out of me."

He smiled but his eyes looked cold. "I thought you were trying to exorcise the demon lover," he said.

It took me a moment to get his meaning. "Oh," I said. "I am. But that doesn't mean I'm going to think he's a murderer."

"What about me? Do you think I could be a murderer?"

I devoutly hoped that no one was listening to our conversation. "Don't be ridiculous," I said.

"I mean it, Anne. Can you picture me killing Leslie?"

"Of course not."

"Why not?"

"Because I know you."

"People probably 'knew' Jack the Ripper."

"Not like I know you and Liam."

He smiled again, and this time his eyes smiled too. "Loyal little Annie."

"The three of us grew up together. We have to be loyal to each other."

The theater lights blinked to indicate that the show was about to start and we turned to face the stage.

It started to rain as we drove home, and I dashed into the house from the car, pausing to wave to Kevin before I closed the door behind me. I washed my face, brushed my teeth, put on my pajamas and got into bed. Instead of shutting my eyes, however, I stared at the window, listening to the rain on the roof. The sound took me back to when I was thirteen years old and Liam and I had been stuck in a thunderstorm and had run for cover to the broodmare's barn. We had been fishing and he was carrying a bucket with our catch in it. Mom always cooked the fish we caught for dinner.

Liam put the bucket down and the two of us stood in the doorway as sheets of rain swept over the farm. I shivered.

"Are you cold?"

We had both gotten wet.

"A little. Thunderstorms always make me shiver."

He turned to me in surprise. "Are you afraid of thunder?"

"I know I shouldn't be," I confessed. "Daddy explained to me about the electricity in the clouds. But I don't like it. It's too noisy and too . . . bright."

At this point a boom of thunder exploded overhead. I jumped. "Come here," Liam said, holding out an arm. I went to him and he put his arm around me and held me close to his hard boy's body. "Is that better?"

I pressed my cheek against his shoulder. "Yes."

"I love storms," he said. "I love the noise and the lightning flashes."

I looked up at him. He was smiling and his eyes were gleaming.

I said, "That's because you're not afraid of anything."

"Do you think so?"

"Of course," I said matter-of-factly. "You're brave."

"Being brave doesn't mean you're not afraid of anything."

"What does it mean then?"

"It means that you *act* like you're not afraid of anything, even if you are."

The afternoon sky lit up and then the thunder boomed. I pressed closer to Liam and thought about what he had said.

"You mean if I pretended that I wasn't afraid of the thunder and lightning, then I would be brave?"

"Something like that."

I felt as if I had disappointed him. "I guess you must think I'm a coward."

"Of course not." He gave me a lordly look. "Girls don't have to be brave, like boys."

"Why not?"

"They just don't, that's all."

I pulled away from him. "I can be brave. I'll show you."

"Don't be a dope, brat. I don't care if you're afraid of thunder or not."

"If you were afraid of thunder would you tell me?"

He thought about that. Then he grinned at me. "Probably not."

"Then, deep inside, you might be as afraid of thunder as I am."

He frowned. "I'm not afraid of thunder."

"That's what you say. But you might just be being brave."

He scowled. "I'm not afraid of thunder."

"That's what you *say*."

He rolled his eyes. Another flash of brilliant lightning lit the courtyard. Behind us, a horse whinnied. "I'm going to check the horses," I said and turned to go deeper into the barn, farther away from the storm. Liam stayed in the doorway.

I thought back on this encounter now as I lay in bed listening to the rain. I had always remembered what Liam said—that bravery is pretending not to be afraid when you really are. Knowing this secret, I had watched him over the years and I suddenly realized that Liam was afraid of his father.

On the surface there had never seemed to be anything amiss between father and son. But I knew that Liam had passed judgment on the senator and, in the conflict that existed between the senator and his wife, Liam was his mother's champion.

I suppose she had been a good mother once, but by the time Liam was a teenager, the booze had won out over her motherly instincts. Any mothering Liam had known had come from my mother, just as my father was more a father to him than the senator had ever been.

Liam disliked and blamed his father. But why did I think he feared him?

The senator held all the power. He held the power to wound and scar his wife, and he was the owner of the thoroughbred breeding farm that Liam loved with all his heart. He had the power and he was untrustworthy.

That must be why Liam had started to buy horses on his own; he couldn't trust his father to safeguard the farm.

At least now, if something happened, Liam would not be left with nothing. At the very worst, he would have a Kentucky Derby winner and three broodmares with their foals. *But does he have enough money to buy a farm of his own? If Buster doesn't make it through the Preakness or the Belmont, will he be able to afford a new place?*

I didn't think so. If the farm was sold, Liam would be jobless.

I was so accustomed to thinking that the Wellingtons had bottomless wealth that it was strange to realize that Liam might be poor.

He could always syndicate Buster for a lot of money. *That's probably what he'll have to do,* I thought. *He'll have to sell shares in Buster.* If Buster did well in the next two Triple Crown races, he could command a lot of money in syndicate shares. Of course, doing this would limit the amount of money that Liam would be able to make in the future.

The rain had lightened up; I could no longer hear it beating on the roof. I shut my eyes to sleep.

I went riding with Kevin the following morning. We rode down to the old four-arched stone bridge that went over Martin's Creek. The morning was a little chilly and I wore a crewneck sweater over my turtleneck. We dismounted on the bridge and leaned against the rail to look at the creek and the surrounding field below us. The now-peaceful scene had been the site of a battle on June 21, 1863 when Confederate artillery had successfully delayed a Union cavalry advance. Many men and horses had died on the bridge, trying to ford the creek. Today, the grass was green and the creek was hidden in a thicket of trees.

Kevin said, "It's been handy, knowing how to ride. I used it in two of my pictures."

"Remember that picture of you in hunt clothes that appeared in *People*?"

"I remember it very well. In fact, I have it framed and hanging in my house."

"It was neat. Rob Roy looked particularly nice."

He said dryly, "Most people weren't looking at the horse."

"I always look at the horse. That's why I'm a horse vet."

He grinned at me. The sun gleamed on his uncovered hair and his eyes were as blue as the sky. "How does a guy get to first base with you, Anne?"

"Liking horses is a good start."

"Tell me about this man you almost married."

"I didn't almost marry him. I almost became engaged to him."

"So tell me about it him."

I tried to conjure up John's face. "There's nothing much to tell. I met him in vet school and we started going out. He's a wonderful guy, kind, generous, loyal . . ."

Kevin said, "You sound as if you're describing a dog."

I laughed. "I liked him very much. I tried to love him, but I just couldn't. End of story."

"You couldn't because of Liam."

I sighed. "I suppose."

"Anne, look at me." Surprised, I turned to him and before I realized what was happening, he had taken me in his arms and was kissing me.

It was a kiss from a man who knew something about kissing. My first reaction was to push him away. I stifled that, though, and let him keep on kissing me, opening my mouth when he asked. When I had had enough, I pushed him away.

"Really, suh," I drawled. "This is a public place after all."

"There's no one here except us and a few hundred ghosts," Kevin said.

I laughed a little shakily. That had been a powerful kiss.

He said, "You have beautiful skin. That's one thing the camera loves—beautiful skin."

"Thank you." I wished he wouldn't compliment me.

"I meant what I said. I could get you a job in pictures."

"Kevin, I didn't spend all those years studying veterinary medicine to become an actress."

"All right, all right. I hear you."

"How much longer are you staying for?"

"I've got to go to New York for a couple of days, then I'm coming back for a week or so. To tell you the truth, I was really very tired after I finished filming my last movie. I need a break from everything."

"Well, it's not too calm around here with a murder investigation going on."

"Yes, but you're here, and that makes it very nice indeed."

"Thank you, sir."

We got back on our horses and returned to the big house where Mary cooked us a wonderful breakfast. Then I headed to the track to work with the horses.

CHAPTER 14

Liam and I drove up to Maryland for the annual Alibi Breakfast, where owners and trainers gathered on the Thursday morning before the Preakness, the second race in the Triple Crown. The breakfast was held at the Pimlico Race Course in Baltimore, and it was traditionally where Derby owners and trainers got together to swap sad stories of why they had lost the Derby and why their horses would most certainly win the Preakness.

I had to make another trip to Nordstrom to buy a linen suit that would be appropriate for the breakfast and ended up with something in fuchsia with a V neck and a short skirt. I saw Liam looking at it, but he didn't say anything.

When Pimlico had been built in 1870 it had been a world-class track, but in later years the neighborhood around it had decayed until the track itself was an urban fortress in a sea of poverty and violence. Still, for one day out of the year, it was once again the focal point of the racing world.

Over the last two weeks, the turf reporters for all the big dailies, as well as the *Bloodstock Journal*, had come to a consensus that Someday Soon's win in the Derby was a fluke. If the early speed had not burned out Honor

Bright and Mileaminute, Someday Soon wouldn't have had a chance. This was the song that Bob Baffert and Sheikh Mohammed and D Wayne Lukas and Prince Salman sang all during breakfast, and it was the song that Liam and I heard when we went down to the stakes barn to visit Buster.

"Do you think he has a chance in the shorter race?" a turf reporter asked Liam as we leaned on Buster's stall and watched him eat hay.

"Sure I think he has a chance. He won the Florida Derby and it was a shorter race than the Derby."

Reporter Fred Isle pointed out, "He wasn't racing against Honor Bright and Mileaminute in the Florida Derby. And he lost to Honor Bright in the Wood."

Liam said, "The Wood was a prep race for the Derby. We're not prepping any more; we're in the real thing. Someday Soon can win the Preakness."

The other turf reporters who were hanging around the shedrow saw Liam talking to one of their number and soon a whole swarm of them had descended on us. Liam introduced me.

"There's nothing wrong with Someday Soon, is there?" somebody asked.

"There's nothing wrong with the horse," Liam replied. "Dr. Foster is an old friend."

"How come my old friends don't look like that?" one of the men joked.

Liam ignored the comment.

I said, "I'm surprised that Someday Soon isn't the favorite for the Preakness. After all, the horse won the Kentucky Derby. And he won it in pretty convincing fashion."

"Your jockey rode a smart race," someone returned.

"Santos kept him out of traffic and he laid off that blistering pace. The chances of your horse having such an easy trip in the Preakness are slimmer."

"I think you gentlemen will be in for a surprise," I said mildly.

We stayed at the stall for about a half an hour, then made our way back to our car.

We had driven up the night before and checked into a hotel. "What do you want to do this afternoon?" Liam asked as we got into his Lexus to go back to the hotel.

"Do you want to get changed and go back to the track?" I asked.

He looked at me gratefully. "You don't mind?"

"Of course not."

We changed into jeans and spent the afternoon hanging around the barn, talking to people and watching Buster.

That evening we went out to dinner by ourselves. Liam took me to a nice restaurant on the harbor and we had a leisurely dinner and went back to the hotel afterward. "Come into my room and we can watch television together," I said.

"Okay."

I stretched out on the bed that was directly in front of the TV and Liam turned it on. "Maybe there's a ballgame on," he said.

The Orioles were playing the Boston Red Sox and Liam came back to the bed and stretched out beside me. I had taken off my sneakers and socks and I wiggled my toes enjoying the freedom.

Liam said with amusement, "Such pretty toes. Somehow you don't imagine your vet having pink toenails."

"A pedicure is one of the finer things in life," I said.

"Do you get manicures and pedicures, Annie?" He sounded genuinely curious.

"You bet I do."

"Let me see your hands."

I held my hand up for him to see. My nails are short, but I had a French manicure.

"Pretty," he said.

"Thank you. I can't have long nails because of my job."

"I don't like long nails."

"Then I'm happy I don't have them."

"I'm so glad that you've been here to share this experience with me, Annie. I'm not great with words, but I want you to know that it means a lot to me."

"I'm glad I'm here too."

"I wish your dad had been able to see this."

"I'm sure he's watching, Liam."

He nodded soberly.

I asked, "Is your father coming for Saturday?"

"Both he and my mother are coming. I think he's mad that he didn't come to the Derby."

"He didn't think Someday Soon would win."

"You got it."

"Kevin told me that he always got along better with your father than you did."

"That's true. They're the same, Kevin and my father. I think they respect each other."

"What do you mean by that?"

"They both always get their own way."

"That could be said of you too."

He shook his head. "The difference is that I count the cost of getting my own way; they don't."

I thought about that. "That may be true of your father, but I don't think it's true of Kevin."

"Please, Annie. Kevin's good looks, not to mention his social status, have always gotten him everything he ever wanted. He wanted to be a Hollywood star and he is." He turned to look at me. "I'm just afraid he may be thinking that he wants you."

His face was somber.

"I think you're exaggerating. Kevin and I are just friends."

"Kevin isn't the kind of man who can be 'friends' with a woman who looks like you do."

"You're prejudiced," I said.

"Don't fall for him, Annie. He's corrupt."

"Puh-leeze," I said. "Kevin may be spoiled, but he's not corrupt."

"He is. I can smell the corruption in him like I can smell it in my father."

He was deadly serious. I said, "I think you're wrong, Liam. You and Kevin were always in competition when you were young. I don't think you see him clearly."

"I think it's you who doesn't see clearly, Annie. I'm worried about you."

He was beginning to get my back up. He was making poor Kevin sound like an ogre. "I think you've lost all sense of proportion on this. Kevin and I have been enjoying each other's company, that's all. We haven't seen each other in ages."

"Has he kissed you?"

I could feel myself flush. "That's none of your business."

"Shit. He has kissed you."

I glared. "Will you watch the damn Orioles and stop

cross-examining me? The more you talk the more you sound like a dog in the manger."

A muscle flickered in his jaw. "I love you, that gives me the right to be concerned about you."

"I love you too, but that doesn't give me the right to criticize whoever you go out with."

"I'm not going out with anyone right now."

"Well, if you were, I wouldn't say bad things about her to you."

"If there were bad things to be said, then you should say them."

"I'd love to see your face if I told you a girl you were going out with was corrupt."

"If she was corrupt, I'd want you to tell me."

"Hah," I said.

He ran his hand through his hair. "This is getting us nowhere."

"Why don't we just drop the subject?"

He glowered at me. "Are you falling in love with Kevin?"

"I don't know yet. And that is the last word I am going to say on this subject."

He looked grim.

Good, I thought. *Let him put that in his pipe and smoke it.*

Silence fell as we both pretended to watch the ballgame. I was terribly conscious of his long body stretched out beside mine in the bed. I wanted so much for him to turn to me, to take me in his arms, to kiss me and tell me he loved me the way I wanted him to love me. Tears pricked behind my eyes. *Oh, Liam,* I thought achingly.

He picked up my hand. "I'm sorry, Annie. I suppose I was prying. But it's only because I care about you so much, and your father isn't here to look after you any more."

"I haven't needed anyone to look after me in a long time, Liam. As I keep telling you, I'm all grown up."

"We all need someone to look after us," Liam said soberly. "It's what makes us human."

I let my fingers curl around his. "You always took care of me when I was small."

"You were always on my side. And there were times when I desperately needed someone on my side."

I thought of the ugly scene that I had once witnessed between Senator Wellington and Liam. The senator's words had been so chilling, so demeaning, that they could be counted as abusive. Liam, who at sixteen did not have his father's facility with language, had been white with shock. I had slipped into the room when the senator left and slid my hand into Liam's.

"Let's go for a walk, Liam," I had said. "Let's get away from here."

He had closed his hand around mine tightly. "Yes, good idea."

We had walked for miles around the farm, hand in hand, neither one of us talking.

"I hate him," Liam had said finally.

"He's not a nice man," I agreed.

"It's hard to accept that such a shit is actually my father."

"What made him so mad at you?"

"He wants Mom and me by his side when he kicks off his reelection campaign. I told him I didn't want to be there."

"That's what made him so angry?"

"One of the things."

"What are you going to do?"

"If Mom goes, I'll go with her."

"Will she go?"

"Probably. Then she'll get drunk."

I squeezed his hand.

"The problem is, he has all the power. He has the money and he has the farm. I love the farm, Annie. I want to make it into a top-notch thoroughbred breeding operation. I've talked about it with your dad and he says I have very good ideas. But if I piss the old man off too much, he won't give me the free hand that I need."

"Stay away from him as much as you can and try to be polite when you're in his company."

"That's what your dad says."

"Daddy gives very good advice."

"So do you."

The feel of Liam's hand around mine brought back that scene with amazing clarity and I looked up at him. "Thank God you bought Pennyroyal."

He looked down at me. "I know. I didn't tell you this, but your dad was the one who advised me to buy a few of my own horses so that I wouldn't be totally dependent on my father. I did a lot of research and I liked Pennyroyal the best of all the mares being sold at Keeneland. Then I paid the farm the stud fee to breed her to Thunderhead."

"Do you board her at the farm for free?"

"Your father said to make sure I paid a boarding fee for all my horses. He said that way it would be clear that they were mine and not part of the farm."

"It sounds as if Daddy was afraid of the same thing you were, that your father would sell the farm."

"Yes. Thank God he gave me that advice. I don't think I would have thought of it on my own."

I smiled at him a little mistily.

"God," Liam said. "I miss him."

I nodded but did not speak. Then I rested my head against his shoulder and he slipped an arm around me and we went back to watching the ballgame.

CHAPTER 15

The day of the Preakness dawned clear and bright. The early odds made Honor Bright the favorite at 2 to 1. Then came Mileaminute, the D Wayne Lukas horse, then Tango With Me, the speed horse. Someday Soon was fourth at 7 to 1.

"We don't get no respect," Liam said when he saw the odds.

I said, "They all think Someday Soon will run out of track. If it was the Belmont, at a mile and a half, he might be the favorite."

"Probably not. Probably Honor Bright would be the favorite for that too."

I put on my lucky pink suit and hat and we drove out to the track, passing through the blighted neighborhood of Belvedere. The track was packed, with over 100,000 people jammed into the stands.

The television network that was broadcasting the event did an interview with John Ford and Liam outside of Someday Soon's stall. "They had to interview us," Liam said. "After all, Buster *is* the Derby winner."

The day flew by. As the time for the race drew near, Liam and I went back to our seats, where we were joined by Senator and Mrs. Wellington. Mrs. Wellington kissed her son. "Darling, I'm so excited for you."

"Thanks, Mom."

Mrs. Wellington had been a beautiful woman, but years of drinking had taken their toll. She was still elegant, but her beauty was a thing of the past.

"I put a bet down on him, Liam," the senator said. "At these odds, I could make a bit of money."

"I hope you do," Liam replied.

"Oh my God," I said. "I forgot to bet!"

Liam laughed.

"Did you bet?" I asked him.

"I certainly did. And from what I gathered from my e-mail, every bettor in Virginia and Kentucky bet on him too."

The Pimlico bugler, wearing a red cutaway jacket and black top hat, blew the call to the post. The horses began to parade past the grandstands and the U.S. Naval Academy Men's Glee Club in dress whites sang, "Maryland, My Maryland."

I stood up on my toes, then back down again. I was so excited I couldn't keep still.

The senator said, "The track has been favoring the inside horses." In fact, the winners of the last five races had all run on the rail. With the track biased for the rail, the inside horses, Honor Bright, Tango With Me and Long Johnnie would have an advantage over the rest of the horses that were coming from the outside.

"I know," Liam replied. "John told Miles not to ride the rail. All of the other horses are going to try to cut in there and if Miles tries it too, he'll get caught in traffic. Better to stick to the outside, where he'll have running room."

To encompass the race's full mile and three-sixteenths, the starting gate was set up just past the final turn. The horses would run past the finish line, around the track, and then come down the homestretch again.

The horses turned around and began to canter toward the starting gate.

"Someday Soon looks great," I said to Liam. "He looks eager."

The starter and the assistant starters began to load the horses into the gate. In less than three minutes, we would know the winner. I dug my nails into my palms. Then they were all in.

The gates opened and the horses sprang out.

Almost the entire field swerved in toward the rail, hoping to get the advantage of the track's bias. Miles Santos and Someday Soon stayed out, about five horses wide. Jorge Chavez on Kerry's Way careened across their path, speeding across six lanes from the ninth slot. At the front of the pack, Tango With Me, Long Johnnie and Honor Bright raced neck and neck, each of the excited horses resisting their jockey's attempt to rate them.

"My God, it's a stampede," Liam said.

Someday Soon was ten horses back and five horses wide. Just in front of him was Pat Day on Mileaminute and on his outside was Gary Stevens on Point Taken. Holding that position, the horses flew past the parking lot on the other side of the chain-link fence.

The time for the first half-mile flashed on the tote board screen. "Jesus," Liam said. "That's two seconds faster than the Derby."

The pack passed the cement barns on the backside and Honor Bright took the lead. Someday Soon was still ten horses back, running in a threesome with Mileaminute and Point Taken

"He's got to get around those horses," I said. "He can't stay stuck there too long."

The field sped by another parking lot filled with yellow school buses. "This is where Santos should make his move," Liam said. "He can't leave it any later than this."

As they watched, Mileaminute swung a little wide, leaving an opening. Santos squeezed through and Someday Soon was free on the track, five horses wide and nine horses behind.

He started to move.

"He's coming!" I shouted. "Oh Liam, he's coming!"

Someday Soon passed Point Taken and then he started picking off the other horses: Tango With Me, who had fallen from the lead, then Kerry's Way, Always Yours and Sentinel Watch. He caught Long Johnnie and Zeus and Kimberly Dan. Then only Honor Bright was ahead of him.

"Come on, Buster!" I screamed. "You can do it, you can do it!"

Liam was shouting next to me, "Go, go, go!"

Ears flat, digging deep, on came Someday Soon. He caught Honor Bright two lengths before the wire and sailed across the finish line the winner.

"Oh my God, he did it. He did it! Buster is the winner!" I was jumping up and down, clapping my hands. Liam picked me up in his arms, taking me right off my feet.

"He did it, he did it, he did it!" He swung me around.

I put my hands on his shoulders to balance myself.

"Congratulations, Liam," Senator Wellington said, holding out his hand. Liam had to put me down to shake

it. Then he embraced his mother. A track official shouldered his way into the box and told us we should follow
him down to the winner's circle.

Someday Soon had beaten fourteen horses for a
chance to compete for the Triple Crown. Liam went over
to him and patted his neck, then he buried his face in the
black-eyed Susans on the victory blanket.

The Preakness presentation platform was filled with
people. Senator and Mrs. Wellington were there as well
as Miles Santos' wife and Lorraine Ford. Charlsie Canty
was interviewing Miles.

"Think you'll be favored in the Belmont?" someone
from the press called to John Ford.

He shrugged. "We'll see."

Above the winner's circle, a painter began painting the
Wellington colors, royal blue and white, onto the weather-
vane jockey.

Liam was interviewed on TV and then the senator,
who was charming and congratulated his son, the owner.
"Liam bred him and raised him and sent him to John
Ford," he said. "All of the congratulations are to go to
him, not me."

I thought it was quite decent of him to admit this and
said as much to Liam.

"I suppose it was," he admitted. "I like it that it's out
in public, that I am the owner, not Wellington Farm."

We went out to dinner with the Fords once again, but
this time we were joined by Miles Santos and his wife as
well as Senator and Mrs. Wellington.

The restaurant put us at a big round table and everyone
ordered a drink. Liam ordered two bottles of wine for the
table. When the drinks arrived, the senator poured me a

glass of Chardonnay. Liam lifted his glass and said, "To Someday Soon."

"To Someday Soon," we all echoed.

Mrs. Wellington said, "Did you ever tell these people that I named that horse for you?"

Liam smiled. "That's right, Mom, you did."

"Where did you get the idea from?" I asked.

"I was reading a book titled *Someday Soon* and I thought it would be a good name for a thoroughbred. I mentioned it to Liam when he told me he was looking for a name for Pennyroyal's colt. He liked it, and that's how Someday Soon got his name."

"It's a great name," I said. "It has presence."

"It was good luck, you naming him, Mom. Maybe I'll have you name all of my horses in the future."

Mrs. Wellington looked pleased. "I'd be happy to."

"When I think of the names that some horses get stuck with," John said.

We spent the next fifteen minutes recalling the most ridiculous names we could come up with as I finished my glass of wine.

The waiter came to take our order and I requested another glass of wine.

The mood at our table was euphoric. I couldn't remember being happier.

We ordered appetizers, then salads, and I had another glass of wine then another. The entree came and I had another glass of wine then another. I was feeling great.

Liam suddenly said, "How many glasses of wine have you had, Annie?"

I smiled at him. "Who knows?"

The senator said, "Leave her alone, Liam. She's having a good time."

"I should have kept an eye on you," Liam said.

"I don't need anyone to keep an eye on me, thank you. I am perfectly able to keep an eye on myself." I spoke slowly and carefully because my mouth didn't feel completely reliable.

Lorraine Ford said, "She's not half as high as you and John were after the Kentucky Derby."

"Thash right," I said.

"She's not driving," the senator said. "Leave her alone, Liam."

"Thank you, shenator."

Mrs. Wellington said calmly, "It's all right to drink on a happy occasion. It's drinking when things are bad that's the problem."

Everyone at the table was silent. They knew they were hearing from an expert. Then Liam said, "All right, but no more, Annie."

"I don't want any more," I told him loftily.

The party continued and I was still feeling very happy. When we broke up to go home, I went with Liam to his car.

"Get in," he said a little grimly as he held the door for me.

I got in.

He went around and got in behind the wheel.

I said, "I felt dizzy when I got up."

"You had too much wine, Annie. You're drunk."

"I am not."

"Yes, you are."

"I have never been drunk in my life."

"Well, you're drunk now. Just what I need. One woman in the family who drinks is enough."

I blinked. "I'm not in your family."

We pulled out into traffic. The dizziness I had experienced when I first stood up returned and all of the lights on the city street were blurred.

I said, "You know, maybe I did drink too much. Everything is blurry."

He didn't reply, but when we got back to the hotel he led me into my room and said, "Are you going to be all right?"

The ride in the car had made me feel sick to my stomach. "I don't feel so good, Liam," I said.

"Come on, Annie. Let's get you into bed."

"Okay." I sat on the edge of the bed and looked at him. He sighed. "Let's take off the jacket, okay? You don't want to sleep in that pretty dress."

I nodded and my fingers fumbled with the buttons.

"Let me do it." He came over and unbuttoned the jacket of my two-piece black dress. He slid the jacket off my shoulder. "Come on, now, give me your other arm." I let him take the jacket off of me.

"Now the skirt," he said. "Stand up."

I stood up and he unbuttoned the skirt and slid it down my legs. "Sit down again," he said and slid the skirt off over my feet.

I was wearing a bra, panties and a short half slip. Liam pulled the covers down on the bed then lifted me into his arms and carried me to the top of the bed. He laid me down, but he did not pull the covers up immediately. I looked up at him. "I'm sorry, Liam," I said. "I'm sorry I drank too much. I was so happy."

"Shh," he said. "It's okay." He sat down on the bed next to me. "You have such beautiful skin, Annie."

He was looking at my breasts.

"You could kiss me," I said.

"I suppose I could do that." He leaned down and kissed me on the mouth, a gentle, loving kiss. I couldn't help the way I responded to him and he straightened up. I had scared him away.

"It's all right," I said. "I'm drunk."

"You are," he agreed. He stood up and pulled the covers up over me. "Sleep it off, tiger. I'll see you in the morning."

I managed to hold back the tears until after he had gone. Then I cried my eyes out. I really was quite drunk.

The next morning I woke with a horrendous headache. "Don't talk to me," I said when Liam called to see if I was awake. "Whisper."

"As bad as that, eh?"

"Yes."

"Are you up to driving home?"

"If you do the driving," I said.

"Okay."

"I'm just going to make a pot of coffee in my room here and drink it. I don't want anything to eat."

"Okay. I'll go down to the coffee shop and give you a buzz when I get back."

"Okay."

I took two Excedrin and drank three cups of coffee. I would have to make several pit stops on the way back to Virginia, but by the third cup I was starting to feel human again. When Liam came to pick me up, I was ready.

"You look white as a ghost," he said.

"Why on earth do people drink? I feel horrible."

"How did you ever come to drink so much wine? I told you that two glasses was your limit. You must have had twice that."

"I don't know how many I had. I just kept refilling my

glass. I was feeling so happy, Liam. You won the Preakness!"

"I was feeling pretty happy too, but I didn't get drunk."

"You got drunk after the Derby. I know because I walked you home."

"You didn't have to put me to bed."

I blushed. "Let's not talk about last night. It was not one of my finest hours."

"Okay. Let's talk about Buster."

"He's a wonderful horse, Liam. I truly believe you have a great shot at the Belmont."

"The Belmont is more his race than the Preakness. I kind of think we got through the hardest of the three races yesterday."

"It's almost awesome— to think that you might have a Triple Crown winner."

"I keep pinching myself to see if I'm awake and not dreaming all of this."

"I know. Daddy would be so proud of you, Liam."

"Buster was his boy. He always thought Buster was going to be something special. He told me to keep him, that he could be a Derby horse. I wish he could have lived to see this."

"Something Special! What a great name. That could be the name of Pennyroyal's new foal."

"I like it. I think I'll get Mom to name the Going West colt that you're working with. She sounded kind of proud that she had named Buster."

"She did. She was great last night, Liam."

"She was."

"You know what's funny?"

"What?"

"When you see your mother and father together, they act like they're married."

"Say that again?"

"I mean, you can sense that there's a bond between them. In spite of all his infidelities, I think they love each other."

"You're a sentimental sap if you think that."

"You don't have to get abusive."

"You don't know what abusive is until you have heard my father in action."

I had heard him in action, and Liam was right. But I was right too. There was a bond between the senator and his wife. I had sensed it yesterday at the racetrack and then again at the dinner. It might not be a healthy bond—in fact, it couldn't possibly be a healthy bond—but it was there.

I said, "Do you think they'll put a sign up saying that Midville is the home of the Preakness winner?"

"I bet they will."

"I think there will be one already there."

Liam continued to drive and I closed my eyes and waited for the Excedrin to kick in.

CHAPTER 16

There was indeed a sign on Washington Street when we drove into town. "In three weeks time that sign will read TRIPLE CROWN WINNER," I said to Liam as we drove by it.

"God, I hope so."

He dropped me at my house and came in to see Mom. She met us at the door. "You won!" She hugged Liam and then she hugged me. "I'm so thrilled for you."

"We're pretty thrilled ourselves," Liam replied.

I wondered if he noticed how he always seemed to refer to the two of us as a couple.

"I have a carrot cake in the fridge," she said. "How about a slice to celebrate?"

"You don't have to ask me twice," Liam said. He put my suitcase down in the hall and we all went back to the kitchen. Mom put the kettle on for tea.

"Do you have anything cold to drink?" Liam asked.

"I have iced tea."

"That would be fine."

"I'll have some too," I said. I was very thirsty. I thought it must be part of the hangover.

"You don't look well, honey," Mom said to me. "You're so pale!"

"She celebrated a little too much last night," Liam said casually.

It took Mom a moment to get it. Then she said, "Oh, you mean she drank too much."

"You got it," I said. "And I can assure you that I'm never going to do it again." I drank my iced tea thirstily.

Mom took out the carrot cake and cut us generous slices. My stomach looked at it and stayed quiet. I accepted a plate. Before I took a bite, I got up and poured myself another glass of iced tea.

"So tell me all about it," she said. "I saw the race on television, of course, but tell me about the stuff I didn't see."

So we told her all about the Alibi Breakfast and the lack of respect shown to Someday Soon by the press and the bettors.

"I bet it will be a different thing for the Belmont," Mom said.

"It's going to be crazy for the Belmont," Liam said. He had some icing on his upper lip, which I pointed out to him. He licked it off.

"Where is Buster going to train?" Mom asked next.

"We're going to ship him to Belmont. John said he'd like to gallop him over the nice wide track there. I think that's what he's going to work on: endurance. He says the speed will take care of itself."

"The Belmont is a very long race for a three-year-old," I said.

"It's a long race for any thoroughbred, no matter what his age is," Liam said.

"That's true."

"What's been going on here?" Liam asked my mother. "Anything new?"

He didn't say it, but we knew he was talking about the case.

"Not that I've heard. I know they've had crime scene people out in the woods where Leslie was found. I don't know what they're looking for."

"They're looking for something that might finger the killer," Liam said soberly. "I hope they find something. I'm sick of being a suspect."

I said hotly, "It's such a shame this had to happen right now, when you're in the middle of a campaign for the Triple Crown. It takes some of the fun out of it."

"The timing could be better," Liam agreed.

"Michael Bates called looking for you, honey," Mom said. "And so did Brent Walker."

I saw Liam's hand go rigid on the table. "Ah," he said sarcastically, "the boyfriends."

"They're not my boyfriends," I said mildly.

"You go out with them."

"I like them both. They're good company."

"You're leading them on, Annie. I never thought you'd be like that."

"Can you believe this, Mom? I go out for a couple of dinners and this is what I get!"

"I think you're overreacting, Liam," Mom said.

"I'm surprised that Kevin didn't call," he remarked next.

I replied smoothly, "Kevin knew I was in Maryland with you. He said he'd call me when I got back."

Liam put down his fork and stood up. "Well, I'd better get out of here before the phone rings again."

I smiled sweetly. "Thanks for taking me, Liam. It was wonderful."

"You're welcome." He stormed to the kitchen door, went out then came back in. "I left your suitcase in the hallway. Do you want me to carry it upstairs for you?"

"No, I'll do it later."

"Okay."

We heard the door close behind him.

"Thanks, Mom," I said. "It was great of you to mention Michael and Brent."

"Anything to help the cause," she said lightly.

"What do you think? Do you think Liam seems jealous?"

"Yes, I certainly do."

"We had such a great time together. I wish he would forget this silly bias he has and see what's right before his nose. We were meant for each other."

"If he can't, though, Anne, you have to be prepared to accept it," Mom said gravely. "You have to be prepared to cut the tie completely if it's necessary."

I sighed. "My brain knows that, Mom. It's my heart that won't accept it."

The phone rang and Mom picked it up. "Hello? Oh, yes, she's here. Just a moment, Kevin."

Too bad he didn't call five minutes earlier, I thought. *Liam would have been here.*

"Hi Kevin," I said brightly into the phone. We talked for a few minutes and then I accepted an invitation to have dinner with him. I said to my mother when I hung up, "Now I just hope Kevin tells Liam that we're going out."

She frowned. "I'm still uncomfortable with you going out with Kevin like this, Anne. Those two boys have been in competition with each other all their lives. It could be dangerous."

I hooted. "Dangerous! You're kidding, Mom."

"No, I'm not."

"I know they were in competition, but brothers are often like that. There was nothing abnormal about their relationship."

"Kevin is very self-centered. He always resented the attention Liam got as the senator's son."

"I know Kevin is self-involved. That's why I'm not worried he'll fall in love with me. The only person Kevin will ever be in love with is himself."

"I don't know, Anne. I just have a very uneasy feeling about you getting in the middle of Kevin and Liam."

"I'll watch it, Mom. If I think Kevin is getting serious with me, I'll back off."

She frowned.

I said, "Liam doesn't like me going out with Michael Bates or Brent Walker but he purely *hates* the idea of me going out with Kevin. Kevin is the one who best fits my purpose."

"Your purpose of making Liam jealous?"

"My purpose of helping him to discover that he loves me."

"He already knows that he loves you."

"That he loves me sexually, I should say."

"Do you think he does?"

I thought of the way he had looked at my breasts. "I think he's on his way."

Mom sighed. "Well, I can't think of anyone I'd rather see you married to than Liam. He's a good boy."

"Then you don't think he killed Leslie?"

"I can imagine Kevin doing that more easily than I can imagine Liam."

"But Kevin has no motive."

"I know."

I frowned. "Do you know what? I don't think it was a good idea for me to eat that carrot cake."

"Why don't you go upstairs and rest. You really do look dreadfully pale."

"I think I'll do that."

I picked up my suitcase and took it up to my new small bedroom. I laid down on top of the quilt in my jeans and knit shirt and in minutes I was asleep.

Kevin called again late in the afternoon to say that he had a reservation at a very nice Washington restaurant and that I should dress up a little. I wore the suit I had bought for the Alibi Breakfast and when he picked me up he looked me over with approval. "Nice suit."

"I bought it in Nordstrom for the Alibi Breakfast. A lot of photographers took my picture."

"I saw you on television with Liam. You were dressed more conservatively."

"My good old pink suit. Liam insisted that I wear the same clothes I wore to the Kentucky Derby. I'm sure I'll have to wear them for the Belmont Stakes as well."

"Including the hat?"

"Including the hat."

"I never knew that Liam was superstitious."

"I'm not superstitious either, but I probably would have done the same on my own. We don't want anything to change. We want everything to be the way it was in the races Buster won."

"Is Liam wearing the same clothes?"

I blinked. "I suppose that he is. He's wearing his blue blazer. I don't know if he's wearing the same tie. He must be."

The drive into Washington took about an hour and the restaurant had valet parking. "This is very nice," I said to Kevin as we came in. It was one of those restaurants that *looks* expensive: the tablecloths were snowy white; there were fresh flowers on each table; there was a setting of elegant china at each place; the chairs looked comfortable. A waiter greeted Kevin by name and showed us to a private table in the corner.

The restaurant was half full and everybody looked at Kevin as he crossed the room. Even in Washington, which was filled with famous people, Kevin commanded attention.

I said, "At least in a place like this people know enough not to come looking for autographs."

"That's one of the reasons I chose it; it also has good food."

I looked at my elegant menu. It was made of parchment and the offerings were in script. I wear glasses for reading, but I can usually see if I need to. I squinted at the menu and it didn't become any clearer.

"Oh dear," I said. "I didn't bring my glasses, Kevin, and this menu is so fancy I can't read it."

"Since when did you start to wear glasses?"

"I got them in college. All of the reading did a job on my eyes. I only need them to read, though, which is why you haven't seen them yet." I looked at him. He was wearing a perfectly tailored gray suit and his hair was neatly brushed. I said, "I bet you don't need glasses."

He looked amused. "I don't, actually."

"Just like you never needed braces."

"I've been lucky."

I nodded. "Do you think you could read me the menu?"

"Sure."

We had a very pleasant dinner. Kevin could be a very amusing companion, and if most of the conversation seemed to revolve around him, I didn't mind. We were drinking our coffee when he said, "Liam doesn't like our going out."

I looked at him warily. "I know."

"I think he's carrying this big brother thing a little far myself."

"I'm not paying any attention to him, Kevin. I hope he didn't upset you."

"Upset me? Of course he didn't upset me. It's just like Liam, though. The minute I have something, he wants it for himself."

This was not how I had read their relationship.

"You and Liam have always been in competition," I said to him lightly. "A lot of brothers are like that."

Kevin's face looked suddenly white, his eyes hard. "Liam and I are not brothers." On the surface his tone was pleasant but the undercurrent was not.

"You were brought up as brothers."

"No. We weren't. Liam was always the son of the owner; I was merely a cousin."

"Kevin, that's not true!"

"Yes it is. Granted I got along better with Uncle Lawrence, but I still wasn't his son, and everyone else on the farm favored Liam."

"That's not true," I repeated, but less certainly than before.

"Liam's mother favored him, your father favored him, you favored him. True or not?"

"Daddy spent more time with Liam, but that was because Liam was horse crazy. You weren't."

"I liked horses well enough."

"Of course you did. And you were great on a hunt. But you didn't live for horses, the way Liam and I did. That's the bond that drew us together, Kevin. Not the fact that Liam was the owner's son."

"I'm not accusing you or your father of sucking up to him, Anne."

"I understand that."

And I did understand—suddenly I understood a lot of things. Kevin was so beautiful and so self possessed that you forgot he had been abandoned by his parents and left with an aunt who drank and an uncle whose life was his political career. Evidently his childhood had left some scars.

He gave me a wry smile. "How did we ever get on this depressing topic?"

"I don't know. Let's talk about something else."

"I had an interesting discussion with my agent the other day. He wants me to do a different kind of movie."

I expressed interest and he spent the rest of the dinner telling me about it. We drove home and Kevin walked me to my door.

"This was very nice," I said to him. "Thank you for the dinner."

"It's like a breath of fresh air, being with you," he said. "You don't have any issues."

I took this to mean that he appreciated my not trying to talk about myself instead of about him. But I didn't want to think unkind thoughts about Kevin. He was what his childhood had made him. I patted him on the arm. "Goodnight."

"Don't I even get a kiss?"

"Sure," I said and put my hands on his shoulders and tilted my face toward his.

He was a very good kisser, but I didn't have that hungry reaction to him that I had had to Liam. Kevin's kiss was pleasant, and I wasn't a bit disappointed when he broke it off.

"Goodnight, sweetheart," he said.

"Goodnight." And I walked into the house.

Mom was watching the news and I talked to her for a few minutes, then I went upstairs to bed.

CHAPTER 17

Jacko and I had started to teach our young pupils to stand in the starting gate and to run straight once they left it. A horse's inclination is to swerve and turn and in general have a good time while running. The young horse has to be taught to run straight. To do this we had three of Liam's grooms, as well as Jacko, riding as we put the horses into sets of four each and had them go down the track.

It was always amusing to watch the youngsters as they tried to master the trick of staying out of each other's way. I was watching four of them coming down the track when Liam appeared beside me. Together we watched as one of the horses swerved in and another veered out, their shoulders colliding as both jockeys used their reins, waved their whips and tried to steer a straight line. Then they all ran in a bunch, bumping into each other, until one of the horses pulled away. He got so excited to be by himself that he started curving left and then right, tacking like a sailboat. The other horses caught up to him of course and then passed him and he bucked and ran after them.

"Don't you just love them?" Liam said.

"When you think of what they have to learn in so short a time, it's amazing," I replied.

"Your father was so fabulous with the young horses. He could be endlessly patient, but he could also be firm. He always seemed to know which he needed to be, too.'"

"Have you found anyone for the job yet?"

I couldn't say "to replace Daddy." No one could replace Daddy.

"I'm having second thoughts about filling the job," Liam said. "If the farm is going to go bust, it won't be fair to have just hired someone."

I frowned. "You're really taking this seriously, aren't you?"

"I am. One of the big dot-com companies that collapsed? Telecom? Dad had tons of their stock. It's a total wipe-out."

"When did you discover this?"

"He told me before we went out to dinner on the night of the Preakness. He said he was glad I owned Someday Soon because he didn't know what was going to become of the horse farm."

"That doesn't sound good."

"No, it doesn't. Apparently he took a lot of money out of the blue chips and put it in this company."

"That's the one that Congress is investigating, isn't it? The one that left all of those people without any pensions?"

"That's the one. Dad knew the CEO—who made a fortune, by the way."

"How could he have been so foolish?"

"People were racking up fortunes on that stock, Annie. Dad just wanted to get in on the fun. He's paying for it now, though."

"Does he have any money left, Liam?"

"He cashed in some more good stocks to help pay for his last campaign."

I was appalled. "Will he have to sell the farm?"

"He might have to sell some of the property. He can sell off five hundred acres and still have the house and two hundred acres—a nice little estate."

"This is awful."

"It is."

"What will you do if he sells the farm out from under you?"

He looked at me somberly. "I was thinking of leasing a farm in Kentucky and standing Someday Soon there."

"Kentucky?"

"That's where the mares are, Annie. If you're standing a stallion you want to be where the mares are. I could charge much more for Someday Soon in Kentucky than I can in Virginia."

"I can't imagine you not being here, at Wellington."

There was a white line around his mouth. "I have a hard time imagining it too. But it might happen."

"Would you have the money to lease a farm in Kentucky?"

He looked at me soberly. "If I win the Triple Crown, and the five million–dollar Visa Triple Crown match prize, I can *buy* a farm in Kentucky."

"Wow. That's right."

"In the meantime, though, because of all of this, I don't think I should hire anyone for Pete's job."

"No, you're right. It wouldn't be fair."

"Do you think you could possibly squeeze two more weeks' leave out of your practice so you can continue to prepare the horses for the Keeneland sale?"

"I'd hate to leave here before the Belmont," I said. "I'll see if I can arrange something."

He put an arm around me and hugged me to his side. "Thanks, Annie."

I leaned against him for a moment, letting my right breast press against his chest. Then I pulled away.

Jacko came up to us. "Do these horses get sillier every year, or is it just me?" he asked.

I looked into his weathered face and smiled.

Liam said, "They didn't look all that bad, Jacko."

Jacko nodded his gray head. "The Going West colt is going to be real good, Liam."

"That's what Annie's told me too. I guess I'll keep him."

"I would if I were you."

"So tell me, Jacko," Liam said. "How much money did you make on Buster?"

Jacko's face split into a giant grin. "A bundle, lad. I made a bundle."

"I don't think you'll get the same odds for the Belmont."

"That won't stop me from betting him," Jacko said loyally.

"I can't believe that I forgot to put down a bet," I said.

Both Liam and Jacko regarded me indulgently. You could almost hear them thinking "*women.*"

I said briskly. "Okay Jacko, time to return this bunch to the barn and bring out the next set."

As Jacko moved off, I turned to Liam. "Do you want to come to dinner at Mom's tonight?"

He gave an exaggerated start. "Don't tell me you're free for dinner? Where are all the boyfriends?"

I smiled innocently. "No one's asked me out yet."

"Well then let me take you up on your invitation fast, before someone steps in and beats me out."

I laughed.

"I understand you went out with Kevin last night."

I said enthusiastically, "We went into Washington. I must say, it's fun going out with Kevin, Liam. He gets the star treatment wherever he goes."

He scowled. "I never thought I would hear such a shallow statement from you, Annie."

I shrugged. "It may be shallow, but it's a lot of fun."

The white line came back around his mouth. "What time do you want me?"

"Six-thirty? Seven?"

"Six-thirty will be fine." He turned away from me. "I have to go. Savannah Road has an appointment."

Savannah Road was the other stallion besides Thunderhead that Liam stood.

I watched him walk back to the truck, followed by the two coonhounds. He walked with all the lithe grace of a cat. Every move he made was so beautiful to me. I loved him so much.

Jacko's voice said, "Which set do you want next, Anne?"

I turned to go back to work.

When I got home, I called Michael Bates and got him in.

"Hi," I said. "I'm returning your call. Mom said you rang while I was away."

"I did. I watched the Preakness on television, though. We had it on at the station. Man, was that exciting."

"I know. I screamed so loud I almost lost my voice."

"I called to ask you out to dinner and a movie."

"How nice of you."

"Yeah, I'm a real prince. Are you available?"

"I could go out tomorrow night."

"I'm on duty tomorrow. What about the next day?"

"Wednesday would be great."

"Wonderful. I'll pick you up at seven. You can tell me all about the Preakness."

"I will. See you in a few days."

I rang off.

"I'm going out with Michael on Wednesday," I told my mother. "Can you be sure to mention it to Liam tonight? You know, casually, the way you did the other night."

"I think I can manage to do that."

There was a look in my mother's eyes that made me feel that I had to justify myself. "I know this seems underhanded," I said. "But I'm fighting for my life, Mom. What's that old saying? 'All's fair in love and war'?"

She smiled ruefully. "I'm not judging you, honey."

"Are you praying for me?"

"I'm praying that whatever will be best for you will happen."

"That's okay," I said. "Liam is best for me. I've known that all my life."

"What are you and Michael doing on Wednesday?"

"Just dinner and a movie. Why don't you come with us, Mom?"

My mother laughed. "I can just see poor Michael's face if I showed up.

"He wouldn't mind."

"He most certainly would. Please don't feel as if you have to be with me all the time, Anne. I'm all right by myself. Honestly, I am."

"You cry when you're by yourself."

"I have to cry. I'm sad. It's good for me to cry."

I hadn't thought of it like that.

"I guess you can't hide from grieving," I said.

"No, you can't. I just have to go through it."

"But I don't want you to go through it alone."

"It's been wonderful having you here, honey. But you don't have to have me tag along on your dates."

"Okay, Mom. I hear you."

"You and Liam should go out together this evening. Your purposes are not served by inviting him to a cozy family dinner."

"What do you mean?"

"I think he needs to see you in different surroundings, Anne. Go out on a date with him. If you stay home you fall back into your old comfortable relationship and that doesn't help."

I thought about what she had said and came to the conclusion that she was right. "But how do I get out of eating at home?"

"I will have a convenient headache and you two will go out to eat on your own."

I said, "Mom, you're a great conspirator."

She smiled. "Thank you, honey."

"With the two of us plotting against him, Liam doesn't have a chance."

My mother laughed. "I hope you're right."

"So do I."

So when Liam came to dinner carrying a bottle of wine, my mother was absent from the scene.

"I'm so sorry, Liam," I said, "but Mom has a rotten headache and is lying down."

I couldn't believe how easily the lie slipped off my

tongue. I had always prided myself on my truthfulness. I had always thought it would be hard to lie. Hah.

Liam looked concerned. "I'm sorry, Annie. We'll make it another time."

I said, "We still have to eat. Do you want to try the Coach Stop?"

"Sure," he said. "That's a good idea."

We parked a block away from the restaurant and walked to the front door. I was wearing black pants, black boots and a pink sweater set. Liam wore khakis and a pullover sweater with loafers.

There were several empty tables when we walked in. The waitress who came to take our order was a girl I had gone to school with.

"Hi Jen," I said. "How are you?"

"Anne! How nice to see you. I didn't know you were still in town."

"I'm staying with my mother for a little while. My father died, you know."

"I know. Everyone in town was so sorry."

Liam said, "You're new here, aren't you?"

I said, "Oh Liam, this is Jen Gayta. We went to school together."

Jen looked a little embarrassed. "I just took this job. My husband got laid off and we need to have some kind of an income."

I said, "I'm sorry. There's a lot of that going around these days."

"Yes, there is. Now, can I get you something to drink before you order?"

I had my usual White Zinfandel and Liam ordered a beer. As Jen moved away Liam said, "Dad isn't the only one who is feeling the bite of this economy."

"No, people are really hurting. Thank God Mom has a real pension coming and not a 401K."

"Your father had a 401K."

"I know, and it's not worth much right now. But Mom can afford to let it ride because she has a job."

"How about you, Annie? What kind of benefits do you have with your job?"

"I have a 401K too."

"Do you have health benefits?"

"Yes. That's part of the package."

"That's good."

"How do you get paid, Liam?" I asked curiously. It was a question I had never thought about before. The Wellingtons had always seemed to me to have a bottomless pool of money.

"I take a salary from the horse business. That's something else your father advised me to do."

"It's a good thing you had Daddy to look out for you."

"Tell me about it."

"So the horse business is making money?"

"It's making money. But I haven't had to pay anything for the use of the land. If I have to lease or buy a farm, I'll have monthly payments to make. I've never had that at Wellington. My father just handed the property over to me and let me do as I liked. I never realized before this how easy he made it for me to succeed."

"He wasn't interested in the farm."

"I've been thinking about this, Annie. I was able to buy Pennyroyal and my two other mares with the money I saved from my salary. I saved my salary because I wasn't paying rent anywhere. I've really been living a privileged life, even though I didn't know it. I just thought it was something that was due to me because I was a Wellington."

"How did you get Thunderhead?"

"I bred Thunderhead, but the stud fee came out of farm income and the mare was a farm mare. Thunderhead belongs to the farm. Damn."

"So if you go out on your own all you'll have is Someday Soon, his mother, two other mares and three foals."

His jaw looked grim. "That's it. Obviously, I will need to buy more horses."

"Why don't you buy the Going West colt? Don't keep him; send him to auction at Keeneland, then buy him back with your own money. I think he's going to be a good one."

"What a devious mind you have."

"I amaze myself," I confessed.

"It's a great idea, though. In fact, I might buy one of the fillies back too."

"It would all be on the up and up if you did it that way, wouldn't it?"

"Yes, because other people will have a chance to bid. If the price goes too high, I'll have to back off."

"Okay, then. It would be a shame if you lost all of the breeding lines you were so careful to get."

"I've been feeling sick about it," he confessed. "I love all my mares. It will break my heart to part with them."

"Could you send some of the mares to the auction and buy them back?"

"I think if I try to do that, I'll be investigated. It will look like a scam. In fact, it may very well *be* a scam."

"Well, it all may come out okay in the end, Liam," I said comfortingly. "Your father won't sell the horses unless he has to."

"I don't think he would. He likes to think of himself as a horse breeder."

"He never really was involved with the horses though, was he?"

"No. My grandfather was big into horses—he bred On Course, the stallion who won the English Derby. He was the one who started me in the horse business. I just took over from him after he died."

"My dad liked working for your grandfather."

"I know. And Grandpa thought your dad was a genius."

I smiled. "He was."

"You won't get any argument from me."

At this point, Jen arrived with our food and our conversation turned to a different subject.

When we got home, Liam got out of the car and walked me to my front door. As I said goodnight to him he suddenly began to glower.

"Do you kiss the boyfriends when they take you home?"

"That's none of your business," I replied mildly.

"Did you kiss Kevin?"

"Let's not get into this again, Liam. I would be happy to kiss you, but you don't want me to. So stop complaining about me and other men."

"Jesus, Annie. You've got me so confused."

This was good news.

"What's to be confused about?" I asked.

"I'm confused about the way I feel about you. You're right. I am being a dog in the manger. I don't feel right kissing you myself, but I don't want you to kiss anyone else."

"Let's just try one little kiss," I suggested. "You can see if it's all that terrible."

"Well . . . okay." He bent his head and I tilted my face up to him. His lips touched mine and, with heroic self control, I responded gently. For a kiss it was short and sweet.

He lifted his head and I smiled up at him and said, "Look. You're still alive."

"I didn't think I was going to be struck dead."

"Sometimes you act that way."

"This was okay," he said.

"Good. Now I've had a busy day and I want to see how Mom is doing. Goodnight, Liam."

"Goodnight, Annie."

I walked into the house, went to the window and watched him return to his car and drive away.

CHAPTER 18

On Tuesday one of the horses stepped on my foot and almost broke it. It was one of the yearlings being silly, and I wasn't fast enough to get out of the way.

Man did it hurt.

Liam had just stopped by a minute before in time to hear me holler and he came running. I was hopping around grimacing with pain.

"What happened?"

"Sparky stepped on my foot."

Liam called, "Jacko, come and take this horse. Annie just got stepped on."

I had been stepped on before, but nothing had ever hurt like this one. "I hope it's not broken," I said worriedly.

I am like that when I get hurt or sick. I always foresee the worst.

"Let's get ice on it right away; then I'll take you to the hospital for an X-ray."

"Okay."

"Come on, I'll carry you out to the truck."

I started to say I could hop, but I bit the words back before they came out of my mouth. It would be nice to be carried by Liam.

"Put your arms around my neck," he ordered.

I obeyed and he bent, scooped me up in his arms and began to walk toward the barn door. He carried me as easily as if I weighed ten pounds.

It was lovely, being held by him like this. The pleasure of his closeness did a good job of distracting me from the pain in my foot. He slid me into the truck's passenger seat, then went around to get in on the other side. He shoed away the Lab who had accompanied him.

"Sorry, fellow, you're going to have to get back home under your own steam." He started the motor and said, "I'm going to take you back to the house and we'll get some ice for that foot. Then we'll go to the hospital."

We arrived at the house five minutes later and he carried me from the truck into the kitchen, where he parked me on a wooden chair. "There are always ice packs in the freezer," he said, taking one out. "You need to take your boot off, Annie."

I bent down and unlaced my boot. I started to pull my foot out of it and winced.

"Unlace the whole boot," Liam said. "Here, let me do it." He knelt in front of me and unlaced my boot. Gently he eased my foot out. "Okay?"

"Okay," I returned.

He peeled my sock off. "It's red," he said.

"It really hurts, Liam. I'm nervous. What if it's broken?"

"It's probably just bruised," he said soothingly. "We'll get it X-rayed, but first I want to put this ice pack on it. Hold on one sec." When he returned he was holding a roll of gauze. "I'll wrap the pack on to keep it in place and then we'll go to the hospital."

What am I going to do if my foot is broken? I thought. *How can I continue training the horses? How can I start back to work again? Will they put it in a cast?*

I asked Liam, "Do they put broken feet in a cast?"

He looked up from his wrapping. "You are incredible. You always imagine the worst. Remember the time you got poison ivy and you thought it was leprosy?"

"I had just read that book. . . ." I justified myself.

"This is probably just bruised. Stop worrying until you find out you really do have something to worry about."

He finished wrapping the gauze. "Okay. We'll leave the sock and boot off." He bent and picked me up again. I slid my left arm around his neck. His body felt so strong and hard against mine. He smelled the way he always did. Put me blindfolded in a room anywhere in the world, and I could pick out Liam by his smell.

He carried me out to the truck and put me on the front seat. A coonhound came up to the truck, looking to get in. "Not now, Sam," Liam said firmly, and closed the door on him. Then he went around and got in the driver's side.

It was a half an hour to the hospital. We didn't talk. Liam drove and I worried about my foot. We went into the emergency room and I had to go into a little office and give all my health insurance information. It was a good time to come in, I guess, because they could take me right away. Liam came with me as we went inside and I sat on one of the beds in a cubicle.

A nurse took my temperature and my blood pressure and told me the doctor would be with me shortly. We waited perhaps five minutes before a young man in a white medical coat came in the room and introduced himself as Dr. Wheeler.

I explained about the horse and my foot.

He felt it and I winced. "We'll get an X-ray," he said. "That's the best way to find out if anything is broken."

They put me in a wheelchair and took me to the X-ray department, where my foot was photographed. Then I was returned to my cubicle, where Liam was waiting for me.

It didn't take long for the doctor to come back. "Nothing's broken," he said cheerfully. "It's just a nasty bruise."

I felt a rush of relief. A bruise I could live with.

"Didn't I tell you so, Annie?" Liam demanded.

"I know. I know."

"The best treatment is what you've been doing," the doctor said. "Ice will help to keep the swelling down."

"You don't need to wrap it or anything?" I asked.

"We don't need to wrap a bruise. Just watch your feet when you're around horses."

"I usually do."

Liam said, "Annie is a veterinarian."

"Really? You look young to be a vet."

"You look young to be a doctor," I said.

He laughed. "Touché. Do you practice around here?"

"My practice is up in Maryland but I'm here for a few weeks visiting my mother. She lives in Midville."

We exchanged a few more pleasantries and then I turned to Liam. He was looking like a thundercloud. I said, "We left my sock and my boot at home, Liam. Do you think you could carry me out to the truck?"

The doctor said, "We have booties I could give you."

"Thank you anyway, but I will carry her." Liam's tone

did not match his polite words. He looked at me. "Are you ready, Annie?"

"Yes. Thank you, doctor."

"You're welcome."

Liam picked me up and we began to walk out of the hospital. "That doctor is probably going to ask you out," he said sourly.

"I suppose I should be flattered that you seem to think every man I meet is after me. But, actually, it's rather annoying."

"You don't realize how beautiful you are, Annie. You were always cute, but you've turned into a beauty. You have to be careful. If you're too nice to a man he'll think you're interested."

"You know what, Liam? I have been dating since I was nineteen years old. I know how to conduct myself around men."

I wondered if he realized how tightly he was holding me.

"Would you go out with that doctor if he asked you?"

"No."

"Why not?"

"I would never marry a doctor. Their hours are as bad as a vet's."

"Aha! So you admit you are thinking about marriage. I thought you told me you wouldn't marry Michael Bates, but you're going out with him."

We had reached the truck but he didn't put me down.

I said, "Every woman thinks about marriage, Liam. I would like to have a big family, so I need a husband. Naturally, I think about the men I am dating in that role."

"Then you *have* considered marrying Michael Bates."

"You can rest easy," I said. "I crossed him off my list of prospects."

"How about in Maryland? Do you have any 'prospects' there?"

"Can we continue this conversation in the truck?" I was having a hard time keeping a clear head with him so near.

"Certainly," he said stiffly, opened the door and slid me in.

"Well?" he said once he was sitting behind the wheel. "Do you?"

"Do I what?"

"Damn it, Annie, don't be cute. Do you have any 'prospects'?"

"I am going out with someone, yes. But it isn't serious."

"It may not be serious on your side but I bet it's serious on his."

"How did you know that?"

"Haven't you heard a word I've said to you? You are a very desirable woman."

"You talk about me as if I'm a femme fatale or something, Liam. I assure you that is not the case at all. And I think we should change the subject."

He started the truck. "Do you want to make a bet that that doctor calls you?"

"You'd lose. If I lived locally, then I agree he might, but he's not going to call for a date with a woman who lives in Maryland."

"You sound very positive."

"I told you, I've been dating for a while."

"Have you ever . . . er . . . done it?"

I wouldn't give him an inch. "Done what?"

"Had sex."

"Yes," I said calmly. I have."

"With the man you were almost engaged to?"

"Yes. And the sex was very good. That wasn't what caused me to break up with him."

He didn't say anything but he didn't look happy.

"Liam, why don't we try just dating? I'm only home for a few more weeks. Let's see if it leads to something."

A muscle twitched on the side of his jaw. "Okay. Let's try it."

I smiled.

"What about taking a picnic lunch down to the swimming hole? That would be fun."

When we were children we had spent many a hot summer afternoon in the pond created by Martin's Creek on the edge of the Wellington property.

"I guess I could manage that."

"I'll bring the lunch."

"Okay. Come by the house and we'll take one of the trucks. Are you sure you can walk?"

"The doctor said walking wouldn't hurt me."

"You could dunk your foot in the pond. The water should be cold enough this time of year."

"That's a good idea."

He dropped me off at home and I limped into the house. Mom was at school and it was quiet. I went upstairs and debated about what I should wear. The day was sunny and warm and I decided that I would wear jean shorts, so Liam could see my legs. I put on a long-sleeved cotton pullover sweater, white crew socks and sneakers. Then I went back downstairs to make our lunch.

I put the lunch basket in the car and drove back to

Wellington, parked in front of the house and got out. Liam was waiting for me on the porch.

"You're limping," he said as I got out of my car and went around to the other side to collect the lunch basket.

"It still hurts."

"Did you take something for it?"

"I took a couple of Advil."

He took the basket from me and we walked over to the truck. Lucy, the Springer spaniel followed us to the truck and I stood aside so she could jump in.

Liam said, "Let me go and collect a ball to throw for her."

"Okay." I got into the truck next to Lucy. Liam came back with a tennis ball in his hand and joined us in the truck. I put the ball in the picnic basket as we drove away.

The swimming hole was in the woods, right where Martin Creek entered Wellington property. It was just a small pond, and the middle wasn't even over an adult's head, but the bottom was soft and the water was clean and clear. When we were small my mother used to come with us to lifeguard, but as we grew older and taller we were allowed to come by ourselves.

"How lucky we were to have this wonderful place to grow up in," I said to Liam as he spread the blanket he had brought on the high grass.

I knelt down on the blanket next to the food basket.

"It's true," Liam said. "Remember the times we sneaked by here on our ponies and took a swim and never told your mother?"

I remembered those days vividly. We would strip down to our underwear, go swimming, then sit on one of the rocks to dry before donning our clothes again and going home.

"Kevin never came with us on those expeditions," I said. "I wonder why."

"He never wanted to leave the house in the summer. He said it was too hot."

I laughed. "And now he's living in southern California."

"He probably moves from his air-conditioned car to his air-conditioned house to his air-conditioned movie set."

I said, "Remember the summer Daddy built us a raft and we played pirate?"

He laughed, and I laughed too. Liam's laughter always affected me that way. He said, "I was the captain and you were my loyal mate."

"I always got the second-place jobs," I said mildly.

"That's because I was older and bigger."

"And bossier."

"That too."

Liam stretched out on his back and put his hands behind his head. The sun was deliciously warm and he narrowed his eyes. I looked at his lean hard body resting so trustingly next to me. I didn't know if all this reminiscing about the past was a good idea or not.

I lay down on my stomach next to him and propped myself on my elbows. "I think Kevin had a very lonely childhood," I said. "Your parents weren't that attentive to either of you and he didn't have the advantage of hanging out at my house, the way you did."

"He never wanted to do any work," Liam said. "He liked to ride, and he's a decent rider, but when it came to currying and brushing the horse after the ride, he'd leave that to the grooms. You know how you and I would hang around when the horses were shod? Kevin never wanted to do that. He didn't like getting dirty."

"He was very smart in school," I said.

"Very. It was the one thing he could beat me at."

He turned his head and looked at me. Our faces were very close. "Are you feeling sorry for Kevin, Annie?"

"I don't feel sorry for him now. He's landed in a field of clover. But I am sorry that he didn't have a more loving childhood."

"He did okay. Even when he was a kid, Kevin was good at looking out for himself."

His eyes were on my mouth and his voice sounded husky. I said, "Do you want to eat?"

He blinked. "Sure."

"I'm afraid we didn't have any cold cuts in the house, but these sandwiches should remind you of the old days."

He bit into the sandwich I had handed him. "Peanut butter and jelly! I haven't had a peanut butter and jelly sandwich in years."

"Is it good?"

"It's terrific."

I unscrewed the thermos of orange juice and filled a glass. It gave me such pleasure, to give him a sandwich and pour a glass of juice for him.

The lock of hair had tumbled down over his forehead and my fingers itched to smooth it back. His fingers looked dark against the white bread of the sandwich. Liam always looked as if he had a tan.

He smiled at me. "This is nice."

"Yes sir, Captain Wellington."

His smile broadened. "Good job, Mate Foster."

We laughed, a low intimate sound. Then Lucy, who

had been investigating the surrounding woods, came up to Liam looking for him to throw something for her.

I got to my feet. "I'm going to go soak my foot."

Liam fished the tennis ball out of the basket. "Come on, Lucy. Do you want to swim?"

I sat on one of the rocks that bordered the pond and took off my shoes and socks. Then I waded in.

The water was cold.

Liam stood on the shore and threw the ball for Lucy, who flew after it, ears streaming back in the breeze she created. Water splashed as she tracked down the ball. Then she had it and was coming back, swimming until she could touch ground and start her tail wagging.

How many times have I watched Liam throw a ball for a dog? Why does watching him now make me want to cry?

I was so close to him. Closer, I thought, than anyone else in the world. And yet I was so far away.

We stayed for another half an hour, then we loaded the picnic basket and the dog back into the truck and went home.

CHAPTER 19

Tuesday night I rented a movie and Liam drove into Mom's to watch it with me. We sat together on the sofa, with a bowl of popcorn on the coffee table, and watched a Julia Roberts film that had just come out on video.

I was so conscious of Liam, whose shoulder was touching mine, that I had a hard time concentrating on the movie. Halfway through the film his hand closed over mine and we watched the remainder of the movie that way.

"That was nice," I said when the film was over.

"Yes, it was." His voice sounded a little huskier than usual. "What do you want to do tomorrow night?"

"I can't do anything with you tomorrow night. I accepted an invitation to have dinner with Michael Bates."

"Cancel it," he said.

"I can't. I don't want to. I want to find out if anything more is happening in the case."

"How about if I tag along with you?"

"No! He won't say anything at all if you're there."

"What more could be happening, Annie?"

"I don't know. That's what I want to find out."

"You're using poor Michael."

"Oh, so now he's 'poor Michael.' You usually talk about him as if he was an ogre."

He was looking very somber. "Do you know what, Annie? If we're going to date then I don't want you going out with anyone else. I'm a possessive sort of bastard. I don't like to share."

The words struck a chord in my mind. Then I remembered. He had said those words, or something very like them, to Leslie the night I had overheard the two of them arguing in the garden.

"All right," I said. "It's a deal. But I can't cancel out on Michael. It would be too rude."

"Okay. Go out with him this once. But that's all."

"I promise."

After Liam had gone home I went to talk to Mom, who had gamely stayed upstairs, supposedly correcting papers, so Liam and I could have the living room to ourselves.

She was reading a book in bed. "How did it go?"

"Good. He held my hand. I think he's starting to look at me as a woman and not as his little pal."

"Well, that's progress."

"I feel encouraged. He's definitely not happy that I'm seeing Michael tomorrow night, but I said it would be too rude of me to cancel."

"It would be."

"I know. Plus I want to pump him to see if there's anything new in the case."

Mom frowned. "You sound very hardhearted, honey."

"Don't you start with the 'poor Michael' too," I said. "He's a grown man and the way I've landed him with company on all of our dates he can't think I'm serious about him. In fact, I'm surprised he continues to ask me out."

"He must like you."

"He's looking to rebound from Kim, which isn't a good idea. He needs some time to heal before he takes up with another woman."

"You're probably right."

"Anyway, I'm only having dinner with him. Liam said I was leading him on, but I'm not. I've never even kissed the man!"

"You don't have to get so defensive, honey. I don't think you're leading him on. But I don't think you should continue to see him just to pump him for information."

"Okay, okay. I think I'm going to bed, Mom. I'm tired."

"Goodnight, honey."

I kissed her cheek. "I'm sorry if I seem to be embroiling you in my love life."

"It's a good distraction for me," she replied. "It gives me something else to think about."

"Good. Goodnight, Mom."

"Goodnight, Anne."

I went across the corridor to my room, took a shower and got into bed. When finally I slept, I dreamed of Liam.

Michael picked me up the following night and as we walked out to his car he said, "I thought we'd go into Upperville. There's a nice restaurant there that you probably haven't been in before."

"Sounds good," I said.

We chatted casually as he drove the few miles it took for us to get to Upperville. Upperville was aptly named since there was more money there than in Midville.

The restaurant was small, with white tablecloths and paintings that were not of horses on the walls.

"It's kind of nice to look at landscapes for a change," I said to Michael.

He agreed. "Midville can overdo it a little on the horsey stuff."

Michael had a reservation and we were shown to our table. A waiter took our orders for drinks.

I said, "So what have you been doing since I saw you last?"

"Nothing as exciting as you," he said. "What a thrill that must have been, to see Someday Soon win the Preakness."

"It was so exciting," I agreed. "I carried on like a four-year-old on Christmas morning."

"And now he only has to win the Belmont and he'll have the Triple Crown. Is that right?"

"It's true that he has to win the Belmont, but not that he 'only' has to win the Belmont. It will be his third race in five weeks, and it's the most grueling of them all. One and a half miles long. There's a reason there are so few Triple Crown winners. I once heard Jim McKay, who has seen years and years of sporting events, say that racing's Triple Crown is the hardest athletic achievement of them all."

"Wow. Do you think Someday Soon has a chance to win?"

"I think he has a very good chance to win."

"That's good. I won a tidy sum of money on him the last time he ran."

"I don't think the odds will be that good this time."

"Probably not."

I said, "Anyway, back to my original question. What have you been doing since I saw you last?"

"Working on Leslie's case and getting nowhere."

Relief washed over me. "It's too old. If there ever was any evidence, it's probably been long gone."

"We did find a few odds and ends in the vicinity of the burial."

"Like what?"

"A bracelet, which Mr. Bartholomew has identified as belonging to Leslie; a hair clip; and a miraculous medal."

My heart plummeted into my stomach. "A what?"

"A miraculous medal. You know, the kind people wear around their necks."

"Oh, yes. That kind of medal."

"Mr. Bartholomew said it didn't belong to Leslie, which wasn't a surprise. Leslie wasn't the kind of girl who went around with medals hanging around her neck."

"No, she wasn't." My voice sounded choked.

"Everyone else was out of town at the race, so I haven't had a chance to show the medal around. Do you know of anyone to whom it might belong?"

"No," I said steadily. "I have no idea."

"Do you know if the senator is back at Wellington?"

"Yes, I believe he came home for a few days."

"Good, then I'll stop by there tomorrow morning. I haven't been able to connect up with him, or with Liam and Kevin."

"Where has Kevin been?" I asked sharply.

"Mary told me he went to New York for a few days."

I essayed a smile. "Well, it doesn't sound as if your investigation is dead at all. You have a hairclip and a miraculous medal to add to the mix."

"The hairclip was probably Leslie's. The medal is interesting, though."

"Was it found right on the grave?"

"No, it was a few feet away. We figured out that it could have come off the killer when he was carrying Leslie to the grave he had dug."

"That's an ugly picture."

"Everything about this case is ugly, Anne. To have a beautiful young girl like Leslie just wiped out like that. My God, she was only eighteen years old."

I bowed my head. "I know."

Michael said, "Hey! We're here on a date! Let's lighten this conversation up, shall we?"

"Okay," I answered. "Tell me about the kind of music that you like."

He responded and we talked about other things while we ate dinner and then dessert. I tried very hard to act normally, but it took tremendous effort and by the time he dropped me off at home, I was so stressed out from the effort that when he bent to kiss me, I jumped.

He said, "Hey, Anne! I'm not going to rape you."

I produced a weak smile. "I'm sorry, Michael."

"What's wrong?"

"Nothing's wrong. I'm just tired, I guess. And I'm worried about Mom."

"Will you jump if I try to kiss you again?"

I should tell him that I'm dating Liam. But then he'll wonder why I went out with him tonight. He'll think I wanted to pump him about the case. I don't want to hurt his feelings. A little kiss can't hurt.

"Sure," I said and lifted my face.

The kiss was a little more intense than I wanted it to

be, but I did my part and smiled when it was over. "Goodnight, Michael."

"Goodnight, Anne. I'll call you soon."

"Okay."

I put my key in the lock and was safely into the house. I stood perfectly still in the hallway for a long time, with the same thought going round and round in my brain. *They found a miraculous medal. They found a miraculous medal. Dear God, they found a miraculous medal.*

"Anne?" My mother's voice came from the living room. "Are you all right?"

Should I tell Mom? The answer was immediate: *No. Don't involve her in this. Don't put her in a position where she may have to lie.*

I put on what I hoped was a normal expression and went into the living room, where Mom was watching TV with a stack of papers on her lap.

"How was your dinner, honey?"

"Very nice. I had duck. I haven't had that in ages."

"Where did you eat?"

I told her.

"Oh yes, I've heard of it. It's pretty pricey, though, isn't it?"

"Very pricey. We'll stick to the Coach Stop."

She laughed.

"Are you watching something good?" A commercial was on.

"I'm watching the Orioles game and correcting papers. They're playing the Yankees."

"Daddy would have been glued to the set if he was here."

"I know. He purely loved baseball."

"Who's winning?"

"The Yankees. Giambi just hit a home run."

"Yuck. Well, I'm going to bed, Mom. I'm tired."

"All right, honey."

I went to give her a kiss and then I went up the stairs to my bedroom. I closed the door, sat on my bed and took out my cell phone. I dialed the number for Wellington.

Thank God Liam answered.

"It's me," I said. "I just got back from dinner with Michael Bates and he told me they found a miraculous medal near Leslie's grave."

Silence.

"Did you hear me, Liam? He's going to be asking everyone in your family if they've ever seen it."

"Do you think it's mine, Annie?"

"You used to wear a miraculous medal. Your grandmother gave it to you for your Confirmation."

"Do you think I lost it while I was burying Leslie's body?"

"Of course not! I don't know how the hell it got there, but it isn't going to look good for you. I think the best thing you can do is to deny it's yours—and get your mother and father and Kevin to deny it too."

"There are bound to be people in town who remember that I wore a medal."

"Some of Leslie's friends might remember seeing it around your neck that summer. You were still wearing it then."

Liam said, "Do you think the cops will put this info in the paper?"

"Probably."

"Shit."

"I know."

"It isn't my medal, Annie. I swear to you, it isn't my medal."

"You don't have to swear to me, Liam. I believe you."

"All right. Let me warn my mother, my father and Kevin. Thanks for the call, Annie."

"Liam . . . do you think Kevin will back you up?"

"We'll see soon, won't we?"

"Okay. I'll see you tomorrow then."

"See you tomorrow." He disconnected the phone.

I got into bed, but I couldn't sleep. Pictures of Liam in bathing shorts in Leslie's pool flashed before my mind. He had worn that medal all summer long. I don't know when he had stopped wearing it. Could I remember seeing it on him anytime after Leslie's death?

I thought and thought and couldn't remember. I had gone away to school and we had seen so little of each other after that.

What was the likelihood of the police finding out about Liam's medal? Michael didn't hang around with Leslie's crowd, so he probably never noticed it. But Justin probably knew. And so would several other people from the old crowd.

What if it was Liam's medal?

It can't be. Liam wouldn't lie to me about this.

How the hell did a miraculous medal, which was an old-fashioned devotion not often seen nowadays, come to be near Leslie's grave?

Maybe Liam still had the medal! I got out of bed, got my cell phone and rang Wellington again. Once again Liam answered.

"Hi," I said. "Do you still have your medal, Liam? If you could show the police that you still have yours, that would disassociate you from the medal they found."

"I think I do still have it, Annie. I'll have to look."

"Look hard," I recommended. "It could be your ticket out of this mess."

"I'll do that."

"Let me know if you find it."

"Stop worrying, Annie. Everything is going to be all right."

"I hope so."

I hung up and went back to bed but it took me two hours before I finally fell asleep.

CHAPTER 20

When I woke up the next morning, I felt as if I had a cloud hanging over me. It didn't take me long to remember the medal. The police would probably show it to the Wellingtons today.

Mom had already left for work and I made myself breakfast. I sat at the table, eating cereal and worrying about the medal. Liam had told me it wasn't his, but what if the police didn't believe him? How many other people in Midville, Virginia went around wearing miraculous medals?

Someone knocked on the front door and I went to see who it was. Kevin was standing there.

"Good morning," he said. "I hope I didn't wake you up."

"I was just eating breakfast. Come on in. Do you want some coffee?"

"Coffee sounds wonderful."

He followed me to the back of the house and sat down at the kitchen table. My hair was hanging loose and I pushed it out of my face as I poured a mug of coffee for Kevin.

"Sexy pajamas," he said with a smile.

They were my oldest and baggiest pair. "I have no one I'm trying to impress," I said.

"Well, that's put me in my place."

It was my turn to smile.

I sat across from him. "Did Liam get a chance to talk to you?"

"About what?"

"About the police's new discovery."

"No, he hasn't talked to me. What have the police discovered?"

I hesitated. *Should I tell Kevin? Will he agree to protect Liam?* I said slowly, "They found something on the ground out near Leslie's grave."

He raised his golden eyebrows. "I haven't heard anything about it."

"You haven't been around these last few days."

"True. What did they find?"

"Liam was supposed to tell you."

"Well, he didn't." He drank some coffee.

"Have you seen him at all this morning?"

"No. He was gone when I got up."

"I think I'd better tell you, Kevin. You should be prepared."

He put his mug down and stared at me. "For God's sake, what is it?"

I took a deep breath. "They found a miraculous medal."

Kevin didn't say anything. He just kept on looking at me. I looked steadily back. Then he said, "Is it Liam's?"

"He says it's not. He was going to look for his, but I don't know if he found it."

"This doesn't look good."

"Liam didn't do it, Kevin!"

He slapped his hand on the table. "Then how the hell did his medal come to be by Leslie's grave?"

"It isn't his medal!"

"Oh, yeah, half of Midville wore miraculous medals that summer."

"You've got to say you don't recognize it," I said intensely. "You can't connect it to Liam."

"You and I are not the only persons who know that Liam wore a medal. It wasn't exactly invisible."

"How many people would remember after all these years?"

"All you need is one person to connect it to Liam."

"Well, don't let that one person be you, Kevin. Please *please* don't tell the police about Liam."

He scowled. "What am I supposed to say? I don't want to be arrested for concealing evidence. It wouldn't look good to my fans."

I wanted to say *To hell with your fans,* but I couldn't alienate Kevin. I said, "Can't you just say you can't connect it with anyone? After all, you have no way of knowing if it's really Liam's medal."

His scowl deepened. "I don't like this, Anne."

"I don't like it either. I can't believe that the police came up with that damn medal."

He asked, "How do you think it got there?"

"I have no idea. All I know is that Liam did not kill Leslie."

"Well . . . I'll think about it."

"You're an actor. You can pull it off."

"I'm not worried about pulling it off. I'm worried about being caught in a lie to the police. My agent would kill me if he knew I was doing something like this."

"Liam's life is more important than your agent."

"Maybe."

I wanted to scream, but I held onto my temper. "All you have to say is that you've never seen it. It isn't Liam's medal so, technically, you really have never seen it. You won't be lying."

"But what if it is Liam's medal? Then I would be lying."

"Then you can say that you thought Liam's medal was different from this one, that you made a mistake. Nothing terrible will happen to you, Kevin, but something terrible might happen to Liam if you say you recognize that medal."

He let out a long breath. "Oh, all right, Anne. I can't out-argue you. I'll say I don't recognize the bloody medal."

I gave him a tremulous smile. "Thank you, Kevin. Oh, thank you."

He finished his coffee. "I came to ask you about the Preakness, but I guess it's not what's at the top of your mind today."

"No, it isn't. But we had a great time. Wasn't Buster fabulous?"

"That he was. I bet a hundred on him and raked in a bundle."

"Great."

"It's hard to believe that Wellington Farm has a horse vying for the Triple Crown."

"I know. But Buster doesn't belong to the farm, Kevin. He belongs to Liam."

He frowned. "How is that? I thought Uncle Lawrence owned all of the horses here."

"He owns most of them, but Liam bought a few of his

own mares and he pays board for them here at the farm. Buster is the son of one of Liam's mares."

"Wow. How lucky is that."

"Yes."

We talked for a little longer and then he got up to go.

"Remember what you promised," I said.

"I remember, but you know what, Anne? I'm beginning to think that old Liam did it."

"How can you say that?" I cried passionately.

"I can say it because I don't see him through the same starry eyes that you do. He's far from perfect, you know."

"I know he's not perfect, but I also know he's not a killer."

"Then whose bloody medal is it?"

"I don't know!"

"I'll protect him for now, because he's my cousin, but I'm not risking my own reputation for him, Anne."

"Okay," I said. "But for now you'll go along with us?"

"If I can do it without an outright lie."

"You're clever, Kevin. You can manage that."

"We'll see," he said grimly.

He left and I sat back down at the table. My hands were shaking. *Please, dear Mary,* I prayed. *Don't let your medal become a trap for Liam. Help us to find a way out of this.*

After awhile I got up and began to put the dishes in the dishwasher. Then I went out to the track to work with the horses.

It started to rain as we were completing our work at the track and when we finished with the horses, Jacko and I went to stand inside the barn to talk.

We were still standing there, evaluating each youngster's progress, when Liam pulled up in the farm's oldest truck. He got out and walked through the rain to join us. My heart leaped in my chest as I watched him come.

Jacko said, "Anne and I are impressed with the Magus filly. She's very intelligent, very calm. And she can run."

Liam said, "She's going to have to go to auction, Jacko. They're all going to go to auction. Dad just told me that he has to liquidate all his assets."

"Oh Liam, no," I cried.

"Yes." He looked bleak. "Our only keepers will be Pennyroyal, My Holiday and Crescent Moon—my mares."

"He's selling all the mares?" Jacko said in horror.

"And the stallions too."

"Not Thunderhead?"

"Yes, Thunderhead too."

Jacko cursed under his breath. "Why would he do such a thing?"

"He needs the money, Jacko. He's in debt and he has to pay it off."

Jacko looked at me. "I'm almost glad your father isn't here to see this."

I nodded. My heart was aching for Liam. He had spent so much time figuring out the right bloodlines for each of his horses; so many happy hours comparing the virtues of one horse as a mate versus another. All of the babies were the products of his careful matchmaking. And the mares! He loved his mares. And Thunderhead, who he had bred himself and now was the sire of a potential Triple Crown Winner. Liam was a hands-on professional, one who was there in the barns every day to form an attachment to the animals. He was emotionally invested in his horses and the loss of them would break his heart.

I said, "If Buster wins the Belmont, you'll have the money to buy some of them back. The sale isn't until July."

The bleak look never left his face. "That's a big 'if', Annie."

"I suppose you'll be letting all the help go?" Jacko asked.

I looked at his grizzled head. Where was Jacko going to get a job to equal this one?

Liam said, "You'll have a job as long as I have horses, Jacko. If Wellington shuts down completely, I'll be starting my own barn."

The relief on Jacko's face was evident. "That's good to know, Liam. Thank you."

Liam looked at me. "Come for a ride with me, Annie?"

"Sure."

We dashed through the rain to the truck. We both climbed in and Liam drove off. Neither of us spoke. Then I said, "I'm so sorry, Liam. This is a terrible blow."

"Yes. It is." He continued to drive. The windshield wipers were working hard; the rain had started to come down fast.

"Are we going anywhere?" I asked.

"No. I just wanted to get you to myself. I'll park by the broodmare pasture."

He parked the truck facing the pasture and we looked at the mares and their foals huddled under the run-in shelter that protected them from the rain and the sun. He said in a choked voice, "I can't believe all this is going."

"I can't either."

We sat together inside the cab of the truck with the rain pouring down outside. "You were afraid this was going to happen," I said.

"I knew there was a problem, but deep down, I never thought it would come to this. To sell all my horses! When Dad said that, it was like a dagger went into my heart."

"Oh, Liam." Tears welled up in my eyes. "I am so sorry, so very very sorry."

"Annie." He turned to me and held out his arms. I slid across the seat and put my own arms around him as his closed around me hard. "I feel like I'm in a nightmare," he said.

My arms were around him, my whole body pressed against his. "Is it a done deal or only a possibility?"

"It's a done deal." His voice sounded muffled because his mouth was pressed against my hair. "He has to have the money. He borrowed money to put into the stock market and now he has to pay it back."

"Is he going to keep the property?"

"He doesn't know yet."

I almost reminded him of his idea of starting anew in Kentucky, but I caught my words back. There would be time to think of the future. Right now he was grieving too hard for what he had lost.

I wondered if the police had come out and shown him the medal.

He said, "I had to see you. You're the only one who understands how I feel about this."

"My heart is broken for you, Liam. But you'll get some of the horses back. I know you will."

"What if Buster doesn't win the Belmont?"

"You'll do what everybody else does, take out a loan."

He said huskily, "You must think I'm acting like a baby about this." His arms never loosened their hold.

"Of course I don't. I think you're devastated, and you

should be devastated. Everything you've worked for for so many years is crumbling around you."

My face was pressed against his chest and I could hear his heart beating under my cheek. It was as if we were alone in the world, with the rain making a drumming sound on the roof and windshield of the truck.

He gave a great shuddering sigh and I pulled away a little to look up at him. For a moment he looked back, then his mouth was coming down on mine.

I closed my eyes and let him kiss me, a long, sweet, gentle kiss. "Annie," he said softly. "I'm glad you're here."

"I am too."

He kissed my cheeks and my forehead and then he came back to my mouth. I was so afraid of scaring him away by showing my neediness that I didn't kiss him back at all. I just received his kiss, as sweetly and gently as he gave it.

He raised his head and cuddled me close. I rested my head against his shoulder. I said, "Liam, did the police contact you about the medal?"

"Not yet. But I left the house right after Dad told me the news."

"Where did you go?"

"I went for a walk. Then, when I couldn't stand my own company any longer, I came looking for you."

"I saw Kevin this morning," I said.

"Oh? Did he ask you for a date?"

"No. But I got him to promise not to say anything about you once wearing a miraculous medal."

I could feel him stiffen. "You got Kevin to lie for me?"

"He's not going to lie. He's going to . . . evade . . . the issue."

"And how the hell is he going to do that?"

"I don't know. Kevin is clever. He'll think of something."

"Is he doing this for your sake?"

"No. He said he would do it because you were his cousin."

Liam snorted.

"He did say that, Liam. Honestly."

"Oh the hell with the medal," he said angrily. "I'm losing my farm."

I reached my hand up and smoothed his hair off his forehead. "If you want to cry, go ahead," I said. "I won't tell anyone."

"I'm not going to cry," he said gruffly.

"You'll be able to buy some of the mares back," I said. "You aren't going to lose them all."

"What about Thunderhead?"

"What if you ask your father not to sell Thunderhead?"

"He was quite clear; he had to sell them all."

"He might be too expensive, then. You'll have Buster to stand at stud. You might have to wait until you can get another stallion."

"It's just that . . . this place is part of me, Annie. It's been my home for all my life. It was home to all of my ancestors. It just stinks that Dad has thrown it away like this."

"I know, Liam. I know."

Outside the rain continued to pour down. After a moment he put his hands on the steering wheel. "I'll take you back to your car."

"Okay."

"I was thinking of flying up to New York to see Buster. Would you like to come with me?"

"I'd love to. When were you going?"

"Let's go tomorrow."

"Terrific."

I ran from the truck to my car and, when I got in, I waited while I watched Liam drive off in the rain. Then I turned the key in the ignition and drove myself home.

CHAPTER 21

We flew out of Dulles the following morning and landed at Kennedy in New York right on time. Liam rented a car at the airport and we drove the few miles to Elmont, where Belmont Racetrack is located.

We checked into a local Holiday Inn then went to the track to see Buster.

He was napping, stretched out on his side with his four legs sticking out in front of him.

Liam said with amusement, "He's really feeling the pressure, isn't he?"

I said, "It's great that he's sleeping like that. Sleep is a great restorative."

Henry, Buster's groom, appeared at the end of the shedrow. "It's just us, Henry, no need to take alarm," Liam said. "We flew up to get a look at the boy."

"Hello, Mr. Wellington." He smiled at me, clearly not remembering my name. "He's been doing great, sir. Mr. Ford is real happy with him."

"That's good," Liam said.

"He certainly looks comfortable," I commented.

"He's a great napper," Henry said. "Even when there's a crowd of newsmen around the stall, he'll still sleep."

"Have there been a lot of reporters?"

"They're all over the lot," Henry said. "Mr. Ford has been galloping Red at five in the morning, just to get away from them." He looked beyond us. "Here comes one of them now."

Liam and I stood there as a tall, thin man in a windbreaker came up to us and introduced himself as John Kerrigan from the *Daily News*. "You must be excited to have a shot at the Triple Crown," he said to Liam.

Liam said, "We're very excited. And it's nice that he's likely to go off as the favorite. He was getting to feel like a stepchild."

Kerrigan looked into the stall. "Yeah, he really looks upset."

Liam almost smiled.

"So you like your chances?" Kerrigan said.

I said, "Our chances are very good—especially if I wear my lucky hat and suit."

The reporter looked interested, so I explained about my pink suit and Kentucky Derby hat. "My only fear is that Liam is going to make me wear it every time one of his horses runs," I concluded.

"Hey, that's an idea," Liam said.

"Now you're a veterinarian, is that right Dr. Foster?" Kerrigan inquired.

"That's right."

"Do you take care of Someday Soon?"

"No, I have a practice in Maryland. But my dad used to break all of Wellington's horses and I grew up on the farm. Liam and I have known each other since we were children."

"Did your father break Someday Soon?"

"He certainly did."

"He must be excited about all of this."

I didn't answer and Liam said, "Pete passed away just before the Derby was run. But I think we both feel that he is with us."

I nodded.

The reporter said, "Have you heard that a horse is being flown in from Ireland to run in the Belmont?"

"No," Liam said. "I hadn't heard. Who's the owner?"

"Coolmore."

"Wouldn't you know it. What do you know about him?"

"He ran one or two big races in Europe and they think he can last the mile and a half."

Liam asked, "Is he a front runner or a come from behinder?"

"He's like Someday Soon. He comes from behind."

"Well, all we can do is run our race. If we do, I think we'll come out on top."

"What do you think is the single most important thing in this race, Mr. Wellington?"

Liam replied without hesitation, "The jockeys. On this long of a race, the jockey is all-important. Only he can judge the pace; only he can know when it's time to make the right move. The trainer can only get the horse ready. Once he turns him over to the jockey, it's all his responsibility."

Kerrigan asked, "Do you think having a Triple Crown winner will help the sport?"

"I think it would be wonderful for racing," Liam said. "It's one of the most difficult feats in all of sports. For example, the British Triple Crown spans five months, not five weeks. It's why it's been decades since the last winner. I hope Someday Soon will break that drought."

There was the sound of rustling inside the stall and then Someday Soon's head appeared over the front door. "Buster," Liam said. "Hey there, boy. How are you doing?"

Someday Soon allowed his face to be rubbed.

"Buster?" Kerrigan said.

"That's his farm nickname. He's had it since he was just a little guy."

We talked for another few minutes and then Liam said to me, "Want to take a walk around and see some of the other horses?"

"Sure," I said.

We said goodbye to Mr. Kerrigan and walked off in the direction of D Wayne Lukas's barn. Liam said, "That was smart, telling him the story about the hat and suit. The press gobbles up things like that."

"I thought it was kind of a cute story. Plus it will explain to anyone who might have noticed that I do have other clothes."

We walked around the barns, admiring the horses, then we returned to Someday Soon, where we found John Ford. "Oh, there you are," he said. "Henry told me you were here."

"We just flew up for the day," Liam said. "I had this yen to see my boy."

"He seems to be fine," John said. "I don't get any sense that he's tired. I haven't been pushing the speed at all; we're just galloping and galloping. And at the end he's still pulling to go."

"That sounds great," I said.

Liam said. "I heard that the Irish are sending a horse."

John replied, "They are. Solomon's Riddle is his

name. I understand he's raced and won at a mile and a half in Ireland."

"So they know he can do the distance."

"Yes. He might be our best challenge. The rest of the horses we've already seen and beaten—except for Star Beta, and I don't think we have to worry about him."

"What else do you know about this Irish horse? Is he here?"

"No, he's not here yet. They're flying him over at the end of the week. That's all I can tell you. Nobody knows much about him."

Liam said, "They must think he has a good chance of winning or they wouldn't send him."

"That's so."

I said, "We took a look at Point Taken and Honor Bright today. They're beautiful-looking animals."

John said, "They're both good horses. But Someday Soon is better."

We all turned to look at Buster. "Not only are you faster than those other horses, but you're more beautiful," I told him.

He pricked his ears as if he agreed with me.

John said, "He's a terrible ham. Every time he sees a camera he poses."

Liam laughed. "Does he really?"

"He does. He lifts his head as if he's looking off into a long distance and holds the pose until the camera is lowered."

I said, "He knows he's special. That's good."

"The TV people are going to film a segment on him this afternoon to be aired on the day of the race. Stick around and you can be in it."

"Buster's going to star in a TV spot?" I said. "If he

likes the still shots he should really hog up the TV camera."

We stayed around the barn for the rest of the afternoon. The TV people did film Liam, "the man who bred and owns Someday Soon," and they talked strategy with John. When they asked him what his instructions to his jockey would be, he replied, "Just keep him within striking range, then let him run."

We got back to our hotel at six-thirty, changed and went out to dinner at a local steakhouse.

"This was a nice break," I said as we sat down with our salads. "I'm glad we came."

"So am I. I wish I knew more about this Irish colt, though."

"You heard what John said. It doesn't matter who else is running, Buster just has to run his own race. Which I'm sure he'll do."

"God, I hope so. That Triple Crown bonus means an awful lot right now."

What will you do if Buster loses? I thought the words but didn't say them. *We'll deal with that when the time comes,* I thought. *Right now Liam has more than enough on his plate.*

We had a good American high-fat meal of steak and French fries and ice cream. We both were silent as Liam drove back to the Holiday Inn.

He had taken two rooms for us and they had a connecting door between them. Liam said, "Do you want to stay here, or go down to the bar next door and watch the TV there?"

"Let's go down to the bar," I said. "It's inter-league play and the Orioles are playing the Mets, so the game will be televised."

"We could watch it here."

"That's true."

"If we go to the bar, you'll order a glass of wine, and you've already had two."

"Good grief, are you my chaperone?"

"Remember how you felt the last time you had too much wine?"

I shuddered. "I was going to drink ginger ale."

"We can get a soda from the machine on the floor."

Clearly, he did not want to go to the bar. "Okay," I said. "We'll stay in."

While Liam went for the sodas, I took off my shoes and propped up two pillows to rest my back. When Liam came back he did the same thing. He poured me a glass of ginger ale and put it on the table next to my side of the bed. Then he poured himself a glass of Coke.

"What time are we flying out tomorrow?" I asked.

"Ten o'clock."

"Good. I'll be home in time to get some work done."

Liam said, "There's something that I ought to tell you."

"What is that?"

"I told the police that the miraculous medal they found was mine."

I froze. "You *what*?"

"I told the police that the miraculous medal they found was mine."

I put down my ginger ale. "In the name of God, why did you do that?"

He looked very grim. "I thought it over and it was impossible to deny that it was mine. Too many people know I wore a medal that summer. So all your blandishment of Kevin went for nothing."

My heart began to hammer in my chest. I felt as if I couldn't catch my breath. I don't ever remember being so scared in all my life. "Don't you get it, Liam? *That medal puts you at the site of the murder.*"

"It puts me at the site of the burial."

"There's not much difference between the two."

He said quietly, "The police were bound to find out, and then it would have looked badly for me. I told the police that I had lost the medal and didn't know how it came to show up at the burial site."

"I thought you told me that you still had the medal," I said suspiciously.

"I forgot that I had lost it."

Something about this wasn't sounding right.

"Is there something involved here that I don't know about?"

He smiled at me. "Loyal Annie. I'm so sorry to disappoint you, but there is nothing else to report."

"What did the police say when you told them it was your medal?"

"They asked me a bunch of questions, but Dad wouldn't let me answer any of them. He's hiring a lawyer for me."

A cold fist of terror squeezed my stomach. "A lawyer?"

"Apparently I'm going to need one."

"What did your mother say?"

"Mom wasn't there. She didn't come home; she's staying with friends in Massachusetts."

"Liam, I don't believe that it was your medal. You were quite sure it wasn't either the last time we talked about it."

He gave me an impatient look. "Why would I say that it was mine if it wasn't?"

"Why did you tell me that you still had it?"

"I forgot that I had lost it."

"I don't believe you."

"Stop being so stubborn, Annie. Your golden boy isn't perfect. I forgot about the bloody medal."

I still didn't believe him, but this argument was getting us nowhere.

I said in a small voice, "Are they going to arrest you, Liam?"

"I don't know. That's why I wanted to get up here to see Buster. I don't know how much longer I'll be free to move around the way I want."

"Oh Liam. I'm so scared."

"Don't be scared, Annie." He reached out an arm to me and I slid over to sit within its circle. "They won't convict me: I didn't do it."

"Look at the cases of all those people who were convicted and now the DNA evidence is showing that they were innocent. Innocent people spent years of their lives in jail, Liam! Don't tell me that you're safe just because you didn't do it."

He said quietly, "Has it ever occurred to you that maybe I did do it?"

"No," I replied immediately.

"Do you really think you know me that well?"

"Yes, I do."

"And you don't think I'm capable of murder?"

"Maybe we're all capable of murder, if the stakes are high enough. But you didn't murder Leslie because she screwed Kevin. It's absurd even to think that."

His arm pulled me closer. "I don't deserve you, Annie."

"Sure you do."

"I missed you. Why did you stay away for so long?"

"I was staying away from you. I was trying not to love you, you see."

"And were you successful?"

"You know the answer to that."

He was silent for a long minute. Then he said, "When I think of my childhood, you were always there."

"I know. We were a great team, Liam."

"We were." I could feel his lips against my hair. "You grew up behind my back."

"I suppose I did."

"I needed a little time to grow accustomed to the fact that you weren't my little pal any more."

"And have you grown accustomed to that fact?"

"I'm getting there."

I looked up to see his face and his mouth came down on mine. This wasn't a tender kiss, it was serious, and I responded immediately. His kiss became harder as he bent over me, pushing my head back into the pillows. I slid my hands up and down his back.

He broke away from my mouth and kissed my forehead and my eyelids. "Annie, how did you get to be so beautiful?"

"I'm glad you think I'm pretty."

"No," he said. "Not pretty. Beautiful."

"Kiss me some more," I suggested and he obliged.

When his mouth lifted again, I said, "Liam did you ever see the movie *Gigi*?"

He lifted his eyebrows in surprise at the change of subject. "Nope."

"It's about an older man and a young girl and about how he comes to realize that she's his one true love."

"It sounds pretty corny."

"It's not! It's beautiful. And the song he sings—it's a musical—when he realizes she's grown up is beautiful. It's sort of like what's happening to us."

"I'm hardly an 'older man',"

"You always thought of yourself as older. You used to boss me around unmercifully."

"Hah," he replied. "You always did exactly as you pleased. You're the most unbossable person that I know."

"I was always pleased to do whatever you wanted."

"You were intelligent enough to know that my way was always best."

I kissed his jaw. "We were a partnership, but you were the senior member."

"I guess I'll go along with that."

We stayed nestled in each other's arms for a few more minutes. Then I said, "I think you should go back to your own room now."

I could feel him stiffen. "Why? I thought we might do a little more kissing."

"A little more kissing will lead to a little more of everything else, and I'm not sure you're ready for that yet."

"I think I'm the best judge of that."

I said, "I think you still have reservations, Liam. I don't want to take advantage of you."

He scowled. "Do you realize how ridiculous you sound? You can't possibly take advantage of me."

"Yes, I can. I know that you want me now, but I have to be sure that it's not a momentary thing. You have to want me all the time, Liam, otherwise it's not good enough for me."

He raked his hair off his forehead. "I don't know what you're talking about."

"I think you do, old buddy. I think you do."

"The only thing in that tirade that I understood was that you wanted me to go back to my own room."

"I do want that."

He straightened away from me and swung his legs over the side of the bed. "Fine. If that's what you want, I'll go."

"It is."

"I think you're making a mistake."

"I don't."

"All right, damn it. I'll go." He shoved his feet into his loafers.

I said, "What time do you want to meet for breakfast tomorrow?"

He turned and looked at me. After a while he said, "We need to be at the airport at nine so let's meet for breakfast at eight."

"Okay, see you then."

He made his way to the connecting door, then he turned and said, "I should have let you have that extra glass of wine."

I laughed. "Goodnight."

"Goodnight," he said grumpily and closed the door behind him.

I lay there looking at the door and wondering if I was crazy. If I had let him make love to me, maybe all our problems would have been solved. But in my heart I just did not feel that it was the right time. I wanted him to want me so badly he hurt with it, the way I hurt from wanting him. I wanted him to run around Paris, like Gigi's Gaston, shouting out how much he loved me. I didn't want any tentativeness at all.

I'm making progress, I told myself. *This kiss was much better than the last one.*

After awhile I put on the ballgame and watched the Orioles get annihilated by the Yankees 12 to 3. Then I went to bed.

CHAPTER 22

When Mom got home from school, I told her about Liam and the medal. "He told me he still had it, then he completely changed his story and claimed the medal they found at the burial site was his. I don't understand him at all."

"Perhaps he's just telling the truth, Anne. He thought he still had the medal and when he looked for it and it was gone he remembered that he had lost it."

"I don't believe that."

"If it was lost, anyone could have found it and put it by the grave to incriminate Liam."

"Whoever buried Leslie thought she'd never be found."

"That's probably true, but the medal was a kind of insurance."

"Mom, you don't think Liam killed Leslie, do you?"

"In my heart? No. I don't."

Thank God.

I said, "He should have kept his mouth shut about the medal. Now he's got to hire a lawyer, and that won't look good."

"Under the circumstances, I think a lawyer is necessary."

It was a warm day and we were sitting in the kitchen with all the windows open. I said, "Damn. Why did they have to find that medal?"

"If you don't think it's Liam's then who do you think it belongs to?" Mom asked.

"I have no idea."

"That's the problem. It's not the sort of thing that people wear nowadays. Liam got it from his grandmother as a gift. That's why he wore it. He would have a hard time denying that the medal was his."

"Well, if the medal is his, then someone else put it there."

"That could be what happened."

We sat talking for a little longer, then Mom said she had to go food shopping. I offered to go for her and she gave me a list. I got in my car and drove to the Safeway.

I was in the frozen food section when I ran into Michael Bates.

"Hi," I said. "It's a surprise to see you here."

"I've been picking up my dinner items," he said, gesturing to the pile of TV dinners in his basket.

"I eat a lot of Lean Cuisine myself when I'm at home," I said. "There just isn't much incentive to cook when it's only for yourself."

"It's about the only thing I miss from my marriage—coming home and finding dinner on the table."

I smiled.

He looked at the fruit and vegetables in my cart. "You look like you're eating healthy."

"Mom believes in having everything fresh. She'd die if she knew I was eating TV dinners."

He laughed. "My mother was the same way."

I said, "I hear that Liam claimed the medal to be his."

He frowned. "Yes, he identified it."

"I don't think it's his, Michael."

He looked wary. "If it isn't his, then why did he say it was?"

"He thought it would look bad if he denied it when everyone knew he wore a medal just like it."

"That doesn't make sense, Anne."

A lady said, "Excuse me," and we moved our baskets out of her way.

"Liam did not kill Leslie, Michael."

"Maybe he didn't, but the only piece of evidence we have points to him."

"You mean the medal?"

"I mean the medal."

"Kevin could have stolen it," I said. "He lived in the same house as Liam. He could easily have lifted it."

"Are you saying that Kevin killed Leslie and left Liam's medal at the grave to implicate him?"

"It's possible."

"If Kevin was going to do something like that, he would have left the medal in the summerhouse."

"Not necessarily."

"I think you're really pushing things here, Anne. I know you're fond of Liam, but evidence is evidence."

"Liam said he lost the medal. Anyone could have found it and used it."

"You started off this conversation by denying that the medal was Liam's. Now you're saying it's his, but it was planted at the grave by someone else. Which is it. Anne?"

"It could be either of those things," I said defiantly.

"It could be, but to be honest, the greatest likelihood is

that Liam buried that body and lost the medal there. The chain was broken."

"He didn't do it, Michael."

"Well, we'll let a jury settle that question, Anne."

A jury! Oh no. I said, "Are you going to arrest Liam, Michael?"

"I can't tell you that, Anne."

I pressed my hand to my mouth. "Oh my God. This is terrible."

"I'm sorry Anne, but that's the way the evidence points."

"You're making a terrible mistake."

"Perhaps we are, but someone killed Leslie and at this point we think it was Liam."

I was silent, my heart thumping in my chest. "I'm so scared," I whispered at last.

"I'm sorry to upset you, but I want to be honest with you."

I nodded.

He said, "I guess there's no point in my asking you out again."

I shook my head. "I can't go out with you anymore, Michael."

"That's too bad. I like you a lot, Anne."

"I like you too, but I love Liam."

"I'm sorry."

"I have to get home now," I said. "Goodbye, Michael."

"Goodbye."

I went through the check-out line, loaded the groceries in the car and drove home to put them away. Then I got back in the car and drove out to Wellington to warn Liam.

I tried the house first and Kevin answered the door. "Hi," I said. "Is Liam here?"

He looked somber. "He was arrested two hours ago, Anne. They took him into town to the police station to book him."

All of a sudden I saw black spots in front of my eyes. "Kevin," I said and reached out my hand. He grabbed me and sat me down in the hallway chair.

"Put your head down," he instructed. I did as he said, trying to breathe evenly. I had broken out into a clammy sweat and I felt awful.

Liam's been arrested! I thought.

"They're not going to keep him," Kevin said reassuringly. "He called his lawyer, who said he would be down to bail him out. He should be home in a few hours."

"I can't believe this is happening."

Kevin said, "Get ahold of yourself, Anne. It's not that bad."

"How can you say that? Liam's been arrested for murder! What could be more terrible than that?"

"They don't have enough evidence to convict him."

"They have that damn medal."

"A single medal is an awfully small thing to convict a man of murder."

"It's the only evidence they have, and it points to Liam. The police are under the gun to arrest someone for Leslie's murder. What if they take this all the way to trial?"

"Liam would be acquitted."

The black spots had disappeared from in front of my eyes and I sat up straight. "Kevin, I am so scared."

"It's a scary situation, I'll give you that. But we'll get the best lawyer available for him, Anne."

"Uncle Lawrence can't afford a good lawyer. He told Liam all of the horses would have to be sold."

Kevin frowned. "Is he in that deep?"

"Apparently."

"Well, I have plenty of money, Anne. I'll make sure that Liam has the best lawyer. So don't worry about that."

I stood up and hugged him. "Thank you, Kevin! Thank you!"

"I doubt that Liam will be so happy to be in my debt, but he'll have to put up with it," Kevin said.

"You're an angel."

"Don't despair, Anne. We'll get him out of this."

Thank God for Kevin, I thought as I gave him a tremulous smile.

"Where is the senator?" I asked.

"He and Aunt Alyssa are in Maine, visiting friends."

"How could he go away when he must have known that Liam was going to be arrested?"

Kevin shrugged.

I said, "The press will have a field day with this, what with Liam being a senator's son and the owner of a potential Triple Crown winner."

"It's going to be ugly."

I said, "I'm going to go into the police station to see if there's anything I can do."

"You'll only be in the way, Anne. Let the attorney handle it."

I twisted my hands. "I have to do *something*, Kevin."

"Wait until Liam gets back. I bet he'll be glad to see you."

"Do you think it will be long?"

"I have no idea how long it will be; but he will be home. Of that I'm certain."

"Thank you, Kevin. You're being very patient with me."

"I'm very fond of you, Anne, but I don't stand a chance against Liam, do I?"

Slowly I shook my head.

"Were you using me to make him jealous?"

My face felt hot. "Kevin, I am so sorry. It was a rotten thing to do. But I was feeling desperate. I love him so much, and he wasn't *seeing* me. He was still seeing the little girl I used to be."

"And did your strategy work?"

"I think so."

"I'm so glad."

I had hurt him. "Kevin, I don't know what to say except I'm sorry. If I thought you really cared about me, I wouldn't have done it."

"Did it ever occur to you that you're as blind as Liam, Anne? He didn't see you clearly; well, perhaps you didn't see me clearly either."

Was he saying he loved me? I felt horrible. I said in a small voice, "It was very selfish of me."

"Yes, it was."

"But I had a good time on our dates, Kevin. I am fond of you. You're one of my best friends."

"Like you're one of Liam's best friends?"

Ouch. "What can I say? I was wrong. I don't blame you for being angry with me."

"I'm not angry. . . . Well, maybe I am angry. But I'm not surprised. It was always Liam for you."

"Yes," I said. "It was."

Outside a car pulled up. Then a door slammed. I clasped my hands to my heart and stared at the door. In less than a minute, Liam walked through.

"Liam!" I flew to him. "Thank God you're home!"

He caught me in his arms. "Hey there, Annie. It's not so bad. I'm out."

My arms were tight around his neck. "They arrested you!"

"They arrested me, but Gil bailed me out. I'm not going to jail. Calm down, Annie, you're strangling me."

"What did you use for the bond?" Kevin asked.

"Dad told us to put up the house," Liam said.

Kevin whistled.

I forced myself to loosen my hold on him. "Where is this lawyer?"

"He went home. He lives near Washington."

"This is a nightmare," I said.

"Tell me about it," Liam said.

"Michael Bates told me that the only evidence they have in the case is the medal. Liam, why did you tell them that the medal was yours? No one could have proved that it was if you'd denied it."

He said steadily, "It was mine. I don't know how it got there, but the medal was mine."

I turned to Kevin. "Do you understand him?"

He said to Liam, "You really did make it easy for them, you know."

Liam shrugged. "I don't think they can convict me on a medal."

Kevin said somberly, "Stranger things have happened."

We were all silent. Then I said, "What does being out on bail mean?"

"It means that if I flee the country, Dad will lose the house."

"Oh my."

Kevin said, "What kind of an attorney is Gil Moran? Is he a criminal attorney?"

"No. He's a corporate lawyer, actually."

"If this case goes to trial, we're hiring you the best criminal attorney in the business. Don't worry about the money. I'll pay."

A muscle jumped in the corner of Liam's jaw. For a long moment he didn't reply. Then he said gruffly, "Thank you."

Kevin nodded then looked down. It was the first time I realized that I was clutching Liam's hand. Kevin said lightly, "I can see that three's a crowd right now, so I'll go out for dinner. Should I call when I'm ready to come back?"

"Do that," Liam said.

We stood hand in hand in the family room waiting for the sound of the front door to close. When it did, Liam turned to me and said, "Let's go upstairs."

CHAPTER 23

Liam's room was furnished with a lovely old four-poster bed. Liam led me by the hand over to the bed, then turned to look down at me. "I'm sorry, Annie. I'm sorry I have to put you through this police business."

It was an odd thing to say, but at the moment its oddness didn't strike me. All I knew was that I was about to get what I had wanted for such a long time.

"I love you," I said. "I have always loved you."

"And I love you."

He bent his head and kissed me. I opened my mouth and took him in. We clung together, our bodies pressed against each other, our tongues intimately touching. He lifted his head. "Annie." It sounded like a groan. "Let's get out of these clothes."

Tight jeans are not the easiest of clothes to shed, but we managed.

"God," he said. "You are so beautiful." He lifted me up and laid me on top of his white chenille bedspread. Then he lay down next to me. I ran my finger over a faint scar on his collarbone. "I remember when you got that," I said.

"I fell out of a tree."

I kissed the scar.

He shuddered. "I want you so much. Do you know what I thought when I was waiting in the police station?"

"What?"

"I was thinking, what if they lock me up and I've never had a chance to make love to Annie?"

"Oh, Liam."

He traced his finger along my jaw. Then he bent and gently kissed each of my breasts. "This is heaven," he murmured.

I buried my hands in his hair and his mouth began to move all over me, stirring up passion everywhere it went.

"Liam," I said. "Oh Liam."

I arched up against his hands and his mouth, answering to the powerful thrill of their touch. My own hands were sliding up and down his shoulders and arms, feeling the strong muscles and smooth skin.

He began to kiss me, again and again and deep inside me the sweet sensation of surrender began to throb. This went on for quite a while.

Finally, "Annie?"

"Yes. Oh yes." I opened myself wide even as I held him tight, arching myself up to receive him. He plunged into me, right into the heart of me, and his coming felt so right, so good. I closed around him, locking my legs around his waist, and we rocked together on the chenille bedspread in the ancient rhythm of love.

I could feel myself softening, could feel the delicious sensation spreading out inside of me, and I lifted my hips to encourage him, holding onto him as I came closer and closer to that moment when an orgasm would roll all through me. . . .

"Annie," he said and I spread to take him even farther

in, my legs high about his waist. And then it came, the shattering moment when we were one in ecstasy, clinging to each other as if nothing else mattered in all the world.

I didn't realize that I was crying until Liam said, "Annie, don't," and kissed the tears on my face.

"I don't know why I'm crying when I'm so happy," I said.

"Annie, I love you. However you want me to love you, I do."

I didn't reply.

"You believe me, don't you?"

"Yes, I believe you, Liam. I think I'm crying because I'm afraid."

"It's not that bad. You heard Kevin. He's going to get me a good lawyer."

"Michael Skakel had a good lawyer, and look what happened to him."

"Maybe he was guilty. I'm not."

"Liam, you can't be so naïve that you believe your innocence will get you off."

"That's why we have the high-priced attorney. Besides, it may never even go to trial."

I looked steadily into his face. "Tell me honestly, did you lose your medal?"

He barely hesitated before he replied, "Yes, I did."

I didn't believe him.

I said, "I couldn't bear it if you went to prison."

He gathered me even closer. "That won't happen, love. I promise. Everything is going to work out okay."

I pressed my cheek into his bare shoulder. "I love you so much."

"It's a miracle, Annie. Having you is like a miracle. I can face anything if I know I have you."

"You'll always have me."

His arms tightened.

The telephone rang.

We both jumped.

"Christ," Liam said. "That will be Kevin."

He went to pick up the phone.

"Hello Kevin. Yes, you can come home now. Annie and I appreciate your tact. Okay. Yeah. See you soon." He hung up.

I said, "I want to leave before Kevin gets here." The thought of facing Kevin's knowing gaze was too much all of a sudden.

"Okay. He's going to be at least fifteen minutes. You have time."

We both got dressed and Liam walked me out to my car. "I hate to say goodbye to you," he said.

"I know."

"When all of this is over we'll get married."

"Okay."

He bent his head and gave me a quick kiss. "Get going or you'll run into Kevin."

"Goodnight," I said, got into my car and drove away.

I didn't say much to Mom. I told her that Liam had been arrested, that he was out on bail, that I had a headache and was going to bed. She didn't try to detain me.

I sat on my bed, the same bed I had had since I was three years old, and stared at the picture of Liam on his pony that adorned the wall. His hair was too long and it fell over his forehead; even at age ten, his nose had been arrogant.

He had been too big for the pony, but he adored her

and had refused to give her up until his feet almost touched the ground.

I knew him inside and out, the way he knew me. That's how I knew he was lying about the medal. But I didn't know why.

I should look at the medal myself.

But could I tell it apart from any other medal? After all, a miraculous medal was a miraculous medal, wasn't it? I had never looked that closely at Liam's. There had never been any reason to.

Maybe Liam was right. Maybe the district attorney would think there wasn't enough evidence for a trial.

I sat there for an hour, my mind going around and around, sometimes going over the intense lovemaking between Liam and me and sometimes going over the police case against Liam. Finally I decided to call it a night, took a shower and went to bed.

I had a nightmare that I was walking through the woods with Liam, and I lost him. I could hear him calling my name, but I couldn't find him. I screamed his name, "Liam, I'm here! I'm here!" but no one answered. *This is a bad dream,* I thought, forced my eyes open and found with profound relief that I was in my own bed.

Thank God. I was trembling and my heart was pounding. I wanted to call him on the phone and hear his voice, but when I looked at the clock and saw that it was three-thirty in the morning I knew I couldn't do that.

When we're married, he'll always be here, I thought.

For the first time I let myself think about what it would be like to be married to Liam. We would start a new farm, either here or in Kentucky. It would be hard work, starting from scratch, but it would be fun. I could work as a local vet and bring money in that way.

I smiled into the dark as I pictured such a life in my mind. We would have a big family. Mom would love having grandchildren.

What would we call our children? *Peter,* I thought. *We'll name our first boy Peter.*

My cell phone rang. I jumped about six feet. I picked it up and said "Hello?"

"It's me," Liam said. "I just got a call from John. Buster is colicking. I'm driving up to New York. Do you want to come?"

"Yes," I said.

"I'll pick you up in fifteen minutes."

"Okay."

I threw cold water on my face, pulled my hair into a ponytail and put on jeans and a striped LL Bean shirt. I went in to tell Mom where I was going and why. I was standing in the doorway when Liam's Lexus rolled up. I ran to the passenger side, opened the door and got in.

"How bad is it?" I asked as we pulled away.

"John said it's mild. The vet gave him Banamine, tubed him with mineral oil, and put him on intravenous fluids. John said he's been pretty quiet since he got the Banamine."

"Did the vet think it was an impaction?"

"That was the likelihood. The problem with a damn colic is you never know for sure."

"Well, the vet did all the right things."

We drove in silence while possible treatments for colic ran through my head, ranging from the relatively benign treatment administered to Someday Soon all the way up to surgery to remove the blockage.

Liam said, "This may mean he can't run in the Belmont."

"It may or it may not. If this is just a minor colic he should recover in time to run. Don't think the worst yet, Liam."

We arrived at Belmont at eleven-thirty in the morning and found a very weary-looking John Ford sitting in a chair outside Someday Soon's stall.

"How is he?" Liam asked tensely.

"He seems to be doing well," John said. "He finished the fluids and the vet didn't put him on new ones."

Liam said, "Let's have Annie take a look at him."

"Sure," John said.

I opened the stall door and went inside. "Have you given him anything to eat?" I asked John.

"The vet said he could have a bran mash, so we gave him that."

"How are you, fella?" I said softly to Buster. "Had a rough night, huh?" I looked at his gums and pinched his skin to check his hydration, which was good.

"When was the last time he had Banamine?"

"Three in the morning."

"And he's gone to the bathroom?"

"This morning at eight."

"What did it look like?"

"It looked pretty loose, but he had that mineral oil in him."

"That's okay. Is he drinking?"

"Just a few sips from his bucket."

"Well, he's had the intravenous fluids, so he's not that thirsty."

I put my head against Buster's side and listened. "I can hear some gut sounds," I said.

"Thank God," Liam said fervently.

"Let me take his temperature just to be certain."

John handed me the thermometer and Liam held Buster's tail aside so I could insert it into his rectum. We waited. When I pulled it out, it was 100 degrees. "It's fine," I announced.

"Looks like you didn't need to make that long trip, Liam," John said.

"I'm glad I came. I feel better now that I've seen him."

Buster was nosing around in his bedding, looking for food. I said, "You could give him a little wet hay, John. Then wait until he goes to the bathroom again."

"Okay," John said.

I had a second thought. "Better check with your vet first. I don't want to do anything he might not approve of."

"Okay, I'll give him a call."

John took out his cell phone and stepped away to make the call. Liam and I stood in front of Someday Soon's stall and watched him.

"Do you really think he's going to be okay?" Liam asked.

"Yes. He had a mild colic but he appears to be over it. He's not looking at his stomach, or pawing the ground. He appears to be perfectly comfortable."

At that moment, Buster lifted his tail. Liam and I stopped breathing. A load of manure came cascading out to land in a pile in the stall. We turned to each other and smiled radiantly.

"Good boy," I said to Buster.

I went over to where John was still on the phone. "He went to the bathroom," I mouthed.

John grinned and spoke into the phone. When he hung up he came to rejoin us in front of the stall. "Great. Two good loads. The vet says wet hay is definitely okay, so

I'm going to find Henry and tell him to start soaking a flake."

"Good," I said.

Two reporters came up to us carrying notebooks. "We hear that Someday Soon colicked last night. Was it bad?"

"No, he seems to be fine this morning," Liam answered evenly.

"Will this affect his start in the Belmont?"

"I don't think so."

They had a dozen more questions and Liam answered them all as patiently as possible. None of the question involved Liam's arrest; apparently that piece of news had not yet reached Belmont.

Liam and I hung around the barn until Someday Soon was fed. Then we watched him eat his wet hay. We waited until he went to the bathroom again, this time with manure that was nearly normal. Then Liam said, "We should find a hotel. I'm going to need some sleep before I make the drive back to Virginia."

I said, "I've been thinking. You should call the police station in Midville and let them know where you are. They might think you've left the country."

He scowled.

"I mean it Liam. I think you should call them."

"All right. I'll call them."

"Did they tell you not to leave the state or anything like that?"

"Not exactly."

"What does that mean?"

"I'll be fine if I just report in. They'll understand when I tell them that Buster colicked. They all probably had bets on him in the Derby and the Preakness."

This was probably true.

He asked, "Do you want to leave early tomorrow, before rush hour starts?"

I nodded. Then I said, "My goodness. What will we find to do to pass the time till then?"

He grinned at me, a bright, lit-up smile that made him look younger than he really was. "Don't worry," he said. "I'll think of something."

CHAPTER 24

We checked into the Holiday Inn but this time we only took one room. I sat in a chair while Liam made his phone call to the Midville police department. They put him through to the chief.

"I just wanted to let you know that I'm in New York, Chief Brown," Liam said courteously. "Someday Soon colicked last night and I drove up to Belmont to see him. I'm driving back to Midville tomorrow morning."

Silence as he listened.

"I *am* letting you know. This was an emergency. Ask any horseman in town about a colic and he'll tell you the same thing. Annie Foster came with me to look at him. She's a vet."

More silence.

"Yes, I'll be leaving early tomorrow. I should be back in Midville by noon. Do you want me to give you a call when I've arrived?"

He shot me an impatient look.

"Okay, I'll do that. Yes. All right. Goodbye." He hung up the phone.

"Was he mad that you left without telling him?"

"What was I supposed to do? Call him at three in the morning?"

"I suppose you could have left a message at the police station. Someone is always on duty there."

"I never even thought of it."

"Neither did I."

"Let's forget about the police, Annie. We have more pleasant things to think about."

I smiled. "What could they be?"

"Let me show you."

I leaned back in my chair. "Why don't you do that?"

He came over to me and held out his hand. I took it and he pulled me to my feet. Then he was kissing me, folding me close against him and kissing me hard. I opened my lips and kissed him back.

It was such heaven, kissing Liam. I could kiss him forever, I thought. After awhile he growled in my ear, "Let's go over to the bed."

With his arm around my shoulders, he picked me up and placed me on the bed. Then he laid beside me, his mouth hungry on mine, his kiss driving me back hard into the pillow.

He kissed my mouth, my face, my throat. He opened the buttons on my knit shirt and kissed me there. I kissed whatever part of him was available at the moment. Then he said, "Let's get undressed."

We stripped off our clothes quickly, then we were naked, our bodies pressed along each other's, his hands hard against my spine, his mouth buried in my hair.

"Annie, Annie, Annie." He repeated my name like a mantra. Then he began to kiss me all over my body. He kissed me until I was trembling, until a hot drenching surge had risen within me and I lifted myself toward him, wanting him, aching for him . . .

"Liam," I cried. "Liam."

For a moment he was poised above me, then I stretched to take him in. He drove in, retreated, then drove in again. He did this until the orgasm ripped through me, causing my whole body to spasm with ecstasy once, then again and again and yet again. My lips opened in a silent scream.

Afterwards, when he lay quiet with his body all along mine, and his head driven into the hollow between my neck and shoulder, I ran my hands over the strong muscles of his shoulders and back, feeling the light sheen of sweat that clung to him. His heart was hammering; I could feel the heavy strokes as I felt the heat of his body and the laboring of his breath.

I love him so much, I thought. *Dear God, don't let anything happen to him. I love him so much.*

He kissed my collarbone. "I love you, Annie."

"And I love you."

"I feel as if I could eat you up."

"You don't want to do that. Then there would be nothing left of me for you to make love to."

He laughed shakily. "That's true."

"Do you know what I was thinking last night?"

"What?"

"That we could name our first son Peter."

He was silent for a moment. Then he said, "I'd like that a lot."

We made ourselves comfortable against the pillows, my head resting in the cradle of his shoulder, and we talked about our future, about what kind of a farm we might have, about our chances for success in the tough business of horse breeding. Then we made love again. Then we got dressed, stopped by to see Buster, who seemed fine, and went out for dinner.

We went to bed early and, after making love again, went to sleep and woke up at four-thirty to get on the road before rush hour. We were across the George Washington Bridge in no time and didn't stop until we were at the bottom of the Jersey Turnpike, where we stopped at a Bob's Big Boy for breakfast. We made it home in less than six hours.

Liam dropped me off at the house, and I went in and put my overnight case down at the bottom of the stairs and went out to the kitchen for something to drink. The morning's *Washington Post* was sitting on the kitchen table and I picked it up. Right there, on page one, was the headline: *Senator's Son Arrested on Murder Charge.*

"Shit!" I said out loud.

I sat down to read the article. It rehashed all of the old stuff about Leslie and emphasized the finding of the medal as the reason for Liam's arrest. "Mr. Wellington identified the medal as his, which led the police to arrest him," I read.

Damn. Why hadn't Liam kept his mouth shut about that medal?

I finished reading the article and sat there, my head in my hands, feeling heartsick. This should be one of the happiest moments of Liam's life. He had a Triple Crown contender in his barn. And he had to worry about being tried for murder. A murder he did not commit.

The press was going to have a field day with this. All of the racing press would be filled with the story of Someday Soon's owner. It was going to be terrible.

Later that afternoon I walked over to the breeding shed

in search of Liam. They were just finishing up a session with Thunderhead and he came out to talk to me while one of the grooms took the stallion back to his paddock.

"Did you see the paper?" I asked.

"Yes. Mary showed it to me. Just what we didn't want."

"Liam, where are your parents? Don't you think they should rally around you while this is going on?"

"I think they're still in Maine. What's to rally around?"

"I presume there will be a hearing or something."

"The lawyer will handle that. My mother and father don't need to be here."

"I should think they'd *want* to be here."

"Well, *I* don't want them, Annie. They'd only be a distraction."

I stared at him in stunned surprise. I knew the Wellingtons had never been a close family, but if ever there was a time for the family to come together, this was it.

"Liam, I'm sure your mother would want to be with you. Have you talked to them? Do they even *know* about your arrest?"

"I talked to my father. He knows."

"And he stayed in Maine?" My voice rose in incredulity.

"Annie." He sounded impatient. "Let it go. I don't need my parents at my side, believe me. I'm a big boy now."

The rest of the men were coming out of the breeding shed. I whispered, "I'm so afraid for you, Liam. I'm so afraid."

He put his arm around me. "Please don't be, Annie. This will be all right. I'm sure it will."

But I did not have his confidence. I think the thing that frightened me the most was the unshakable feeling that he was not fighting for himself. He just seemed so passive, so ready to let this thing happen to him. It was not like Liam to be this way. I didn't understand what was wrong with him.

"I do have some good news," Liam said now.

"What?"

"Kevin is going back to Hollywood. We have the house to ourselves."

This was good news.

"Another reason not to wish for the swift return of my parents," Liam said.

I hadn't thought of that.

"Can you move in?"

"I hate to leave Mom by herself."

"If you were going back to your job when you planned you'd have left yesterday."

"I guess that's true."

He bent his head and nuzzled my temple. "Move in with me, Annie, darlin'. Please."

"Okay." I was so easy.

We were standing there in each other's arms when a police car pulled up.

"Christ," Liam said. "I forgot to call the police to tell them I was back."

"Oh Liam!"

The chief himself got out of the car. He was a man of about fifty-five, tall and broad shouldered with a shock of gray hair. He came up to us. "I thought I told you to call me when you got back to the farm."

"I know, I know," Liam said. "I'm sorry, Chief. We had a breeding session, and I just plain forgot."

"It's important, Liam. You're out on bail on a murder case."

I must have made some kind of a sound because both men suddenly looked at me. I said, "Sorry."

Liam said, "Look, Chief. I have a horse running for the Triple Crown in less than two weeks. I'm not going anywhere."

"That's probably true, but I have to go by the rules, Liam. I want you to keep me apprised of your movements in the future."

"Okay, I'll do that."

I said, "Exactly where was that medal found, Chief Brown?"

He looked at me. He had faded blue eyes. "Now why would you want to know that, Anne?"

"Liam and I used to ride all through those woods. He could easily have lost the medal on one of our rides. Was it on the track that goes by Leslie's gravesite?"

There was a long silence. Then he said, "Yes."

"Liam and I often rode that path. The medal could have come off at any time."

There was a long silence. I could feel Liam looking at me.

I said, "I will be happy to testify to that fact in a court of law."

The chief said heavily, "I'm sure you will, Anne." He turned to Liam. "You heard what I said."

"I heard you, Chief."

We stood together and watched the police car drive away.

Liam said, "That was clever of you, Annie."

"Well, one of us has to be clever. It seems to me you've been bungling this from the word go. I still don't understand why you confirmed that that medal was yours."

"It was."

I let out a frustrated puff of air.

"I know you're annoyed at me, but let it go. With you to take care of me—as well as Kevin's expensive lawyer—everything will be all right."

It occurred to me that negativity might not be what Liam needed just now. I forced a smile. "I'm sure you're right."

"So how about you going home, packing up your bags and moving in with me?"

"Give me one more night with Mom."

He sighed. "Oh, all right. Kevin's not leaving until tomorrow anyway."

I smiled. "You and I. Together. I can't wait."

He gave me his best Liam smile, the one that set off bells in my heart. "I can't either."

I got into my Toyota, backed out of the parking spot, turned, waved and drove away.

CHAPTER 25

I stopped by the big house on my way home to say goodbye to Kevin. He wasn't there, but he pulled up as I was turning away from the door.

"Kevin," I said. "I've come to say goodbye. Liam told me you were leaving."

"I'm catching a flight tomorrow morning. Come on in and we'll have a farewell drink together."

"Okay."

We went into the kitchen and Kevin poured us both a glass of Chardonnay from the bottle in the refrigerator. We sat at the kitchen table.

"Will you be starting another movie?" I asked.

"Next week."

"You keep a crazy schedule."

"At least I'm not operating on colicking horses at three in the morning."

"Touché."

"So are you and Liam going to get married?"

"If he isn't convicted of murder."

"Don't look so bleak, Annie. That isn't likely to happen."

"That's what he keeps saying. I wish I could be so sure."

"We'll get him a terrific lawyer. Don't worry."

"If only Liam hadn't identified that damn medal."

Kevin said, "You know how proud Liam is. He didn't want to be caught in a lie. Someone was bound to identify the bloody thing as his and he didn't want to look as if he was hiding something, as if he was afraid. So he went ahead and identified it himself. It's just the sort of thing he would do."

It disturbed me a little that Kevin knew Liam that well.

"How do you think it got there?" I asked him.

"I have no idea."

"I told Chief Brown that Liam and I used to ride along that path a lot, that it could have fallen off at any time."

"Is that true?"

"Yes."

It was certainly true that we had ridden along that path. "A lot" might be pushing it a bit.

Kevin said, "That's the sort of thing a good lawyer can make quite an issue of."

"Do you think so?"

"Absolutely."

I took a drink of my wine. "Do you know what I find really strange about all of this, Kevin?"

He smiled faintly. "You appear to find the whole matter of Liam's arrest strange, Anne."

I waved my hand. "I know. But it's really strange that his mother and father haven't come home. Liam says that they're still in Maine. Isn't that odd?"

Kevin poured himself some more wine. "It's not strange at all. The last thing Uncle Lawrence wants is to find himself in the middle of a murder investigation."

"But Liam is his *son*!"

Kevin said slowly and clearly, "Uncle Lawrence does not want to get himself photographed with Liam while Liam is under arrest for murder. It won't look good to the voters."

"That's outrageous."

Kevin shrugged. "Maybe, but that's how it is."

"What about Mrs. Wellington?"

"I wonder if she even knows about the arrest."

"*What?*"

"I wouldn't put it past Uncle Lawrence to keep the matter from her. It wouldn't be hard. She doesn't read the newspapers."

"Why would he do that?"

"So she wouldn't demand that they come riding to Liam's rescue, of course."

I remembered what Liam had said to me: *My father knows.*

Liam knew. He knew why his father hadn't come home and he knew that his mother had not been informed. This was terrible.

"I think Senator Wellington is despicable," I said heatedly.

"He's better than my father," Kevin said. "At least he gave me a home."

In all these years, it was the only time I had ever heard Kevin mention his parents.

"Do you ever hear from your parents?" I asked diffidently.

"I heard from my father after my first successful film. He wrote me a letter of congratulation, said he would look me up the next time he was in Los Angeles."

"What did you do?"

"I wrote back and told him I had no interest in seeing him—ever."

I thought of all the words I could say about forgiveness, about water under the bridge, about healing the wounds. I said instead, "I don't blame you."

He said, "My mother died ten years ago from a drug overdose."

"Oh, Kevin," I said. "I'm so sorry."

"Yeah. Wellington was far from perfect, but I was lucky to have it."

"How come you and Liam never got along?"

He shrugged. "Personalities. Each of us wanted to be top dog, I guess. I felt I had to earn my right to be at Wellington by being the best, and Liam just naturally wanted to be the best because it was his nature. We were in constant competition."

We sat in silence for a few minutes, sipping our wine. Then Kevin asked, "Now it's your turn to tell me something. Why did you pick Liam? I never had a chance with you. It was always Liam. Why?"

"I can't explain it," I said slowly. "All I know is that from our first pony ride together, we both knew there was a connection between us. At first it was the horses; then it grew to be everything else."

"It's a very uncommon thing, you know, this . . . connection . . . between you and Liam. I envy you both. It must be wonderful to be able to count on another person the way you two do."

I put my hand over his on the table. "You'll find someone of your own, Kevin."

He smiled crookedly. "There's only one Anne."

"You'll find your own Anne."

He turned his hand so that it was grasping mine. "I don't think so, darling."

"Sure you will," I said bracingly. I squeezed his hand then freed mine. "By the way, do you know exactly where in Maine the Wellingtons are staying?"

"I think they're staying with the Osbornes. Why?"

I waved an airy hand. "Oh, I just wondered."

He fixed me with a piercing blue stare. I smiled. "Whereabout in Maine do the Osbornes live?"

His eyes got bluer. "Anne, don't meddle in this business."

I opened my own eyes wider. "Whatever can you mean?"

"You know exactly what I mean. You're thinking of calling Aunt Alyssa and telling her that Liam's been arrested."

I gave up all pretense of innocence. "Well, I think she has a right to know that her only son—her only *child*—is in danger of his life! I think it's outrageous that the senator hasn't told her."

"You don't know that."

"You just said before that he probably hadn't!"

"I was guessing, for God's sake! Who knows what he's done?"

"Well, I think you've guessed right. I don't think she knows. And I think she should."

"Liam won't appreciate you getting involved, Anne. If he wanted his mother to know, he would have told her himself."

"Liam is behaving like an idiot. He needs someone to look after him, and that someone is me."

"Anne, did it ever occur to you that Liam doesn't want his mother to know? He might not want to stress her. He might be afraid it would push her into another binge of drinking."

I had to admit that this aspect of the situation had not occurred to me. I frowned.

Kevin went on. "You can't judge other people by what you would want for yourself. *You* would want to know if your son was in trouble, but maybe it would be too much for Aunt Alyssa. Maybe both Uncle Lawrence and Liam know that."

Reluctantly, I had to agree that Kevin was making some sense.

I scowled. "I just have this gut feeling, Kevin, that she should be told."

"She'll have to be told eventually, certainly. But leave the when of it up to the judgment of her husband and her son."

There was a long silence as he looked at me. Finally I lowered my eyes and sighed. "Oh all right, you win. I won't meddle. For now."

"That's a good girl."

I got to my feet. "Well, I have to be getting home."

He rose too. "I'll walk you to your car." We walked together through the house out to the porch and down the steps to my Toyota. Kevin put his finger under my chin and tilted my face up. "Goodbye Anne. If ever you need me, just call."

I smiled. "Thank you, Kevin." I received his gentle kiss, turned and got into my car and drove away.

Mom was cooking dinner when I got home. As I made salads I told her about our trip to New York and Someday Soon's recovery from colic. Then, as we sat eating, I told her about Liam's invitation to move in with him.

"We're going to get married, Mom. It's not like we haven't made a commitment to each other," I said.

"You and Liam made a commitment to each other when you were children," Mom said. "I have no objection to you moving into Wellington, Anne."

"I just wish I didn't have to desert you."

Mom smiled. "I have to learn to live alone, honey. It's been wonderful having you, and you've helped me over a bad patch, but I have to do the rest on my own."

"Are you sure it's okay?"

"I'm sure."

Tears misted my eyes. "You're such a trooper, Mom."

Tears sparkled in my mother's eyes. "I know."

We both sniffled and laughed and blew our noses with our paper napkins.

We were halfway through our chicken when I told my mother about Mrs. Wellington's ignorance of Liam's arrest.

"That's terrible," Mom said.

"That's what I think. I was even ready to call and tell her, but Kevin talked me out of it. He said that I might push her into a relapse."

"He's right that it isn't your place to interfere, Anne. But I don't think it's right for her family to keep her in the dark."

"I don't either."

"It would look better for Liam too, to have his family around him. To have them staying away like this makes it seem like they think he's guilty."

"God, Mom. What if they don't come to the Belmont?"

"It won't look good."

"Kevin's lawyer is going to have to talk some sense

into the senator, make him understand how it will look if he doesn't show up."

"When is this lawyer of Kevin's coming on the scene?"

"Soon, I hope. Kevin gave his agent the job of finding 'the best'."

We cleared away the dishes, then went inside to the living room and turned on the television. A&E had a rerun of *Law and Order*.

I used to like watching *Law and Order* but tonight I found it terribly depressing. All the discussions about plea bargains and murder charges vs. manslaughter charges and jail times . . . it all made me feel very gloomy. I was very glad when *Everybody Loves Raymond* came on and I had something to make me laugh.

It was a funny feeling going up to bed, thinking that tomorrow night I would be sleeping with Liam. *Poor Mom,* I thought. Her future held only emptiness on the other side of the bed.

This business of the murder charge had to be resolved. Liam had to go free. He had to! The alternative was simply unthinkable. I got into bed and thought about it for an hour and a half before I finally fell asleep.

CHAPTER 26

The following morning I had breakfast with Mom and kissed her as she left for work. I sat over another cup of coffee and cried a little because I felt as if I was deserting her. Then I went upstairs to pack.

The wardrobe I had brought with me was not extensive. It consisted mainly of jeans, knit shirts, sweaters, two pairs of nice slacks, my trusty black dress, the suit I had worn to the Derby and the new clothes I had bought for the Preakness Alibi Breakfast and the concert with Kevin. After I had packed, I picked up the phone and dialed my practice in Maryland. Fortunately, the head partner was in the office.

"Hi Doug," I said. "It's Anne. I have some news for you. I'm getting married."

"Uh-oh," he said. "To someone in Virginia?"

"That's right."

"Damn," he said. "Does that mean you'll be leaving us?"

"I'm afraid so."

"How soon?"

"I'll stay until you can hire someone to replace me."

"You're going to be hard to replace, Anne. The clients love you."

"Thank you, Doug. That's nice of you to say."

"Who's the lucky fellow?"

"Someone I've known since I was six years old."

"Wow."

"Yeah. It took a while, but I finally got my man."

He laughed. "Are you coming back when you said you would?"

"Yes. I'll be back the week after the Belmont, and I'll stay until you get someone to replace me."

Doug said suspiciously, "This fellow you're marrying . . . it isn't by any chance the guy who owns Someday Soon, is it?"

"As a matter of fact, it is."

"Anne, hasn't he been arrested for murder?"

"He didn't do it, Doug. He'll be acquitted."

"My God."

"Don't worry about me. I know what I'm doing."

"I hope so."

"I'll see you in about ten days."

"Okay."

We hung up.

Good God. Even Doug, who never looked at a newspaper, knew about Liam's arrest. How was it possible that his mother didn't know?

I carried my good clothes on hangers down to the car, then I came back and got my suitcase. At the last minute, I sat down at the kitchen table and scribbled a note to my mother. I propped it against the sugar bowl, then I went out to my car.

Sam and Freddy, the two coonhounds, were curled up on the front porch when I arrived at the big house. The front door was unlocked and I went in to see who was inside.

Mary was in the kitchen, cleaning up after breakfast.

"Anne, honey," she said. "I hear you're comin' here to live." She came to give me a hug.

Mary is a very big woman. I almost disappeared inside her arms and her bosom. When I reappeared I grinned up at her. "I'm glad you're happy."

"We've been waitin' for this for years—you and Liam."

"I've been waiting too. I finally convinced him."

"Now we jest have to get rid of the po-lice."

"We will, Mary. I'm sure of it."

She nodded emphatically and asked if I wanted anything to eat. I declined and went to get my clothes out of the car. I brought them into the house, up the stairs and into Liam's room.

It was a plain room, with that attractive walnut four-poster bed and two walnut end tables. The rug was a faded red and blue oriental and the tall windows had dark wood cornices and pale flowered draperies. Over the bed hung a picture of one of Liam's ancestors. There was a large chest of drawers for Liam's clothes and a bookcase and two chairs.

I wondered where I was going to put my stuff.

Maybe I should just stay packed up until Liam got home, I thought. Maybe this would work better if I moved into one of the guest rooms.

I decided I would go and see how the yearlings were coming along.

When I got back to the house at about four o'clock, Liam was there. "Hey you," he said as I came up onto the front porch. He put his arms around me, and kissed me deeply.

"Wow," I said breathlessly when he finally lifted his head. My feet were dangling a few inches short of the floor.

"You're here," he said. "You're really here."

"I'm really here, but I think I'd feel better if I was standing on the ground."

He slid my body along his as he let me down.

"Very sexy," I said.

"I aim to please."

"I didn't unpack because I didn't know where to put things."

"Hmm," he said. "Let's go upstairs and look."

We went hand in hand up the stairs and into his bedroom. He looked at my suitcase and at my clothes lying on his bed. "The clothes on the hanger can go in my closet."

"I didn't know you had a closet. I didn't see one."

"It's inside the bathroom." He opened the door to the old-fashioned bathroom and there was a sliding door on the right that opened to reveal a closet. The sliding door and the closet were obviously a modern addition to the room.

It was not a large closet, but Liam did not have a lot of clothes.

"Goodness, but your wardrobe is sparse," I said.

"I have a few good suits and a blazer. And I have some shirts. The rest of the time I live in jeans or khakis."

"Well, it looks like there will be room for my dresses." He went and got them and hung them up. One item taken care of.

"What about my underwear? And my shirts and my jeans and stuff?"

"That is a problem. My dresser is filled."

"Maybe it would be better for me to use one of the guest rooms."

He glared. "You're staying here with me!"

"Oh well. I suppose I can live out of my suitcase."

"Not at all. We'll just move a dresser from one of the guest rooms in here."

I looked around. Like all the rooms at Wellington, Liam's bedroom was quite large. "Okay, that would work."

"Let's go and shop for one."

We tried three guest rooms and picked a dresser from the red room. The two of us moved it down the hall into Liam's room where we found an open space along the wall to place it. Liam had to move a picture, that was all.

Liam sat in one of the chairs and watched while I unpacked. He told me about his conversation with John Ford as I went back and forth from my suitcase carrying underwear and pajamas and socks and shirts and so forth.

"John was really pleased with this morning's workout. Buster was full of run at the end of it—just what John wanted to see."

"He doesn't seem to have been affected by the colic then?"

"Not at all."

"That's great."

"I thought we'd go up to New York on Wednesday. What do you think?"

"It's fine with me. Do you think you'll have a problem with Chief Brown?"

"I think the residents of Midville would lynch Chief Brown if he tried to keep me home."

I laughed. "You may be right."

"What do you want to do about dinner tonight?"

"Why don't we drive into the Safeway, buy a nice juicy steak, and cook it here?"

"That sounds great."

"I'll check the larder and see what else we might need. Mary only does breakfast and cleaning when your father's not here."

The phone rang. Liam went out into the hall to answer the upstairs extension. He was gone for a while. I had finished putting my clothes away when he came back.

"That was Kevin. He's found me a lawyer. His name is Abraham Kessler and he'll be calling here at nine tonight."

"I've never heard of him."

"Neither have I, but that doesn't mean anything. It's not an area in which I have any expertise. Kevin says he's one of the top ten trial lawyers in the country."

"Well, that's certainly a good recommendation."

He sighed and lowered himself into a chair.

I went to him and sat on his lap. "I'm so sorry, Liam. This should be such a happy time for you. You should be thinking of nothing except Buster and his chances for the Triple Crown and instead you have this terrible thing hanging over you—like the sword of Damocles. It just stinks."

He rested his cheek against my hair. "It does."

I could feel his heart beating against my face. I said in a muffled voice, "Liam, don't you think you should ask your parents to come home? It doesn't look good for you, their staying away like this. It looks as if they think you're guilty."

I could feel him stiffen. "We've been over this before, Annie. I don't want them around."

"I wish you would reconsider. Even my mother said she thought it looked funny not having them here."

He was silent.

"Will they be coming to the Belmont?"

More silence.

"Liam, if they don't it really won't look good."

"Maybe they'll come for the race."

"They have to. Talk to your father and tell him that. Please."

"Okay. I'll talk to him."

Tension I didn't even know I was feeling drained out of my body.

"Do you know what might be nice?" Liam asked.

"What?"

"It might be nice to invite your mom to share the steak with us."

Tears stung my eyes. "Oh, Liam."

"Is that 'Oh, Liam' yes, or 'Oh, Liam' no?"

I sniffled and blinked. It's 'Oh, Liam,' yes."

So we went into town, bought a steak and a few other groceries at the Safeway and stopped by Mom's. At first she refused to come, but when she realized that we really wanted her, she relented. She insisted on driving her own car, however, so that Liam wouldn't have to drive her home.

Liam grilled out on the back patio and Mom and I cooked rice and green beans inside on Mary's immaculate stove. We had a very enjoyable dinner. Mom told some funny stories about school and Liam filled her in on

Buster's progress. We all talked about the Triple Crown and what it would mean if Buster won.

"I wish Pete could be here," Liam said, voicing the thought that was in all of our minds.

"He would be so proud of you, Liam," Mom said. "You bred that horse and you bred his sire. You did a brilliant job."

"Thanks, Nancy. I appreciate that."

The New York lawyer called at nine o'clock and Liam spoke to him for twenty minutes, then Mom went home. Liam told me about the call as we cleaned up the kitchen and at ten o'clock we went upstairs to bed.

CHAPTER 27

On Saturday evening, exactly one week before the Belmont, Senator and Mrs. Wellington arrived home. Liam and I were having dinner in the kitchen when they walked in.

"How cozy you look," Mrs. Wellington said as she came to kiss first Liam and then me.

"Would you like something to eat? There's some more chicken in the pot," I replied.

"No, thank you." Her eyes went to the wine bottle. "Perhaps a glass of wine."

Liam and his father shook hands and the senator smiled at me. "How are you, Anne?"

"Fine," I returned.

Mrs. Wellington fetched a glass from one of the cabinets, turned and asked her husband if he wanted wine as well. When he said he did, she took down another glass.

When both the elder Wellingtons were seated with their wine, Liam's mother turned to him. "I understand that you have been arrested. I cannot believe it, Liam. They have no evidence! It's just ridiculous. Your father tells me that Kevin has found a top lawyer for you and you should be acquitted easily. But still—to have to go through that charade! I don't understand it at all."

Both men were silent.

I said, "They don't exactly have no evidence, Mrs. Wellington. They have the medal."

She had been lifting the glass to her lips, but now she went completely still. She looked at me. "Medal? What medal?"

Liam and his father sat like stones.

I looked into her glittering blue eyes. "They found Liam's miraculous medal near Leslie's grave. That's why they arrested him. Didn't you know?"

She put her glass down. She was paper white and her hand was trembling. "No. I didn't know."

Liam said, "I identified the medal as mine. It's not that big a deal, Mom. Annie is going to testify that we often rode along that path and that I could have lost it anytime. Or, whoever did kill Leslie could have stolen it from me and planted it. It's too fragile a piece of evidence to convict me."

Mrs. Wellington looked at her husband.

"Liam is right," he said to her. "There is very little chance that he will be convicted."

"You never told me about the medal," she said.

"He won't be convicted, Alyssa."

"But suppose he is?" she whispered.

"He won't be."

I found it strange that Mrs. Wellington had known about the arrest but not about the medal. I asked, "How did you find out about Liam's arrest, Mrs. Wellington?"

"I heard it on the radio yesterday," she replied.

She heard it on the radio! I stared at the senator. He did not look back.

Liam said, "Mom, there's nothing you can do. Just let events take their course and everything will be all right. Okay?"

She looked at him, her face stricken. For the first time I thought that she looked old.

"Oh my darling. I am so afraid."

Well, I could sympathize with that.

"Don't be. It will all work out."

I said encouragingly, "This lawyer is one of the ten best in the country, Mrs. Wellington. Kevin did a good job."

"Bless him," she said.

I said, "We were just going to have tea and dessert. Why don't you join us?"

"That would be very nice," Senator Wellington said heartily.

"I have some good news for you," Liam said. "Annie and I are going to get married."

"That's wonderful!" Mrs. Wellington said. "I'm so happy for you both."

"Congratulations," Senator Wellington said to his son. There were kisses and hugs all around.

"And Annie has moved into my room until she has to go back to Maryland to her job."

"We're delighted to have her as our guest," the senator said with charming courtesy.

"Have you set a date?" Mrs. Wellington asked.

I said, "I promised my practice that I would stay until they got someone to replace me, so I can't think of dates until they do that."

"And I can't get married while I have this murder charge hanging over my head," Liam said.

"Sure you can," I replied. "These things sometimes drag on forever."

"I'm not marrying you until my name is cleared."

I pushed out my lower lip, like a little girl who isn't getting her way. "I wish Daddy was here. He'd tell you to make an honest woman of me."

"You are an honest woman."

"Not in the eyes of the Church. I can't go to communion when I go to Mass."

He scowled.

"It's true."

"You're the best person that I know."

"But I'm sleeping with you and we're not married."

"We'll get this business with Liam fixed up in no time, Anne," the senator said gruffly. "Abraham Kessler is an excellent attorney."

"You've heard of him?" I asked eagerly.

"I certainly have," the senator replied. "Kevin came through big time."

"He certainly did," Liam said wryly. "Now he'll always be one up on me."

"Liam!" I protested.

He gave me a crooked grin. Then he turned to his father. "Did you have a good time up in Maine? How was your golf game?"

The two men talked while Mrs. Wellington sipped her wine, looking pale and fragile. I loaded our dinner dishes in the dishwasher and filled the kettle with water for tea.

While I was waiting for the water to boil I uncovered the angel cake that Mary had made that morning. It had some kind of a caramel filling that was truly heavenly.

"Who would like a slice of Mary's angel cake?" I said.

The senator and Liam said yes, but Mrs. Wellington

shook her head no. The kettle whistled and I filled the
china teapot and put a teacup in front of all four places at
the table. Then I gave out the cake, sat down and began
to pour the tea.

Right in the middle of the senator's describing a hole-
in-one he almost made, Mrs. Wellington said, "If it
wasn't for the medal, they wouldn't have arrested you. Is
that right, Liam?"

"I don't know about that," Liam began, but I cut in
over him.

"That's right, Mrs. Wellington. And do you know, he
identified the medal the minute he saw it? 'Here's the
medal, Mr. Wellington.' Boom! 'Oh yes, that's mine.'
Surprise! 'You're arrested.'"

The senator said stiffly, "If it was his, someone was
sure to identify it."

"Maybe, maybe not. But by identifying it, he handed
himself over on a silver plate."

Then we heard the clatter of something falling and we
all looked. Mrs Wellington had dropped her fork on the
floor. "Oh, how silly of me." She bent as if she would get
it.

"Don't, Mom. I'll get it."

She looked awful, as if she might faint.

"Can I get you something, Mrs. Wellington?" I asked.
"A glass of water?" She looked as if what she really
needed was smelling salts.

"No, oh no. I'll be fine."

"I think you should lie down," I said firmly. I looked
at her husband. "Why don't you take her upstairs and see
that she lies down? She's going to faint any minute."

"I think you're right," he replied. "Come along,
Alyssa. Let's go upstairs."

She stood up, but she swayed. Liam was by her side in a flash. He bent and picked her up. "It's okay, Mom. I'll carry you. Lead the way, Dad."

I sat by myself at the table as the three Wellingtons left the room, contemplating the scene I had just witnessed.

Mrs Wellington had known about Liam's arrest when she entered the room. She had not become distraught until she learned of the existence of the medal. What could that mean?

The likeliest explanation was that for the first time she realized there was actually some evidence connecting her beloved son to the murder. She had been resting secure, believing that there was nothing other than speculation to tie Liam to the crime. Then she had found out about the medal.

Liam and his father had probably tried to keep the information away from her because they feared she would fall apart. She was certainly a fragile flower.

I was very glad she wasn't my mother.

Liam came down to rejoin me at the table and poured himself a cup of tea.

"How is your mother?"

"She's okay. Upset. Dad's going to stay with her for a while."

"I still can't believe she had to learn that you were arrested from the radio."

"You saw how she fell apart just now. Is it any wonder that we tried to keep the news from her?"

"I would hate to be a person that people felt they had to keep things from."

"Mom has always been fragile. You know that. It's just the way she is."

His face looked shadowed and tense. I patted him on

the hand. "Well, at least they're here. That looks good for you."

"I wish they weren't here," he said savagely. "I wish they were back in Maine playing golf."

That note of savagery disturbed me profoundly. I didn't know how to account for it. After a moment I said quietly, "I wish I could be alone with you, too."

He took my hand and held it so tightly it hurt. He didn't speak.

"Is there something you want to tell me, Liam?" I asked softly.

He shook his head. "I can't, Annie. I can't."

"All right."

He held my hand to his mouth. "I love you."

"I love you too."

"Can we go upstairs?"

"Absolutely."

"Now?"

"Sure."

We left the tea and cake on the table and went up the stairs to our bedroom. There was an element of desperation in Liam's lovemaking that night that had not been there before. He held onto me the way a drowning man might hold onto a flotation device. I didn't understand what was happening, but I did know that it had to be connected in some way to the visit of his father and mother.

I drew him as deeply into me as I possibly could, wanting to take all his pain, his need, wanting to give him the closeness, the oneness, the reassurance that we were there for each other, two persons in one body. When it was over we lay pressed against each other, our hearts hammering, our breaths hurrying, and Liam said, "Annie. My other self."

I turned my head and kissed his cheekbone. "I wish I could help you."

"You do help me. Just by being here, you help me."

"That's good."

"One day I'll tell you. But I can't now."

"Okay."

We lay quietly for a little while. Then I said, "I'm going to have to clean up that kitchen. I can't leave the cake and tea dishes out for Mary to find in the morning. The dishes have to be put in the dishwasher and the cake has to be put away."

He groaned. "We have to get up?"

"You can stay in bed if you like, but I have to get up."

"Yeah, and what kind of a heel will that make me look like?"

"The worst sort."

"That's what I thought."

"We can catch the news, then."

"Great."

I handed him his jeans. "Here you go, buddy."

He accepted them and sat on the edge of the bed to put them on.

CHAPTER 28

Senator Wellington hustled his wife away the following day. She didn't want to go, but he bullied her into it. What surprised me was that Liam stood by and made no effort to stop it.

"Will you be coming to the Belmont?" I asked as they stood outside the car.

"Of course," the senator replied smoothly.

"Anne, dear, come and give me a kiss," Mrs. Wellington said.

I went over to her. She put her arms around me and said in my ear, "Have you seen that medal, dear?"

"No," I replied.

"Go and look at it," she said.

"Alyssa, we're waiting for you."

She released me. "We're so happy about you and Liam."

I looked into her face and nodded.

Then they were in the car and driving away. Liam put an arm around my waist. "Dad said he thought he could let me have a few of the mares after all. Isn't that great?"

I thought it was odd. Something about this whole visit

was odd. I was going to get a look at that medal the first chance I could.

Jacko and I worked with the yearlings in the morning, then in the afternoon I drove into town to the police station. I was hoping I would see Michael Bates on duty, but someone else was in the office when I walked in.

"Hi," I said. "I'm Anne Foster. I'm Liam Wellington's fiancée."

"Hi there Dr. Foster," the young policeman behind the desk replied. "What can I do for you today?"

"I'd like to see the medal that's the evidence in the case against my fiancé. I've never had a chance to look at it and I'll be testifying about it so I thought I should see it."

He frowned. "I don't know if I should just show it to you."

"Why on earth not? It's a matter of public record, isn't it?"

"Well, yes."

"Do you want to ask someone?"

"The chief isn't here just now."

"I promise you, I just want to look at it. I'm not going to try to steal it or anything."

"Well . . . I guess it's all right."

"Sure it is."

"It's in the evidence safe."

"If you'll go and get it, I'll wait here."

I waited in the small, bare waiting room, my heart pounding. There was something fishy about this medal. There must be, or why had Mrs. Wellington told me to look at it? After what seemed like an eternity, the policeman came back carrying an envelope in his hand. He brought it over to me. "Here it is," he said, and slid a medal out onto his hand.

It was gold. That was all I saw. The medal was gold.

Liam's medal had been silver.

What the hell was going on here?

"You can see where the chain was broken," the policeman pointed out helpfully. I looked at the tear in the delicate chain.

"Yes," I said faintly. "Yes, I see. Thank you very much, Officer. I appreciate your help."

I stumbled a little as I went down the front step of the police station and I caught myself at the bottom. My mind was in a whirl.

Liam had lied. He had known that the medal wasn't his and he had lied.

Who did the medal belong to?

I thought of Mrs. Wellington, of how her husband and son had struggled to keep the news of Liam's arrest from her; of how the senator had whisked her away this morning; of how she had asked me to go and look at the medal.

Could the medal belong to Mrs. Wellington?

But that didn't make sense. I certainly couldn't picture fragile Mrs. Wellington killing Leslie.

Nothing made sense.

What was I going to tell Liam?

Clearly, this was the secret he said he couldn't tell me. And now I knew it. Would he be upset if I told him? Would he be angry?

I had to tell him. This was not something I could keep to myself. I walked to my car, my heart thumping.

It isn't Liam's medal. It isn't Liam's medal.

But whose medal was it? Who was he protecting?

His father?

I got into the car and drove back to the farm. For almost the first time in my life I had a dilemma I couldn't lay before my mother. This was something that had to stay between Liam and me.

I cooked a pot of pasta for dinner, then Liam asked me if I wanted to take a walk to check on the mares and foals. We put on jackets against the evening chill and walked hand in hand down the path to the big pastures that housed the mares and their babies.

It was a beautiful night. The stars were clear in the sky and the moon gave enough light for us to see our way. The air smelled of grass and horse and earth.

"I'm going to hate to see all this go," Liam said.

"You'll have a new farm," I replied.

"We will," he replied. "And it will be easier now that Dad has said I can take some of the mares with me."

A bribe, I thought cynically.

"Which ones will you take?" I asked out loud.

"I'll have to think about it."

"How many did he say you could take?"

"He didn't exactly give me a number."

"You'd better pin him down to a number, so you know what you're talking about."

"You're probably right."

I looked up at the stars. *If only people were as clear and straight and true,* I thought.

One of the foals decided he wanted to nurse and nudged his mother. She curved her neck to nuzzle him.

Liam said, "I might take Ring Of Kerry. She's had some very nice foals."

Better say it out here, I thought. *Under the stars.*

My heart began to pound. "Liam," I said. "When I was saying goodbye to your mother yesterday she asked me to go and look at the medal at the police department. I had never seen it, you know."

His hand went rigid in mine.

"I went today."

He didn't say anything.

"The medal at the police station was gold, Liam. Your medal was silver."

Still he didn't say anything.

"That's not your medal," I said. "You identified it as yours, but it isn't. That's what you couldn't tell me, isn't it?"

Silence.

I looked up at the sky and let the silence build.

Finally he said, "My mother asked you to go and look at it?"

"Yes. When she was hugging me to say goodbye. She asked me if I had seen it and when I said I hadn't she asked me to go and look at it. So I went."

"Shit."

"She didn't know anything about the medal until I mentioned it to her. I let the cat out of the bag, didn't I?"

He dropped my hand and leaned against the fence. "Yeah," he said. "You did."

"So what's going on, Liam? Are you going to tell me now?"

He looked at me, his face bleached white by the moon. "How much have you guessed?"

"I've guessed that you're covering for someone, but I don't know if it's for your mother or your father."

He laughed bitterly. "Try both of them."

My mouth dropped open. "What?"

"Christ, Annie, I can hardly believe it myself. When I saw my mother's medal I almost fainted."

"So it was your mother's medal."

"Yeah. Grandma had given one to her as well and she usually wore it. I couldn't believe it when I saw it. I knew it was damning evidence, though, so I thought I would say it was mine until I could find out what was going on."

The June night was cool because of radiation cooling, but the chill I felt had nothing to do with the weather. He knew it was damning evidence. He had kept telling me it wasn't important.

"So what did you do after you got home from the police station?"

"I called my father and told him what had been found. I told him what I'd done. I told him I expected to be arrested."

"What did he say?"

"At first he said he had no idea how my mother's medal had come to be at Leslie's grave site. I told him that wasn't good enough, that if that was all he could tell me, I'd tell the police who it really belonged to. After a great deal of heated discussion, he came clean."

There was silence. Out in the field the horses moved slowly around. I didn't say anything.

"This is so hard for me Annie."

I put my hand over his on the fence.

He drew a deep breath. "Did you know that Leslie was having an affair with my father?"

"Good God. At the same time she was with you?"

"That's right."

"Did you know that?"

"Of course not. But my mother did."

"Oh."

"Yeah. The night of the party Mom was very drunk—and very angry at Leslie. Dad had always kept his affairs away from Midville. At home he played the faithful husband and Mom could hold up her head. She was furious that he had broken that rule with Leslie. At some time during the party she accosted Leslie and asked if she could talk to her in the summerhouse. Leslie went with her. The conversation did not go well. Basically, Leslie said it wasn't her problem if Mom couldn't keep her husband faithful. Mom was drunk and livid and she picked up the baseball bat and bashed Leslie over the head with it."

I stared at Liam in stunned amazement. "Your mother killed Leslie?"

"That's right."

"But she's so fragile . . ."

"Not apparently with a baseball bat in her hand," Liam said grimly.

"I can't believe this."

"It took me a while too."

"All these years, while people were suspecting you, it was really your mother!"

"The last person anyone would suspect."

"But how did your father know this, Liam? Did she tell him?"

He looked at me in irony. "Who do you think buried Leslie? Mom?"

My eyes popped. "Oh my God. Your father buried her?"

"That's right. Mom went and found Dad and told him what she had done. They waited until the party was over, then they got one of the farm trucks, loaded up the body and drove it out into the woods. Dad dug the grave and buried the body. Mom was there; that's when she must have lost the medal."

"I can't believe I'm hearing this."

"You can imagine how I felt. They're *my* parents."

"You can't take the rap for this, Liam. It's outrageous that your parents should expect you to."

"The alternative is that Mom would go to prison for murder and Dad would go for being an accessory."

"So it's better for *you* to go?"

"Dad said they won't let me be convicted."

"Great. They'll step forward after we've all perjured ourselves by swearing that your mother's medal is your medal—so we'll go to prison for perjury!"

"Oh God, I don't know. It's all such a mess, Annie. I don't know what I'm doing any more."

"I'll tell you one thing, Liam. I don't think your mother intends to let you take the fall for her. Once she finds out that the medal is hers, I think she intends to claim it."

"Dad won't let her."

"This may be one time when your father can't stop her."

"Dad can always control Mom."

"He couldn't control her drinking and he couldn't control her killing Leslie."

He didn't say anything.

"Where did your parents go?"

"To the Georgetown house."

There was a stand of trees in the pasture and a bird began to call from them.

"What do you want me to do?" I asked.

He rubbed his hands across his eyes. "I don't know."

I said quietly, "I hope you're not going to ask me to perjure myself."

A second bird answered the first.

He sighed. "No, Annie. I'm not going to ask you to perjure yourself."

"It was always impossible, Liam. The medal was the evidence. You couldn't look at it, and swear on a bible that it was yours. That's just crazy."

"I was hoping they'd throw the case out before it came to trial," he said.

"You're the one who said the evidence was damning."

He sighed again. "I know."

I said, "I think you and your mother and your father should sit down with this fancy lawyer of Kevin's and tell him the truth. Let him work out a deal for your parents. Your mother certainly wasn't mentally competent when she hit Leslie that night. She might have to serve some time, but I'll bet it won't be very much."

He shuddered. "To think of my mother in jail!"

It might sober her up. But this was an unkind thought.

"And Dad. He'll lose his senatorship."

"He participated in a crime, Liam. Leslie lost her life. Someone has to pay for that."

"I know. You're right, Annie. It's just . . . hard. They're my parents, you know?"

"I know. And I'm sorry. I'm sorry it's ended this way."

His shoulders slumped. "So am I."

The two birds were now singing together.

I took his hand. "Let's go home, honey."

His fingers curled over mine. "I'll call Dad tomorrow morning."

"I think that would be best."

"Kessler has his offices in New York. Maybe we can see him while we're there for the Belmont."

"It would be great for you to see the Belmont with this monkey off your back."

"Yes. It would."

We started to walk back toward the house.

He said, "Do you know, maybe it will be nice to make a fresh start somewhere else, just the two of us."

I reached up and kissed his cheek. "I think it will be very nice."

We went back home, and got into bed, and comforted each other.

CHAPTER 29

L iam called his father the following morning and spent half an hour on the phone with him. When he hung up he looked grim. "He doesn't want to go see Kessler."

The selfish bastard. "What does he expect you to do?"

"He wants me to wait and see if they'll throw the case out for lack of evidence to prosecute."

"No," I said. "That's not good enough. Even if they do that—which they won't—you'll spend the rest of your life with people thinking you killed Leslie. Call him back and tell him that I'm going to the police and telling them that it isn't your medal."

"Annie, I don't want you getting into the middle of this."

"I am in the middle of it, Liam. Your mother asked me to look at that medal. She was asking me for help. Well, I'm going to give it to her. I'm going to tell the police that the medal isn't yours. I can't tell them whose it is because I never saw your mother wearing it, but I can tell them it isn't yours. I imagine there are a few people left who will remember that your medal was silver."

"Maybe we should just wait . . ."

"No. I am not playing around with your life."

"All right. I'll call my father again."

The phone was in the hallway and Liam sat on one chair and I sat on another as he called.

"Dad? It's me. We've hit a snag. Annie is going to tell the police that the medal isn't mine."

"No, I can't stop her. She says she's doing what Mom wants."

"Dad, Annie is her own person. She has to do what she thinks is right. I *want* her to do what she thinks is right. I don't want a relationship like the one you have with Mom."

"No, she isn't going to tell the police the medal is Mom's. She's just going to say it isn't mine."

"I have no idea what I'm going to say about why I identified the medal as mine. I'll think of something."

"All right. Yes. Okay. Goodbye."

He hung up.

I said, "Did he want you to browbeat me into keeping quiet?"

"Something like that."

Mary was in the kitchen and I got up to talk to her. "Mary, do you remember the miraculous medal that Liam used to wear?"

"The one his granny gave him? Sure."

"Do you remember if it was silver or gold?"

"It was silver."

"Thank you," I said and went back out into the hall.

"Mary just told me that your medal was silver."

He puffed his cheeks out and exhaled.

"I don't know how you thought you were going to get away with this. The moment I saw the medal in court, I would have jumped up and screeched that it wasn't yours."

"I was just so horrified. I wasn't thinking clearly."

"And your father took advantage of that."

"Yeah. He did."

"Let's go into the police station and talk to Chief Brown."

Liam said, "I actually do have my own medal. I found it right after all of this stuff started."

"Great. Take it with you."

He sat for a long moment staring at the floor, his hair hanging over his forehead. "Annie, how the hell am I going to explain the fact that I identified the medal as mine?"

"I don't know."

"Maybe we shouldn't go rushing off to the police on our own. Maybe we should talk to Kessler first."

I thought about that. My own desire was to get Liam cleared as soon as possible, but there was so much involved here that perhaps he was right. "It wouldn't hurt to give him a call."

We spent the rest of the day waiting to get in touch with Abraham Kessler in New York. When Liam finally got him on the phone he explained what had happened and, after a moment's hesitation and after making sure the attorney-client privilege applied, he admitted that the medal belonged to his mother.

When Liam hung up he turned to me. "Kessler is sending someone from his office to go to see Chief Brown with us tomorrow."

A weight lifted from my shoulders. "That's great. Is he flying down?"

"He'll be coming into Dulles tomorrow morning. We can pick him up."

"This was the right thing to do," I said.

"I think so. I told him the medal was Mom's. I thought it was important he realize just how delicate things are."

"Good move."

He smiled at me. "Let's get this taken care of tomorrow, then go up to New York for the Belmont."

I smiled back. "I can't wait."

Stephen Waller was a very smart-looking young man in a gray pinstriped suit, white shirt and gray tie. His handshake was firm and his smile was professional. He gave no hint that he thought it was a waste of his time to come all the way to Virginia simply to accompany us to the police chief's office.

We explained in the car what we wanted, but he had already been briefed in New York. "Basically, you want to tell the police that the medal is not Mr. Wellington's, and that is it. You don't want to say anything else."

"That's right," Liam said.

"Okay. Leave it to me."

We drove to the police station and went in together. I was wearing a blazer and a skirt I had borrowed from my mother and Liam was wearing a blazer and a pair of gray slacks. We had made an appointment with Chief Brown the previous day.

Michael Bates was in the outer office when we went in. I gave him a brief smile. Stephen said, "We have an appointment with Chief Brown."

The woman at the front desk said, "I'll let the chief know you're here."

Then we were being shown into the chief's office.

Chairs were found and we all sat down. Stephen introduced himself as Liam's attorney.

"My client has come here to make a simple statement, Chief Brown," he said. "Liam."

Liam said, "The miraculous medal you found near Leslie's grave is not mine, Chief Brown."

The chief looked thunderstruck. "What!"

I said, "I came to look at it yesterday. I knew as soon as I saw it that it wasn't Liam's. Liam's medal was silver. The one you have is gold."

The chief raised his voice. "If it isn't yours then why the hell did you say it was?"

Stephen said, "We did not come here to address that question. We came here to inform you that the medal is not Mr. Wellington's. This information can be corroborated by Dr. Foster and by Mary Lincoln, the cook at Wellington, both of whom remember the medal as being silver. Plus, Mr. Wellington still has his medal. Liam?"

Liam took a silver medal out of his breast pocket and put it on the table.

The chief slammed his hand down on his desk. "This is outrageous."

Stephen stood up. "I expect all charges to be dropped against my client by the end of the day."

"I'll file new charges against him for the obstruction of justice," the chief snarled.

"I wouldn't clutter up this case any more than it already is," Stephen said coldly. "Liam, Anne, it's time to go."

We went back through the outer office and out into the warm sunshine. My face broke into a smile as soon as the door had closed behind us.

"Thank you," I said to Stephen. "Will they really drop the charges against Liam?"

"They'll have to. Without the medal, they have no case."

I hugged Liam's arm.

He said to Stephen, "Everyone is going to want to know why I identified the medal as mine."

"You answer, it was a mistake; you found your medal in your drawer."

Liam nodded soberly.

We went out to lunch at the Coach Stop then we drove Stephen back to the airport.

"It was a long way to come just to babysit us through a visit to the chief's office, but we appreciate it," Liam said to him as they shook hands. "I wouldn't have known what to say to the chief about why I identified the medal as mine."

"That's why Abe sent me," Stephen returned comfortably. "Just keep saying 'It was a mistake,' and don't let anyone rattle you."

"Okay."

We drove back to the farm talking about what might come next in the case.

"They'll try to identify the real owner of the medal," I said.

"If Mom and Dad just keep quiet, everything should be all right. There's no reason to trace the medal to them."

I looked at Liam's profile. His mouth looked somber. I wasn't as sanguine about his parents' safety as he was. The police were going to look for a reason for Liam's lying and chances are they would deduce he had been trying to protect someone.

To be honest, I wasn't as anxious to see his parents get away with murder as he was. Leslie's life had been snuffed out. Someone should pay for that.

We had planned a mini race for the yearlings at the farm that afternoon. Liam was trying to decide which horses to bid on at the Keeneland sale in July, so we had picked eight of the best youngsters and decided to run them for a half a mile to see which looked the most promising.

It was a warm afternoon as we took the horses out to the training track at about three o'clock. We had saddled up in the barn area and the grooms who were riding guided the youngsters along the farm road as Liam and I rode in one of the farm trucks. Jacko was waiting for us up at the training track and he opened the gate for the horses to let them into the track area.

Once their feet touched the track, the youngsters knew where they were. A few of them got excited and started to act up. Their riders cantered them up the track to relax them and then brought them down toward the starting gate.

They did me proud. Every one them of them walked into the starting gate and stood for the few seconds it took for Jacko to get them off.

"Good job," Liam said to me.

I smiled.

The horses broke. I would like to say they broke cleanly, but that did not happen. They bounced off each other at the start, but then they did get the hang of running forward and it began to look like a race and not a melee.

One youngster went right to the front and stayed there.

"Winky hates to be behind," I said.

"Look at Red," Liam said.

I looked at the chestnut colt running along on the outside. He was passing another colt. "Ummm," I said. "He
has a beautiful stride."

The race was over and no one was hurt.

"Thanks everyone," Liam said to the grooms. "Walk
them out and give them baths."

Liam and I went back to the barn with the horses, and
Liam went around to each one, feeling their legs to make
sure there was no swelling or heat.

He lingered over one filly in particular.

"She ran well today," he said to me.

"She ran very well. She would have done better if she
hadn't been bumped so badly at the start."

"Her sire is Native Son."

"She could go for a bit of money."

"She could. But her dam is one of our own mares,
Milky Way. I like her a lot—it's why I bred her to Native
Son—but she doesn't have a reputation. That could hold
the price down some."

I nodded.

We talked about the other horses, about the ones that
Liam would like to try for, about the ones he was most
likely to be able to afford. Then, when they were all
cooled down and ready to eat, we took the truck back to
the house.

The phone was ringing as we came in the front door.
Liam went to answer it.

"Hello. Oh, Stephen. Hello. Yes. Yes, that is good
news. Thank you very much. Yes. Thanks for calling.
Yes, I'll do that. Okay. Goodbye."

He hung up and turned to me. "That was Stephen Waller. The charges against me have been dropped."

I flew across the hallway and into his arms. "Thank God. Oh, thank God."

He held me tightly.

"Thank you, Annie," he said huskily. "I'd backed myself into a corner and I didn't know how to get out."

"Thank your mother," I replied. "She's the one who told me to go and look at the medal."

His arms tightened even more. "She must have known what you'd find."

"I'm sure she did. She must know her medal is missing."

"Oh Annie." A shudder went all through him. "What a mess this all is."

"You're out of it, Liam," I told him. "Nothing you can do will affect the outcome of this case. Your part in it is over."

"I guess it is," he said wonderingly.

"Just think—you can go to New York without having to report your actions to the police chief first."

He smiled down at me, his blue eyes bright. "That is a great feeling."

I smiled back. "Do you want to go out to dinner to celebrate?"

"Sure. Do you think word has gotten around town that I've been exonerated?"

"Are you kidding?"

"It'll be great not to feel that people are wondering if I'm a killer or not."

"Let me call Mom and tell her the good news, then we can get changed and go out."

"Okay. Let's make it an early night, though. I have lots of things I want to do to you later on."

I smiled up into his wickedly sparkling eyes. "Let's do that," I said. "Let's do that."

CHAPTER 30

We left for New York on the Wednesday before the Belmont. We flew from Dulles to Kennedy where we rented a car and drove straight to the racetrack.

It was a madhouse. Triple Crown fever had hit Belmont with a vengeance and for the first time in the series of races Someday Soon was the focal point of press attention.

John Ford was going nuts.

"I have to run him at four-thirty in the morning if I want any privacy," he complained to Liam. "The press swarm over every move that we make."

The press certainly swarmed over Liam and me the moment we arrived. They had heard that the charges against Liam had been dropped and were full of curiosity about what had happened. We were standing in front of Someday Soon's stall when the questions started.

Liam followed Stephen's advice and said, "I made a mistake. It wasn't my medal after all. I found my own medal in my drawer. And that is all I have to say on the subject."

"How could you make a mistake on such an important matter?" one reporter called.

"I just did," Liam replied. A light breeze blew his hair over his forehead and he brushed it back.

"How could you not know your own medal?" another reporter asked incredulously.

I moved closer to Liam's side.

"It was a mistake," Liam repeated.

"It's nice that the charges were dropped in time for the Belmont," the *Daily News* reporter said.

Liam smiled faintly. "It certainly is."

A candy wrapper blew along the shedrow and John scowled mightily and bent to pick it up.

The *Bloodstock Journal* reporter asked, "What about this Irish horse, Mr. Wellington? What do you think about him?"

"I know very little about him," Liam replied.

"He's run a mile and a half in Ireland. And won. So we know he can go the distance."

"Someday Soon can go the distance," Liam said.

"But he's never done it."

"He'll do it on Saturday," Liam returned.

The *Bloodstock Journal* reporter asked next, "What's this we hear about your father selling his farm?"

A few of the reporters turned to look at the man asking the question. Obviously not everyone had heard that rumor.

Liam's mouth set in a grim line. "He may be selling some of the horses."

"Will you continue to train there if that happens?"

Liam shrugged. "We'll cross that bridge when we come to it. Right now I am focused on Saturday. I'll worry about what comes after, after."

"Solomon's Riddle and Point Taken have had some

very impressive workouts," the *New York Times* man said.

"Good for them," Liam returned. "But workouts have to translate into racing results and we'll see about that on Saturday, won't we?"

The *Daily News* reporter called, "What will you do with the Visa Triple Crown match prize if you win it?"

Liam grinned. "What any horseman would do—buy more horses."

Everyone laughed.

"Hey Dr. Foster," somebody called. "How are you keeping your job? You've been spending an awful lot of time with Someday Soon."

Liam said, "As soon as Dr. Foster's practice can find a replacement for her, we will be getting married."

He sounded so proud saying that; I had to blink.

The newsmen sent up a chorus of congratulations.

Liam reached out to take my hand.

Cameras clicked.

I curled my hand around Liam's and smiled.

All of this is because of Buster, I thought with some wonder. *All because of one horse, Liam and I are suddenly newsworthy.*

Finally the reporters ran out of questions and drifted away. Liam and John Ford got into a deep conversation and I went to watch Buster eat his hay.

His bright chestnut coat gleamed with grooming and with health as he reached his elegant neck down and grazed on the pile of hay in the corner of his stall. So much was riding on those four slender legs, I thought. The hopes of the thoroughbred world for another Triple Crown champion and Liam's hopes for the championship and the money that came with it.

I wondered about this Irish colt. We had beat just about all the other horses that would be running in the race, but this Irish colt was the unknown. The reporters had said he was big, too. Big and strong and he had won at a mile and a half.

You can do it, Buster, I thought fiercely. *I know you can do it.*

Liam said, "Ready to go, Annie?"

I turned to him with a smile. "Sure," I said, and we went off to the car.

There was a party that night in the Garden City Hotel for the owners and their guests. Most of the other owners brought an entourage; we brought John Ford and his wife. Liam hadn't talked to his father since our trip to the police station.

I wore the dress I had bought for the concert with Kevin and Liam had brought his tuxedo. The room we were in was elegant, with waitresses passing hors d'oeuvres and a bar dispensing drinks. I was very anxious to meet the Coolmore people to see if we could find anything out about their horse, but they weren't there.

"They keep to themselves," John told us when I commented on their absence. "I wouldn't exactly say they're secretive, but they're close to it."

All anyone wanted to know was did we think that Someday Soon was going to capture the Triple Crown.

"We like his chances," Liam kept replying.

"He's as ready as he'll ever be," John Ford said.

The owner of a lightly regarded runner shook Liam's hand. "Well, I hope he does it. It would be great for the country to have a Triple Crown winner just now."

"Wow," I said when the man walked away. "That's a

lot to lay on Buster's shoulders. Now he's running for the good of the country."

Liam grinned. "It *would* be a boost for the country. Everyone—even non-horse people—gets excited over a Triple Crown winner."

A number of the same people who had been present throughout the other two triple crown races were present at the Belmont party: Bob Baffert with Sheikh Mohammed and D Wayne Lukas with Prince Salman to name two. New to the gathering was trainer Nick Zito with Star Beta, a New York–bred horse who was said to be good at a distance. We had a chance to talk to Zito at dinner, as we were seated with him.

As a trainer, Zito was based at Belmont, so he had a bit of an advantage over everyone else in that he trained on the track all the time. Star Beta had done very well in his last outing, coming off the pace to win convincingly and thus earn himself a ticket to the Belmont.

"He's one of those late bloomers," Zito said. "He wasn't ready for the Derby, but he's ready now. And he's rested, while the rest of these colts have two tough races behind them. I think he has a really good shot at pulling off an upset."

This kind of talk made me very nervous. How many times in the last twenty years had a horse made it through the Derby and the Preakness only to fall in the Belmont? Too many times to count. And it always seemed to be some horse that came out of nowhere to take it away.

I smiled at Zito, a trim-looking man in his fifties. "Your colt has never run in this kind of competition though."

"He ran fast enough," he replied, quoting me some impressive numbers. "I think he deserves to be in this company."

Liam said, "What do you know about the Irish horse?"

"He's big," Zito replied. "Have you seen him?"

"Not yet."

"He's seventeen hands, at least, and powerful. He reminds me a little bit of Secretariat."

"Great," I said sourly.

"They're keeping him under wraps, but a few of the boys got a peek at his workout the other day and it was very impressive."

"Someday Soon has been working well too," I said defensively.

Nick flicked John Ford an amused look. "Yeah, at four in the morning, when Johnny runs him."

"I can't stand all those reporters hanging around," John said.

"You should be more like Baffert. He loves 'em."

"He can have them."

Liam said with mock seriousness, "A lot is riding on this race, John. Some fellow told Annie and me that the good of the country depended upon Someday Soon winning the Triple Crown."

John snorted.

Nick laughed. "Well, I will tell you this. If I don't win, then I hope that you do. It would be nice to have a Triple Crown winner again. But that doesn't mean that I'm not going to do my damndest to beat you."

"Fair enough," Liam said.

With all this talk of viable rivals, my stomach was in a knot and I couldn't eat. What were the chances of Buster being able to pull off three wins in a row? No horse had done it in over two decades. And these two powerful new rivals had not had to run two exhausting races within a few weeks of the Belmont. Star Beta had had one "tune-up" race and God knew when Solomon's Riddle had last run.

The more I thought about it, the more depressed I became. Were we asking too much of our gallant boy? Since Affirmed had last won the Triple Crown in 1978, eight horses had made it two thirds of the way, but couldn't quite finish. Was Buster going to be number ten?

The difference to Liam's future would be enormous. Not only would the Triple Crown bring him millions, it would make Buster worth millions at stud. Without it, Buster was just another very good racehorse. "What are you looking so worried about?" Liam asked me in a low voice.

I forced a smile. "I get nervous hearing about all of these rivals."

"Just remember, Buster is the horse to beat. He's the one with the credentials. The others are chasing him."

I nodded and sat up straight. "You're right."

He gave me a crooked grin. "I get nervous too."

We were both glad when the party was over. There was so much stress attached to the race on Saturday that the festivities just weren't much fun. All I wanted was for the race to be over—and for us to have won, of course.

We were quiet in the car on the drive back to our hotel.

"I wish the damn race was tomorrow," Liam finally said.

"I know," I replied.

"We should be lapping up all this attention. It's great for business."

"It'll be good for you when you go out on your own.

You'll have had a lot of exposure. Very few owners are also the breeders."

He nodded. "What if Buster doesn't win, Annie? What do I do then?"

"You can always stay on the farm for a while, can't you? Your father isn't talking about selling Wellington."

"No."

"You'll still have Buster, and your mares, and you have enough money to buy some more. We'll do okay, Liam. It just won't be as big a start as you'd like."

"It will be tight. Very tight."

"That's okay. I can always get a job as a vet and help out."

He drove for a while in silence. "It could be worse. At least I'm not being charged with murder."

"It could be a lot worse," I said fervently.

We got back to the hotel and went upstairs. I asked him to unzip my dress and he did and then his hands held me and his mouth came down to kiss my bare back. "Do you know what?" he asked.

"What?"

"My future looks bright just because I have you."

I turned my head and looked at him over my shoulder. "I feel the same way about you."

He turned me around and took me into his arms. "I am such a lucky, lucky man."

"Everything is going to be fine, love," I said. "Even if Buster doesn't win, we'll work things out."

He bent his head and kissed my throat. "I don't want to stay on the farm, Annie. I don't want to be beholden to Dad anymore."

"Okay," I said. "Then we'll rent someplace."

"Ummm," he said. His lips moved lower.

I closed my eyes.

"Did I tell you today that I love you?"

"I don't believe that you have."

"I love you."

"I love you too."

"Why don't you take this very pretty dress off? If I take it off I'm afraid I'll rip it."

I smiled up at him. "Okay."

I stepped out of my dress and went to hang it in the closet, then I peeled off my panty hose. While I was doing this, Liam was shedding his tuxedo.

"Don't just throw it on a chair," I scolded. "You may have to wear it again." In my underwear I went and picked up his tux from the chair and hung it on a hanger and put it in the closet with my dress.

Liam turned down the bed. "Come here," he said, holding out his arms.

I went to him.

We melted together with the familiarity of old lovers but with the passion of new. Holding each other, we came to rest on the bed, our arms and bodies entwined, our mouths exploring each other. Never would I get enough of the feel of him, the smell of him, the touch of him. Here was my world, here in the arms of this man. His possession of me was the most thrilling, ecstatic moment of my life, when all my vulnerable innermost being opened for him, shuddering in ecstasy, giving and trusting and holding nothing back.

"Annie," he groaned. "Oh Annie. I love you so much."

"I love you too."

His body was burning with heat and his face was driven into the hollow between my neck and my shoulder. I rested my lips on the top of his damp black hair.

"I love to make love with you," I said.

"Words cannot describe how much I love to make love with you," he said. "I've thought of taking Viagra so I could do it all day long."

I chuckled. "You definitely don't need Viagra, love."

"If I was going to do it all day long, I might."

"Well, you're not going to do it all day long. You have other things to do, and so do I."

He sighed. "Damn."

We stayed like that for quite a while. Then I said, "My leg is going to sleep."

He shifted his weight off it. "I suppose the rest of you wants to go to sleep as well."

"You got it."

He yawned. "Okay. You can get up.

"Thank you." I got out of bed, collected my pajamas from the drawer and went into the bathroom. When I came out Liam was lying in bed, his arms crossed behind his head.'

"The bathroom is all yours," I said.

"Do you know what, Annie?" he asked.

"What?"

"It would really be wonderful if Buster won the Triple Crown."

I went to kiss him.

"It would."

CHAPTER 31

I woke up at four-thirty on the morning of the Belmont and looked at the clock. It was pitch dark outside.

Four-thirty, I thought. *John will be taking Buster for a walk around the track.*

I couldn't go back to sleep. I pictured the scene in my mind, the horse with an exercise rider aboard and John Ford up on a stable pony, the chill dark air, the moon, Buster stamping the ground, eager to run, the struggle to hold him to a walk, to let him stretch his legs without losing any of the precious energy he would need that afternoon. Then, afterward, the walk back to the stakes barn, where Buster would be safely tucked behind a police barricade as he ate his breakfast and snoozed over his hay.

I lay quietly until seven o'clock, when Liam said, "Are you awake?"

"Yes."

"Me too. I kept waking up all night."

"I've been awake since four-thirty."

"The day is finally here."

"I know."

I leaned up on my elbow and looked down at him. His hair was hanging in his eyes and he had a stubble of beard on his face. I said "We have to have our picture taken with Buster at nine o'clock. You have some work to do before then, chum."

He raised his hand and ran it over his jaw. "Are you going to wear your lucky suit?"

"Of course."

He gave me a comical look. "Once I get out of bed, this day has officially started."

I pulled the covers off him. "Don't be such a wimp. Get up."

"Okay, okay." He climbed out of bed and headed for the bathroom.

We got dressed and stopped in the coffee shop for some breakfast.

I had coffee and some toast. Liam, who was so professedly nervous, had eggs, bacon, potatoes and toast. If the man ever stopped eating, then I would know there was something seriously wrong with him.

We arrived at the barn at a quarter to nine and showed our credentials to get past the police barricade. John was waiting for us, dressed nicely in a gray suit with a dark red tie. Liam also wore a suit and I wore my suit but not my hat. At nine o'clock the photographer showed up.

We posed in front of the barn and at the last minute, Buster obliged by poking his head out of his stall door.

"That horse is such a ham," John said. "I can't believe it. I swear, he knows there's a picture being taken."

We all laughed and the photographer got a merry threesome with a beautiful thoroughbred looking on, ears pricked, eyes curious. You would never in a million years think that we were on the brink of the biggest race of his young life.

The photographer put down his camera and Buster disappeared back inside his stall.

Liam shook his head. "He really is a ham."

"No question about it," John said.

Liam had picked up the newspapers at the coffee shop and now we sat down on chairs in front of Buster's stall and read what the pundits had to say about the race.

I read *Newsday* first, a column by Andrew House.

"The American Triple Crown is not just difficult to win, at times it seems almost impossible. Since 1978 nine horses have reached the threshold, with wins in the Derby and the Preakness: Spectacular Bid, Pleasant Colony, Alysheba, Sunday Silence, Silver Charm, Real Quiet, Charismatic, and War Emblem, and Funny Cide, only to be defeated by the interminable Belmont. Will Someday Soon be able to break this curse and come home a winner today? I'd like to think he will, but I have my doubts.

In both the Derby and the Preakness he was the benefactor of a blistering front pace that burned out his competitors and left the field open for a come-from-behind specialist like himself. But the Belmont has added two other specialists like this: Solomon's Riddle and Star Beta. And both of these horses are more rested than Someday Soon, who is coming off the punishing double of the Derby and the Preakness in five weeks. And Solomon's Riddle has proven he can go a mile and a half; something no American three-year-old has yet done.

The Belmont looks to be a very different race from the Derby or the Preakness. When Someday

Soon makes his move this time, he'll have company. My money is on the Irish horse to win. I think we're going to have to wait for another year to have a Triple Crown winner.

Part of me was furiously indignant at what House had to say about Buster and part of me was scared that he was right. I said to Liam, "This guy from *Newsday* is picking the Irish horse."

"The *Times* is going with Buster," he replied.

I was very glad to hear that. It made me feel better to know that such a bastion of respectability was behind us.

"The hell with the newspapers," Liam said. "Let's go for a walk."

We wandered around as the crowds streamed in. By the time the first race started, people packed the grandstands, the lawn by the rail at the final turn, the clubhouse and the paddock.

We had lunch in the restaurant—Liam never misses a meal— and went back down to the stakes barn to be with Buster. TV cameras were everywhere, as reporters tried to get interviews with trainers and jockeys and owners.

The day had started out sunny but it became progressively more overcast as the afternoon went on.

"I hope it doesn't rain," Liam said for perhaps the tenth time.

"Rain wasn't in the forecast." I made the same reply I had been making all afternoon.

Finally it was time to move to the paddock. Buster's groom, Henry, and John took hold of his bridle and led him out of his stall, past the police barricades. Liam and I followed, the security guards trailing us, and we started the walk toward the paddock, where we would saddle up.

The reporters came behind and cameramen raced ahead, maneuvering their equipment to get a shot of Buster as he was led forward.

When we reached the paddock area we led Buster into stall six. There was a fence in front of the stall and the area behind the fence was packed with people who had come to watch the potential Triple Crown champion be saddled.

The clerk of scales called the riders for weigh-in, and they went one at a time. When Miles Santos, Buster's jockey, stepped on the scale, his valet handed him his saddle and cloth. The clerk noted the weight. "He needs a pound," he said, and a lead pad was tucked into Miles' saddle to bring the weight up to level.

Then Miles brought the saddle over to Buster's stall and John saddled him up.

"He looks wonderful," I said to Liam.

He did. He knew what was coming and he was tossing his head, eager to be out of the stall, eager to be out on the track and running.

John was talking to Miles Santos. "Just don't let him get buried too far behind. He's had stamina built into him. Put him in a place to run and he'll do the rest."

The bugler blew the call to the post and the grooms led the horses into the walking ring. John gave Miles a leg up and the horses paraded once around the ring. My eyes went to Solomon's Riddle.

He was a magnificent-looking animal, a huge red horse with powerful muscles. He looked like he could run all day and all night. I swallowed and looked back at Buster. He was shaking his head up and down. He wanted to run. "Good boy," I whispered. "Good boy."

"Come on," Liam said. "Let's get to our seats."

We got back to our seats just as the horses were coming out of the tunnel onto the track. The minute the first horse, Honor Bright, put his foot on the track, the sun broke through the clouds and shone brightly on his bay coat. The crowd roared.

One by one the rest of the field appeared on the track and were taken up by their lead ponies. Then, as they began to walk down the field, a Broadway actress sang "New York, New York."

Buster was behaving very well, and when he began to canter he went quietly along with his lead pony. As the horses galloped up the field past the final turn to warm up, a maintenance worker drove the starting gate onto the course right in front of the grandstand.

Belmont racecourse was a full mile and a half around and the horses would make one full circle of the oval to complete the race.

At the top of the turn, the horses turned and began to come back down toward the starting gate where the starter and his assistants awaited them. The noise of the crowd was deafening.

Take it Easy with Shane Sellers aboard wearing red and green silks went in first on the rail. The rear door closed behind him. Next to load was Point Taken, with Gary Stevens aboard.

The noise of the crowd was painful. I shouted to Liam, "How can the starters even hear each other?"

He shrugged.

Risky Business went into the gate next. Then came Solomon's Riddle. The big red colt tried to back up when the assistant starters came for him, but when they grabbed him he came forward and let himself be loaded. Buster was in the post position next to Solomon's Riddle and we could see the bright royal blue and white silks of Miles Santos as our boy went quietly into his slot and had the door closed on him

Finally all the horses were in the gate. I could feel my heart thumping inside my chest in the brief seconds while we waited for the starter to send them off. Then the bell rang and the gate sprang open and the horses lunged forward together.

The crowd, impossibly, became even louder.

The field stayed close together as they passed the clubhouse stands for the first time, then as they went around the clubhouse turn the horses began to differentiate themselves. Runforyourmoney with Jose Velazquez aboard took the lead, followed closely by Take It Easy. A little bit back off the pace were Honor Bright and Point Taken. Then, running easily, side by side across the track were Buster, Solomon's Riddle and Star Beta.

"He's in good position," John shouted to Liam. "As long as Miles doesn't fire him too soon."

Down the backstretch they ran, at the far side of the oval, away from the noise of the crowd. I lifted my binoculars and looked at Buster. He was running under a hold from Miles, but Solomon's Riddle was under a hold too. Both jockeys were waiting to make their move.

At the mile mark Runforyourmoney faded from first place and Take It Easy took over. Honor Bright and Point Taken moved closer to the front. A few more strides and Honor Bright had the lead; Take It Easy began to fade.

The horses hit the final turn and Buster began to make his move. So did Solomon's Riddle and Star Beta. Buster and Solomon's Riddle, who had been running side by side, moved as one as they accelerated on the outside of the track. Star Beta made his move on the inside.

"Here he comes!" Liam said.

No one who saw that Belmont Stakes will ever forget it. Buster and Solomon's Riddle came off the turn and galloped straight into the wall of sound of the crowd. They caught and passed Runforyourmoney and Take It Easy. They had now run the distance of the Kentucky Derby but had a full quarter-mile to go.

The two horses, running like mirror images, passed Point Taken and Honor Bright and were now out in front of the track, with nothing in front of them but the finish line. Side by side they ran, head to head, shoulder to shoulder, eye to eye.

"Jesus!" Liam screamed. "It's like Affirmed and Alydar all over again!"

Then, as the finish line approached, one nose poked out in front of the other, then a half a head. Then they were across the finish line and sweeping along in front of us, and the crowd went absolutely manic.

When I watched a rerun on TV later that night all the announcer could do was scream hysterically, "We have a Triple Crown winner! We have a Triple Crown winner!"

Liam and I were hugging each other and pounding each other on the back and jumping up and down.

"He did it! He did it! He did it!"

Then John and Liam were hugging and Lorraine and I were doing a kind of a jig.

Security men appeared in the box to escort us down to the winner's circle.

Liam and I held hands as we made our way through the crowds. The first thing Liam did when we got into the winner's box was go up to Buster and kiss him.

I patted his sweaty neck.

Liam shook Miles' hand. "Good job."

The reporters had surrounded John and were bombarding him with questions.

A TV camera appeared in front of us. "How does it feel to have a Triple Crown winner, Mr. Wellington?" a reporter asked, holding a microphone to Liam's face.

Liam shook his head. "I'm still in a state of shock, I think."

"You bred Someday Soon, didn't you?"

"I was there when he was born," Liam replied.

"Wow. This must be really exciting then."

"It surely is."

They were calling Liam over for the trophy presentation. Cameras flashed. TV cameras rolled. Buster posed with his blanket of flowers. The crowd was somewhat quiet.

Then the president of Visa got up to present the check for the five-million–dollar Visa Triple Crown match prize.

Liam looked dazed as he accepted the money. We had talked about it, but actually to have it in his hand seemed unbelievable. The whole thing seemed unbelievable.

Buster had won the Triple Crown.

John said, "Let's get him back to the stable."

Henry began to lead Buster out of the winner's circle, preceded by a phalanx of security men. He skittered a little as he went, scattering the press who had been behind him.

We crossed back through the tunnel to the paddock area and from there to the stakes barn, where the police barricade was still in place. There Henry gave Buster a bath and turned him over to one of the hot walkers to walk him until he was cooled off. Then John and Lorraine and Liam and I trundled off to the press conference that had been arranged by the track.

When the press had finally finished asking their questions, we all went back to Buster's stall, took beers from a cooler and sat down on bales of hay to toast each other.

"That was the most unbelievable race," John said.

"It was like a replay of Affirmed and Alydar," Liam said.

"Buster just had the bigger heart," I said.

John took a swallow of his beer and nodded slowly. "I think so. They were eye to eye and Buster just wouldn't give up."

"He reached deep," Liam said.

"Yes," John said. "He did."

"It's still hard to believe, though," Liam said. "My little Buster has won the Triple Crown."

"It's going to be crazy around here," John said. "What do you want to do with him? He needs a break from racing for a while."

"We'll ship him home to Virginia for a month or so. He can relax out at pasture for a while."

"Good. We'll aim to have him ready for the Saratoga session."

We talked for half an hour while Buster ate his hay and occasionally popped his head over his stall door to see what we were doing. Liam gave him a Mrs. Pasture's cookie.

We made a date to have dinner with John and Lorraine and then got in the car to go back to our hotel. We didn't say much on the ride home; it seemed that everything had been said already. When Liam let us into our hotel room, we just stood there for a moment, facing each other. Then Liam whooped and grabbed for me. I started to laugh. He waltzed me around the room, bumping into furniture on our way.

"We won, we won, we won," he chanted as we swirled around.

"Buster is the best horse in the whole world," I said.

"He is." He stopped waltzing and regarded me solemnly. "He was smaller and lighter than that other horse, but he wouldn't give up. He just wouldn't be beaten."

"He has the heart of a lion."

"I'm so proud of him."

"You should be."

He smoothed his hand over the jacket of my pink suit and smiled. "You may have to wear this suit for the rest of his racing career."

"I don't think this suit has anything to do with Buster's winning."

He looked alarmed. "Does that mean you won't wear it any more?"

I laughed. "I'll wear it if you want, but I truly think Buster can take care of business without my pink suit."

"It's best not to change anything," Liam said.

I shook my head. "I can't believe how superstitious you are."

"I don't believe in messing with a winning combination."

I slid my arms out of the jacket. "Well, I have no intention of wearing this suit out to dinner. Do you want to take a shower first or can I?"

"I have something else that I'd like to do first."

I looked at my watch. "We don't have time."

"Yes we do." He took the jacket from me and laid it on a chair. "Winning the Triple Crown has made me horny as hell. How about we call John and say we'll be an hour late?"

I looked up into his narrowed blue eyes. I felt that look all the way down in my stomach. "You don't think he'll mind?" I asked weakly.

"I'm sure he won't. I'll call him now." He went over to the phone on the desk next to the bed. I looked at his back, at his broad shoulders and narrow waist and hips. I listened to the deep murmur of his voice as he spoke to John.

You are like putty in his hands, I told myself.

He turned away from the telephone and started back toward me. "We have an hour," he said, still with that narrow-eyed intent look.

I inhaled a little unevenly. "Okay."

He began to unbutton my blouse. "Let's start by getting the rest of the lucky suit off."

I let him finish unbuttoning and pull the blouse out of my skirt. When he took it off I had only my bra on. "Let me unbutton your shirt," I said.

We helped each other get undressed and then we made our way to the king-sized bed. Liam had been telling the truth when he had said he was horny; he was fully erect right from the start. He tried to hold back and wait for me, and I tried to meet him as quickly as I could. When at last he was buried deep within me, we both knew the rushing ecstasy of orgasm and afterward we hung on to each other with the mixture of triumph and gratitude we knew from our other encounters.

He kissed my temple and said, "I don't want to go out to dinner. I want to stay right here."

"I know," I murmured. "But we can't stand John up. He just trained Buster to a Triple Crown for you."

He sighed. "You're right."

We cuddled even closer.

"I need a shower," I said.

"Me too."

"I'll go first."

"Okay."

Neither of us moved.

Liam's stomach growled.

"That's it," I said. "You're hungry. I'm getting up." I pulled away from him and swung my legs over the side of the bed.

"I guess it is getting late," he said.

I shook my head and headed toward the bathroom.

CHAPTER 32

We stopped by to see my mother on the way back to the farm from the airport. She was having dinner and, after the hugs and kisses and exclamations, we joined her for a cup of tea.

"Midville is going crazy," she told us. "There are signs and flags all over town."

"It's great for the whole Virginia horse business to have a Triple Crown winner," Liam said.

Mom said, "The bar at the Jockey Club has invented a new drink—the Someday Soon."

Liam laughed.

I said, "I suppose that's a compliment."

"I'm sure it's meant to be," Mom said.

She wanted to know all about the Belmont and we told her everything that had happened.

"Some of the papers had picked the Irish horse," I said. "It was a little scary—they were making him out to be so great."

"He turned out to be pretty great actually," Liam said. "He only lost by a nose."

Mom said, "I thought I would have a heart attack, watching those two horses come down the stretch like that. Then, when Buster stuck his nose out in front! It was just wonderful!"

"Liam kissed him," I said.

"He deserved to be kissed," Mom said.

I sipped my tea. "He's coming home tomorrow. Liam's vanning him down from Belmont. He deserves a few weeks off before he has to start training for the Saratoga season."

Mom said, "I'm surprised your parents weren't there, Liam."

Liam and I avoided looking at each other.

"I think they were visiting friends," Liam said.

"But to miss the Triple Crown!"

"I'm sure they caught it on television."

Mom frowned.

I said, "I'm going to have to go back to work tomorrow. I got a call yesterday on my cell phone from Doug congratulating me on Buster's win and begging me to come back. The extra vet is gone and they're still interviewing for my job. They're swamped."

Liam scowled. "You didn't tell me that."

"I'm telling you now."

"You don't have to go tomorrow!"

"Yes, I do. They need me, Liam. And until they hire someone to replace me, it's my job—my responsibility. I have to go."

"Damn," he said.

"That's the way it is."

"I suppose so," he said grumpily.

Mom said carefully, "Are you going to continue to practice after you leave this job, Anne?"

"Of course I will, Mom. I didn't go through all that training not to use it."

Mom looked relieved.

We talked for another half an hour or so and then left to drive back to the farm.

We said goodbye to each other that night as if we were never going to see each other again. We had become so close in the last few weeks, so used to having each other around, that this coming separation was really painful. When I drove away from the farm the following morning, I had tears in my eyes.

Once I plunged back into my practice, however, I hardly had time to breathe, let alone dwell on missing Liam. The first day I was back we had two colic surgeries. Then we had a horse with an infection that went into the blood and turned septic. The clinic was filled to capacity and on top of that we had all the usual calls for lameness and injuries and runny noses and the like. Plus I was scheduled for two pre-purchase exams. It was crazy.

I talked to Liam every night when I finally got home, or I called him from the clinic when I got a break.

"It sounds to me as if they need two vets to replace you," he said when I explained to him what was happening.

"I think you're right," I said. "The practice is really growing."

It was on the second night I talked to him that he gave me the news. "The police were out to talk to Mary this morning. They brought Mom's medal and wanted to know if she recognized it."

"Oh no. What did she say?"

"What could she say? She said it looked like Mom's."

"Oh, Liam."

He sounded grim. "I suppose it was inevitable that

something like this would happen. They must have started asking themselves who I could have been trying to protect."

"I shouldn't have mentioned Mary as backing me up in identifying your medal. It put her name in the police's mind."

"You couldn't know that would happen."

"It never crossed my mind."

He sighed. "I know."

"Have you heard anything from your parents, Liam?"

"They called me to congratulate me about the Triple Crown. Mom sounded really happy. Dad was . . . reserved."

Screw him, I thought.

"How is Buster?" I asked.

"He's settling in just great. You'd think he never left."

"Do you have a lot of people who want to see him?"

He laughed. "Just about everybody from within a twenty-five-mile radius has come calling. If they have cameras, he poses. Otherwise he just keeps on eating."

I laughed. "He's wonderful."

We talked for some more and then we hung up without saying anything more about Mary's identification of Mrs. Wellington's medal. But I lay awake for a while that night, wondering what was going to happen next.

The police asked Liam if the medal he had identified as his actually belonged to his mother. Liam said he didn't know. They asked him if his mother had had a medal and he said yes but that he didn't know if the one the police had was his mother's or not.

"It was the best I could do," he said to me over the

phone. He sounded wretched. "They asked me if Mom's medal had been gold and I had to say that it was."

"It's all right, darling," I said to him. I wished with all my heart that I was there with him, that I was not so far away. "You did the best you could for her under the circumstances. There was Mary's evidence, and they'll talk to other people who will remember that your mother had a gold medal."

"I suppose."

"Have the police talked to your mother yet?"

"I don't think so. I called Dad and told him what was happening here and he got the lawyers involved right away. I don't think the police have been able to talk to Mom yet."

I said what I could to cheer him up, but I wasn't sure it helped. I wished desperately that this whole business of Mrs. Wellington and the medal would just be over. It was like Chinese water torture for Liam to have it carrying on like this, drip by drip by drip.

Ten days after I returned to Maryland, Doug finally hired a vet to take my place in the practice. Since he could start right away, I was free to return to Virginia. I called Liam and my mother with the good news, called my landlord to cancel the lease on my condo, packed a suitcase and headed south.

I arrived on a hot summer afternoon. The dogs were all stretched out in the shade of the porch, sleeping. They opened their eyes when I arrived, wagged their tails, then closed their eyes again.

"Hello to you too," I said.

I carried my suitcase into the house, which was empty. Then I went upstairs to Liam's room and plunked my suitcase on the bed. The air conditioning was on in the house and it was cool inside. I went back downstairs to the kitchen for a glass of water, then I went to look for Liam.

I found him with the yearlings. The Keeneland sale would be in a week or so and this time of year the farm's focus was on the yearlings.

"Annie!" He grinned when he saw me and held out his arms. He looked wonderful, I thought. He had a baseball cap on over his black hair, he was tanned from being out in the sun, and his knit shirt and jeans clung to his long, fit body. I hugged him, taking in the scent of sweat and sun and horse that clung to him, and was dizzy with happiness.

"Home for good?" he said.

"Home for good," I answered.

"Nice to see you, Anne," Jacko said.

"Nice to see you too, Jacko," I replied.

We looked at the yearlings, all of whom looked splendid, then Liam said, "Come and have a peek at Buster."

We got into my car and drove out to the stallions' paddocks, and there he was, the Triple Crown Champion, turned out in his own black oak-fenced paddock, his chestnut coat bright under the summer sky.

Liam whistled to him and his head lifted and his ears perked up. He looked at us for a long minute, then he went back to grazing.

"He looks great," I said.

"John doesn't want him to get too fat, so I have to be careful with the grass. But he does look good."

"He needs a break, mentally and physically."

"I think so too."

We stood for perhaps fifteen minutes, just watching

our boy enjoy himself. Then we got into the car and went back to the house.

The next morning I went into town to see my mother. She wasn't home so I parked in front of her house and walked up to the main street to pick up some candy. I was standing in front of the confectioner's shop when I ran into Michael Bates. He was wearing his uniform.

"Hi Michael," I said.

"How are you, Anne?" he replied. "I thought you had gone back to Maryland."

"I did, but they found someone to take my place in the practice so now I'm back home for good."

"Liam must be happy about that."

"Yes," I said. "He is."

We exchanged a few more pleasantries, then we parted and I didn't think anything more of the conversation until later in the afternoon when Liam and I got back to the farmhouse to find Michael waiting for us. "Michael," I said in surprise.

He was looking very grave. "I'm not here in an official capacity, Anne, I'm here as a friend." His eyes moved to Liam. "I just thought you'd like to know that we arrested your mother this afternoon for the murder of Leslie Bartholomew."

Liam's face went white.

"What happened?" I said.

"Perhaps we could go inside," Michael said.

Without answering, Liam opened the front door.

"Come into the family room," I said, and led the way into the comfortable room that held the television set. We all sat down, Liam and I on the sofa, Michael on a chair facing us.

Michael said, "Chief Brown went up to Washington today to interview her and he took me with him. We met with Mrs. Wellington, the senator and her attorney. The Chief wanted to ask her how her medal came to be at the crime scene."

Liam and I nodded.

"It was not an easy interview. The Senator and her attorney kept interrupting and refusing to allow her to answer. Finally the Chief lost his temper. 'That medal is yours, Mrs. Wellington,' he roared. 'Everyone knows it is yours. Your son lied to cover up the fact that it is yours. Your maid and your friends say that it is yours. I want to know what the hell that medal was doing next to Leslie Bartholomew's gravesite.'

"Well, the senator started yelling, the lawyer started spouting law, and then Mrs. Wellington held up her hand. 'That's enough,' she said calmly. 'I will tell you how that medal got there, Chief Brown. It got there because I killed Leslie and it came off when I was burying her body.'"

Liam groaned. "Oh my God."

My mouth fell open. "She said that?"

"Yes, she did. The senator and the lawyer tried to shut her up but she wouldn't stop. 'I'm sick of being quiet,' she said. 'I've lived with this terrible thing for all these years and I can't live with it any more. It's poisoning me. And it's coming out, Lawrence. The medal has been found. How to explain that except by the truth?'"

Liam dropped his head into his hands.

I said, "So she confessed."

"She confessed."

"Did she say why she did it?"

"She said that she was drunk and that she knew Leslie

was having an affair with her husband and that she was jealous. She didn't mean to kill her, she just struck out blindly. She was very drunk."

Liam raised his head. "Surely that is diminished responsibility."

"I would think so," Michael said.

I said, "So she's been arrested?"

"Yes. But I'm sure her attorney will arrange bail."

Liam said flatly, "Did she say she did this all by herself?"

"Yes, she did," Michael answered. "But I don't think anyone believes that Mrs. Wellington was capable of moving a dead body by herself, let alone burying it."

"It seems unlikely," Liam said, still in the same flat voice.

Michael got to his feet. "Well, that's the reason I came by. I thought you should know what really happened right away, not what the gossip will conjure up."

"Thank you, Michael," I said with genuine gratitude. "We appreciate your thoughtfulness."

"Yes." Liam held out his hand. "It was very good of you."

When Michael had gone, we turned to look at each other in silence. Then Liam said, "I can't believe she confessed."

"It must have been preying on her mind for all of these years," I said. "Who knows? Maybe it's one of the reasons for her continued drinking."

"But even if they established that it was her medal that was found by Leslie's gravesite, they had no way to connect Mom to the murder itself. All she had to do was keep quiet."

"I guess she couldn't do that anymore, Liam."

There was a long silence.

Then he said, "I guess not."

He was very quiet all night and when we went to bed he just wanted to hold me. I didn't think Alyssa Wellington had been much of a mother, but she was the only mother Liam had ever known and I guess the thought of your mother going to jail was pretty horrible. I tried to give him what comfort I could, and thanked God I had the wonderful mother that I did.

The next day, Alyssa was out on bail and I started talking to Liam about looking at horse farms in Kentucky. "There's nothing you can do about your mother's situation; there's no point in letting it paralyze your own life. You said you wanted to have your own farm, well now is a good time to look. If there are repairs that need to be done we'll have time to do them before the winter."

Once he started talking to real-estate agents, he began to perk up.

"What about our getting married?" he said to me. "Do you think we could just have a small wedding, with immediate family and a lunch or something?"

"An excellent idea. It wouldn't look too good for us to be planning a big wedding right now anyway."

So that was what we did. We had a small wedding in St. Margaret's Church, then afterward about twenty-five of us went back to Wellington for a catered lunch. Liam and I went to Bermuda for a week on our honeymoon, which was wonderful. When we got home, we got down to the serious business of hunting for a farm.

In the autumn, the plea bargain between the State of Virginia and Alyssa Wellington was finally arraigned and Liam's mom got three years behind bars. I thought that she had gotten off pretty easily and hoped that the years away from alcohol might break her of the habit.

Senator Wellington never came into the picture at all, even though everyone knew that he must have been the one who buried the body. But Alyssa stuck to her guns that she did it alone, and he got away scot-free. Well, maybe not. The chances of his winning another election look pretty slim.

In early December, Liam and I moved into our new farm in Paris, Kentucky. We had twelve beautiful thoroughbred mares, all in foal to good stallions, three really nice yearlings who would be turning two, and Someday Soon, the Triple Crown winner, Breeder's Cup winner, and Horse of the Year. Not to mention all the dogs from Wellington. And true to my word, I got a job with one of the local veterinary practices.

Our first Christmas in our new home was very happy. My mother came for the holiday and helped us decorate the tree and put the presents under it. On Christmas Eve, as we cuddled under the covers in our own bed, in our own bedroom, on our own farm, I whispered to Liam, "I am so happy."

He smoothed my hair off my cheek. "That's wonderful. Because I'm happy too."

I rested my head against his chest.

"Poor Mom," he said. He had visited her the previous week.

"I know. But it won't be that long before she can spend Christmas with us, like my Mom. And maybe by then we'll have a grandchild for her to play with."

"That would be nice." I could hear the smile in his voice.

Thump, thump, thump. I listened to the beat of his

heart. It was as vital to me as the beat of my own heart, I thought. Life without Liam was unthinkable.

"I think you're going to like the present I got you," he said. He sounded anticipatory, like a small boy.

"I'm sure I will," I said. "How come it isn't under the tree?"

"I don't want you to see it until tomorrow."

"Wow. Now you've really got me curious."

"Good."

"I'm afraid I got you a rather ordinary present."

"That's okay. I'm sure I'll like it."

I pulled away so I could look into his face. "What could it be?"

He grinned. "You'll see tomorrow morning."

I loved it when he grinned like that.

I reached up and kissed his mouth. "I love you."

"Now, that is something I never get tired of hearing."

"Okay," I said. "I love you, I love you, I love you, I love you."

"Still not tired."

I laughed. "Enough, you glutton."

His face sobered. "It's my turn then. I love you, Annie. I love you so much."

His head and shoulders were looming over me. "Oh, Liam," I said. "Oh, Liam."

We loved each other with all the youth and passion that was in us and afterwards we lay pressed against each other, hearts pounding, breaths coming fast.

"Nothing in the world is better than that," Liam said into my ear.

"Not even winning the Triple Crown?"

He laughed. "Not even winning the Triple Crown."

"Wow."

We held each other for quite a while, then my eyes began to close. It had been a long day; I had made a lot of barn calls.

"Annie," Liam said. "I think you should put your pajamas back on before you go to sleep or you're going to be cold."

I forced my eyes open. "What?"

"Sit up."

I sat up and he began to put my arm into the sleeve of my pajama jacket. I blinked and said, "I'll do it. I have to go to the bathroom anyway."

When I returned from the bathroom wearing my pajamas, Liam had straightened the bed and folded back the quilt for me. I crawled in. He came around to my side, bent over me and said, "I'm going to do a little rearranging of the presents under the tree. You go to sleep and I'll see you in the morning."

"Okay."

He kissed my cheek. "My Annie."

My eyes were shut, but I smiled.

He went out and softly shut the door behind him and I went to sleep.